PRAISE FOR VICTOR METHOS

A Killer's Wife

An Amazon Best Book of the Month: Mystery, Thriller & Suspense

"*A Killer's Wife* is a high-stakes legal thriller loaded with intense courtroom drama, compelling characters, and surprising twists that will keep you turning the pages at breakneck speed."

—T. R. Ragan, *New York Times* bestselling author

"Exquisitely paced and skillfully crafted, *A Killer's Wife* delivers a wicked psychological suspense wrapped around a hypnotic legal thriller. One cleverly designed twist after another kept me saying, 'I did not see that coming.'"

—Steven Konkoly, *Wall Street Journal* bestselling author

"A gripping thriller that doesn't let up for a single page. Surprising twists with a hero you care about. I read the whole book in one sitting!"

—Chad Zunker, bestselling author of *An Equal Justice*

AN
UNRELIABLE
TRUTH

OTHER TITLES BY VICTOR METHOS

Desert Plains Series

A Killer's Wife
Crimson Lake Road

Other Titles

The Hallows
The Shotgun Lawyer
A Gambler's Jury
An Invisible Client

Neon Lawyer Series

Mercy
The Neon Lawyer

AN
UNRELIABLE
TRUTH

VICTOR METHOS

 THOMAS & MERCER

Text copyright © 2021 by Victor Methos
All rights reserved.

Published by Thomas & Mercer, Seattle

www.apub.com

Amazon, the Amazon logo, and Thomas & Mercer are trademarks of Amazon.com, Inc., or its affiliates.

ISBN-13: 9781542022668
ISBN-10: 1542022665

Cover design by Christopher Lin

Printed in the United States of America

Dedicated to all the prosecutors and criminal defense attorneys fighting it out in the trenches.

1

Holly Fallows screamed until she went hoarse.

The pain was so excruciating it didn't feel like her body was causing it. More like something had taken possession of her and was trying to tear her apart from the inside out. Her neck was stabilized on a backboard, and several nurses, doctors, and paramedics rushed her through the hospital corridors. All she could see was fluorescent light after fluorescent light as her croaky screaming bounced back at her from the walls.

"Am I dying?" she cried. "Am I gonna die?"

No one would answer her. It amplified the terror and constricted her throat so much she couldn't breathe.

"My dad doesn't know where I am! I have to call my dad. Please let me call my dad. Please!"

No one talked to her; no one looked at her or even acknowledged she was there. They were shouting about trauma, fractures, and internal bleeding. Someone was yelling about x-rays and CAT scans. Another person held gauze against a wound in her leg, and the gauze had soaked red with blood. It felt like the hospital corridors were closing in to crush her, and she shouted, "Someone answer me. Please!"

They rushed her around a corner, and two other men joined the crowd before they pushed through some double doors into an open room. Holly's nose had been broken so badly she couldn't smell, and when one of the nurses barely tapped the nail on her index finger, the bloody sliver of nail slid off.

As she was wheeled past a smooth metal cabinet, she caught a glimpse of herself and thought she looked like a nightmare. Exposed flesh, dried blood, and splotches of darker black blood from wounds she couldn't even see.

The images and sounds she'd been fighting came to her now. Dense forest, laughing, screaming, and blood.

Something black from head to toe that looked like it was part of the forest rather than a man. And then, with the black figure almost upon her, she had a single choice: die, or jump off a canyon precipice and have a chance of surviving.

She'd made the decision in a split second. She didn't know if her sister was still alive, but her father relied on them to take care of him. Without Holly or April, their father would be put in some moldy room in a care center basement and die alone. Holly wouldn't let that happen. He'd given up everything to raise them as a single dad, and they had always intended to take care of him in his old age. Holly had to survive for him.

She was thinking of her father when someone said, "Breathe deep."

Something went over Holly's face, and she fought. She tried to claw at it, but her arms were being held down. As she cried and struggled, she slowly felt a calming sensation loosen her muscles. The calm washed down to the tips of her toes, and she slept.

2

Dylan Aster sat next to his client at the defense table and thought about how being in a courtroom waiting for the jury to return with their verdict felt like waiting for a doctor to come back with your test results. The air had some sort of vibration to it. Edginess, maybe. Or boredom. He couldn't tell anymore.

The defendant, Gerald Dean Weaver, was tapping his fingers against the tabletop to some tune. The prosecutor, a chubby man named Ian, flicked lint off his beige suit. Dylan glanced back and saw his law partner, Lily Ricci, sitting in the spectator benches. She winked at him, and he grinned and turned back around. Glancing out the windows, he saw a rust-colored moon from the lunar eclipse that had begun a bit ago. The Las Vegas Strip wasn't far from the courthouse, and the glimmering neon glow in the distance made it look as if part of the city were on fire.

The jury had been in deliberation for seven hours. When the judge had suggested they break and come back in the morning, the foreperson had insisted they could reach a verdict with more time. Now, apparently, they had.

The bailiff, a man whose forearms were bigger than Dylan's head, leaned against the judge's bench and silently mouthed the words, *What number?*

Dylan mouthed back, *Forty-four.*

Trial number forty-four and, if he won, his forty-fourth straight not-guilty verdict. Defense attorneys and prosecutors liked to tout their "undefeated" records at trial, but the truth was that prosecutors routinely dismissed or offered good deals on the cases they were likely to lose at trial, and private defense attorneys could fire their clients. Dylan, on the other hand, had racked up most of his verdicts as a public defender for Clark County before he and his partner went out on their own. Public defenders couldn't fire clients or dismiss cases. He took the worst of the worst cases, the unwinnable cases, to trial and had never lost.

"We should win, right?" Gerald whispered, leaning toward him. "That cop totally lied. I think I wanna sue."

Dylan leaned over as well and said, "Gerry, lemme tell you the first rule of criminal law: everybody lies. Defendants lie because they have to, cops lie because they *think* they have to, and witnesses lie for reasons they don't understand. No one's gonna care that he lied on some drug case, and even if they did, how much money you think a jury's gonna give you?"

The door leading back to the deliberation room opened, and the bailiff bellowed, "All rise for the jury."

Twelve men and women entered and didn't look at either the defense or the prosecution, but it didn't matter where they looked. Dylan could feel their energy. It almost radiated off them. They were going to acquit Gerry, and he surmised there had been only one hold-out, the elderly woman at the end. She had given Gerry a dirty look during jury selection, the grimace on her face saying she wanted to— good Lord—be absolutely anywhere but a courtroom, and someone was going to pay for it. But when the other jurors didn't budge, she probably knew it would be too much effort to keep fighting, and the path of least resistance was to acquit.

The judge said, "It's my understanding the jury has reached a verdict in this matter?"

The foreperson, a lithe woman in a black skirt and white blouse, stood. "We have, Your Honor."

"What say you?"

The foreperson raised the verdict form and read, "We the jury, in the matter of *the State of Nevada v. Gerald Dean Weaver*, on count one, distribution of a controlled substance, find the defendant, Gerald Dean Weaver, not guilty."

Gerry let out a long breath and had to put his hands on the table, seemingly to keep from falling over. The judge asked everyone to remain standing as the jury filed out, then thanked Dylan and Ian for their hard work and told Gerry he was free to go.

Gerry hugged Dylan, then shook his hand, and then hugged him again.

"I still wanna sue the cops," he said.

"Let it go, Gerry. You just dodged ten years at Low Desert Plains. Go get a beer and celebrate."

Gerry waved to Lily on his way out as Ian gathered his papers and briefcase and came over to the defense table. "He's guilty as sin, you know that, right?"

"How 'bout a beer on me to make up for it?"

"I'm going to bed, Dylan. You should get some sleep, too. And buy a new suit, for hell's sake. You look like you slept in that one."

Dylan grinned as he gathered his papers and lawbooks. He dressed like this purposefully, acutely aware of what impression he wanted to make with the jury. The better the prosecutor dressed, the worse he did. Who didn't love an underdog?

"Forty-four," Lily said on the way out. "I think that's gotta be a record for the state."

Dylan shrugged. "It was nothing. They didn't have a good case."

"They had a great case. You just outworked him. Ian doesn't want to work that hard."

Dylan usually felt a surge of adrenaline after a trial, but he didn't feel it now. He felt nothing but fatigue and a dull sense of dread that he would have to wake up tomorrow and start preparing for the next trial without any rest in between.

"Harry's?" he asked. After a verdict, he liked going to Harry's, a bar in Clark County that catered mostly to lawyers, judges, and cops. Workers in the same factory.

"No, Jake's expecting me. Late dinner."

He checked his watch. "Yeah, I guess I better get home, too."

They reached the elevator, and the police officer who had arrested Gerry was already waiting there. The officer was tall and skinny with a thick mustache and had glared at Dylan angrily several times during the trial. No one said anything as they got onto the elevator. Lily hit the button for the first floor, and they stood in silence as the elevator started to move.

"I don't know how you do it," the officer finally blurted out. "I don't know how you live with yourself, getting dirtbags like that off."

The elevator dinged, and the doors opened. Dylan turned to him. "Some unsolicited advice? Don't stay a cop too long. It'll taint how you see people, and you'll be cynical the rest of your life."

As he stepped off the elevator, the officer said, "Same to you, Counselor. You defend 'em too long, you'll become like 'em."

Lily must've been able to tell it bothered Dylan, because she put her arm around his elbow. "He's a little man upset that someone challenged his authority, Dylan. Ignore him. What we do is important."

They got outside, and Dylan took a hit of the night air. It was warm, like the air in an oven, and had a hint of exhaust, but it was better than the stale air of the courtroom.

"You sure no beers?" he said.

"Jake got a promotion at the investment firm and I have a whole romantic evening planned. With all the trials I've been doing the past few months, we haven't had a date in a while."

She told him she'd see him tomorrow at the office and went to her truck across the street. Dylan watched as she got in and drove away. He waved to her as she sped past the courthouse to make the light at the intersection.

He sighed and looked across the street. People were still pulling over and taking photos of the ruddy-brown moon while it lasted. It had tinted the sky red in a way he'd never seen before.

He stared at it awhile and then went to his car.

3

Kelly Whitewolf woke to her cell phone vibrating on the bed. She had fallen asleep watching a true-crime documentary, and the TV was still on, the volume turned down. Blurry eyed, she picked up her phone and saw that the ID said *Hank Philips*. She turned the TV off and answered.

"What time is it?"

"Not so late I feel bad calling," he said.

She inhaled deeply and sat up in bed. The room was bathed in dull crimson, and it took a moment for her to remember there had been a blood moon. She felt the empty side of the bed, and the sheets were cool to the touch.

After the birth of the twins, her marriage had fallen apart. She and her ex had rushed into it so quickly; they weren't prepared for how much stress children would bring into the relationship. So she had been a single mother ever since her girls were six months old.

Kelly wondered what it would be like to wake up next to someone else that you knew would be there during the day to help you when you felt overwhelmed.

"Kelly, you there?"

"Yeah, yeah, hang on." She sat up in bed, then went to the espresso maker she kept on her dresser and turned it on. "What's up?" she said once the familiar filtering sound started and she could smell the coffee.

"You're gonna wanna come down to the station. We got . . . well, it's a damn massacre, Kelly."

"What do you mean?"

"Just what I said. It's four kids up Coyote Canyon. One of them lived, but she's in the ICU at Roosevelt. Banged up real bad. The other three are . . . I mean, I've never seen anything like it. Well, almost."

Hank Philips had been a police officer for twenty-four years, sixteen of those in the Robbery-Homicide Unit of the Jackson County Sheriff's Office. For him to say he'd never seen anything like it sent a cold shiver through her.

"We got an AP down here at the station."

"That fast?"

"He was pulled over by a patrol on I-15 for speeding. When the uniform got him outta the car, he said the guy was drenched in blood. I just left the room he's in, and the uniform wasn't kidding. He's covered from head to toe."

"I'm coming now."

She peed, jumped in the shower, and then threw on a black suit. She guzzled a double espresso before opening a drawer that held her gold badge, *Jackson County District Attorney's Office* engraved across the top.

Sometimes she carried a concealed firearm as well, but she decided to leave it at home tonight. As the first female district attorney for Jackson County, she had gotten more than her fair share of threats. Some of the good ole boys didn't like the idea of a woman, especially a Native American woman, putting them away.

Though the county was small and in the middle of an isolated swath of desert in northwestern Nevada, it was growing exponentially. She had petitioned the county council to give her five more prosecutors, but so far they kept citing budgetary concerns and stalling. None of them actually wanted to publicly refuse law enforcement a request for more personnel, but they also had their own pet projects they wanted to fund instead. The entire council was made up of the exact types of people Kelly disliked: people that would say anything to get what they wanted.

She tiptoed past Aunt Noya's room and into her children's bedroom. Bethany and Bella were sleeping soundly on their backs in the bunk beds. Bella had a pink stuffed bunny wrapped in her arms, and Bethany had an arm hanging down from the top bunk as she drooled onto her pillow. Kelly kissed each of them, then left a note on the fridge for Noya saying that she had to run to work and would be back when she could.

It was tribal custom for the elders who could no longer take care of themselves to move in with younger relatives that could care for them. But she had to admit that Noya had helped her far more than she was able to help her aunt.

When Kelly's mother was murdered on a cold November night when Kelly was only twelve, it was Noya who took her in and explained the life cycle and why her mother could never really be gone. Noya's words that night and on countless others were the only things that had kept the trauma from burying itself so deep Kelly might never have been able to get it out.

The Sheriff's Office wasn't too far from her house. A square brick building that looked like it had been office space in the sixties, it felt like an old glove to her sometimes. She had started her career here two decades ago as a deputy, and she remembered those days in a police cruiser fondly, though at the time, working the night shift and going to law school during the day, all she could think about was becoming a prosecutor.

She went inside and found no one staffing the front desk, so she headed down the hall to the interview rooms. A deputy, a gal named Cindy, came out of the break room, smiled, and held out a Styrofoam cup filled with coffee.

"Fresh," she said.

Kelly took it without stopping and said, "You're the best."

She marched down a long hallway to the first interview room and looked through the one-way glass, ignoring Hank and his partner, Sil, who were speaking quietly a dozen feet away.

The man behind the glass was sitting down. He was thin, with brown hair, a sallow face that was almost sickly pale, and large brown eyes that Kelly instantly thought held a lot of sadness. He rocked slowly back and forth. She noticed all this in a blink, but what really struck her was the blood.

Hank hadn't been embellishing. It looked like the guy had bathed in the stuff. Blood dried a crimson brown, but if someone tried to clean it with, say, bleach or strong soap, it dried to a dull gray because the hemoglobin was destroyed. This blood was deep red, which meant there had been a lot of it and he hadn't tried to clean it up.

His clothes consisted of a plain white T-shirt and jeans, but she almost couldn't see the white in his shirt because of the blood. His hands were coated in it and his hair matted with it. His face was smeared, as if he'd picked up bloody mud and spread it over his exposed skin.

"Holy hell," she whispered.

Hank came up next to her and looked in. "Yeah . . . but he said it wasn't entirely his fault."

"How?"

Hank put his hands in his pockets. "Says a demon told him to do it."

"A demon?"

He nodded. "That's what he said. But here's the part you need to see. Some crime scene photos from something you'll remember."

He handed her a file, and she opened it. Inside were glossy photos from a case she had thought about every day since she had closed the file and sent it to the basement to be locked away in the open-unsolved racks six years ago.

"It's almost exactly like—"

"I know," she quickly interjected. She glanced at Sil. "He know?"

"Nope. Just me and you."

She closed the file and tapped his chest with it, leaving it against his heart. "No one can know about this, not yet."

"I know."

"Hank, I'm serious. This doesn't go anywhere but you and me. It was our mess, and I need time to make sure this is him."

He nodded and looked back at the man sitting in the interview room. "You really think this guy could've—"

"Yes," she said, before digging out a clove cigarette from her purse. Hank took out a lighter and lit it for her. She blew out a puff of smoke before saying, "Anyone is capable of doing anything, Hank. They just need to be put in the right circumstances."

4

The red tinge of the blood moon had faded to the color of copper by the time Dylan stopped at a drive-through before heading home.

Home was a flat rambler on the outskirts of Clark County in a small town called Janesville. His father had built it with his own hands.

His father had been a large man, tall and muscular, and Dylan remembered him as a giant. Not only in size, but also in remoteness, unreachability. The image entered his mind of the last time he saw his father: lying in a hospital bed with tubes coming out of him. The doctor telling him and his mother that the bullets had done too much damage to his lungs and kidneys and that they couldn't get a transplant fast enough to save his life.

Dylan brought the food inside, where the television was blaring. His twelve-year-old sister, Markie, sat on the couch watching cartoons. Her face was stained red with punch and whatever food she had eaten recently.

"Hi, Dylan!"

She had the widest smile, and her eyes always glimmered when he came home. He put the food down on the table and took her chubby face in his hands and kissed her forehead.

"Where's Mama?"

"She's watching her shows."

Dylan went into the master bedroom and found his mother in a bathrobe on the bed. Her eyes were glazed over from the antipsychotics that seemed to do little more than force her to sleep sixteen hours a day.

She didn't acknowledge Dylan until he said, "Brought dinner, Mama."

"What'd you bring?"

"Chicken."

"Be right there."

She reached for her walker, and Dylan brought it over to her. He helped her out of bed and into the dining room. "Markie," he called as he set out the food, "come eat."

Markie got up, her eyes glued on the television as she walked. She bumped into the side table and said, "Oww."

Dylan chuckled.

"Don't laugh at her, Dylan. She don't like it."

"She knows I would never laugh *at* her."

Once they'd each selected pieces of chicken and fries, his mother folded her arms and said grace, ending it, as she always did, with the words, "And bless Papa that he knows we love him and will see him soon."

The "and will see him soon" always bothered Dylan as a kid. Did his mother know something about when death would come calling, or was her mental illness affecting her ability to accept that her husband was really gone?

After dinner, Markie sprawled out on the couch again, laughing at a cartoon shark chasing a dog. Dylan's mother had taken her pills, the medications that slowed her schizophrenic episodes but made her extremely drowsy, and was snoring from the bedroom. He checked on her, then went back out to his sister.

"Time for bed, Markie."

"No, Dylan, no. I wanna watch this. This is the best part."

Dylan took a deep breath and sat down next to his sister. She attended a special-needs school that inexplicably started the day at seven in the morning, rather than the nine o'clock start time of the regular county schools nearby.

In the ceiling near the corner, he saw a crack. Something he'd been meaning to learn how to fix for weeks. Today, with his forty-fourth straight jury trial win, he had no doubt there wasn't a trial lawyer in the state that could match his record. The partners at the big firms who barely knew how to speak to a jury without fumbling over their words—and had their paralegals do all the real work—were pulling down six and seven figures. Meanwhile, he didn't have enough money to hire someone to fix a crack in his ceiling. The perceived injustice of it made him bitter, and he couldn't think about it often.

He put his arm around his sister as they watched the cartoon—exhaustion allowing him to keep his eyes open only a few minutes before he drifted to sleep.

5

After a few busy weeks of client meetings and court appearances that drained him to the point he thought about taking some time off, Dylan woke like he did every morning: to the sound of his alarm clock. He hated that sound. It made him grate his teeth and reminded him of days as a teenager, getting up early to work menial jobs before going to high school classes.

He turned the alarm off, went to the mirror in the bathroom, and noticed the scar on his neck. Unlike the alarm, it was something he was able to ignore most days. He ran his fingers over it and felt how it rose a little on his skin. Just slightly, but enough for him to notice.

After showering and getting dressed, he checked the calendar on his phone and saw a court hearing at two. He made breakfast for Markie and left a plate on the dining table for when his mother woke up. Markie gave him a hug at the door and said, "Love you!" before running out to catch the bus. Dylan watched until she got on, and she turned and waved to him. He smiled and waved back.

She had been a surprise child for his parents. Their father had died before her first birthday, and she had never known a man in her life other than Dylan. Most days, he felt he wasn't good enough, that she deserved a better father, but he did the best he could. He made sure Markie had breakfast every morning, and no matter how consuming a case he was on, he was home to give her dinner whenever possible.

But he'd received an offer from a large firm in Los Angeles that had been following his trial victories and had called him out of the blue for an interview. He'd done a phone interview and two personal interviews and received the offer last week. He was dreading telling his mother. Any change in her life seemed to throw her off balance, like she could no longer think rationally until she grew accustomed to the change. He didn't know how severe the reaction would be when he told her they were moving to LA. Or that if she refused to go, he and Markie would move anyway and he'd send money back to her.

He drove the forty minutes to the law offices of Aster & Ricci. Before he pulled into the underground parking lot, he saw that a line had formed outside the Clark County District Courthouse doors across the street. People waiting for a bailiff to unlock them.

The Biltmore Building had six floors, and he and Lily took up two offices on the third floor. He took the elevators up and said hello to their receptionist, whose hair had been dyed green today from deep brown, before going into his office and shutting the door. The windows looked out at the courthouse, and he stood there a moment and watched the line of people. It never ceased to amaze him that the justice system worked at all, considering how many people had to go through it every day.

A feeling often came to him lately when he stood here staring out at the courthouse. Something he hadn't felt before, and it was bewildering why he was feeling it now: boredom.

His phone vibrated in his pocket. It was a number from the District Attorney's Office.

"This is Dylan."

"Dylan, hi, this is Jessica Yardley."

He sat down in his executive chair and kicked his feet up on the desk. Last year, they'd been on opposite sides of one of the most interesting cases he'd worked on: the Crimson Lake Road Executioner.

"Long time no see. How's the zoo of the DA's Office?" he asked.

"Believe it or not, I'm actually glad I didn't retire. How are you?"

"Same old. So do we have a case together, or did you just miss me?"

"Actually, I'm calling for a personal reason. I have a friend who's a public defender for Jackson County. You there much?"

"Few cases a year, I think. Why?"

"She caught a complex case a few weeks ago, and she reached out to ask if I knew anybody she could speak with. It could potentially be certified as a capital case, and she's never handled a death penalty case before."

"What is it?"

"Apparently a triple murder. It's starting to get some media attention, so I'm sure you'll hear about it."

Dylan had handled a triple murder before: a man who'd shot up a gas station while attempting to rob it. Dylan had settled the case with a plea deal that saved the man's life but landed him in prison without parole.

There was almost always overwhelming evidence in multiple-homicide cases, which made them among the most difficult for defense attorneys to win. Dylan felt a flicker of excitement he hadn't felt in a while.

"Huh. Yeah, I'm happy to talk to her. Gimme the number."

He wrote down the information on a legal pad and said, "So why you asking me?"

She chuckled. "You just like to hear compliments, don't you?"

"They don't hurt."

"You know what I think about your work. She sounded scared, so I wanted the best defense attorney I knew."

He grinned and wondered if he was blushing. Compliments had always been awkward for him, probably because he had so seldom received them growing up. His father was the type who thought giving any type of recognition or affection to a child made them weak, and his mother had gone through long periods where she wasn't lucid. He had raised himself and Markie without much parental guidance.

"Okay, yeah, I'll give her a call." He leaned back in the chair. "When you quitting prosecution and joining Lil and me?"

Jessica chuckled. "Maybe in another life. I appreciate this, Dylan."

"No prob."

He hung up and looked at what he had written on the pad. *Madeline Ismera*. He picked up the phone again.

"Hello?" a soft female voice answered. He introduced himself, and she said, "Oh my gosh, thank you for calling. Jessica said she would reach out to you." She sounded incredibly young, and he remembered when he was just starting out and how overwhelming the system had felt.

"Happy to help. So, sounds like you got something interesting."

She sighed. "Arlo Ward. He was arrested a few weeks ago. He's accused of killing three people in Coyote Canyon. I mean, like, really violently killing them. There was a fourth victim who survived. So there's rumors they're going to make this a capital case because of how brutal it is, and I've never handled one. Apparently, you're not required to have much experience in this state to do one, so they just gave it to me."

Dylan knew precisely why she had gotten the case. Most counties didn't have a permanent public defender's office and instead put out bids every year, which meant the DA's Office had a lot of input on who got the contracts, how they were managed, and which attorneys got the call. They wanted someone on this who would plead it out quickly. Madeline would be a perfect choice.

"You can pass on it. Let one of the other PDs who has more experience handle it."

"I wish. I'm two years out of law school, and my only income is this contract. You turn down cases, and pretty soon, you're not in the rotation anymore. Especially if I bail on one this huge."

"What's wrong with their case?"

"What do you mean?"

"They gave this case to you hoping you'd plead him out fast, which means they're nervous about something. Do you know what it is?"

"Well, Arlo is . . . unique. He has schizophrenia. A really severe type with auditory and visual hallucinations."

"Yup, that would do it. He might not be competent to stand trial, and a case that's going to get this much media attention will have the public out for blood. Putting him in a hospital where he might be released one day isn't going to play well in the news. Who's the prosecutor?"

"The DA is handling it herself. Kelly Whitewolf."

Dylan whistled. "She's a pit bull."

"Well, that makes me feel better."

He grinned. "Normally an aggressive prosecutor is a terrible hand to be dealt on a case like this, but she's smart, too. She'll know he might not be competent and will probably offer a decent deal."

There was a slight pause, and he knew exactly what she was thinking. She wanted him to take a look at the case.

"Could you . . . maybe just read the police reports and tell me what you think? I know who you are. I mean, every defense attorney does. It would really help Arlo if someone with your reputation took a look at it."

"I got a friend up there in Jackson. He's good. Let me give him a call."

"Oh, okay. I was kinda hoping you'd do it, though."

"Madeline, I am so swamped right now. I have a federal conspiracy trial coming up that has two hundred hours of surveillance recordings and sixty witnesses. There's no way I could get involved with a triple homicide right now."

Lily walked into his office and raised her eyebrows when she heard "triple homicide." She sat across from him and put her arm on the back of the chair next to her.

"Oh, okay," Madeline said. "I totally get it. Yeah, if you could have your friend call me, I would really appreciate it."

"Sure thing."

He hung up and put his phone on the desk.

"Triple homicide?" Lily asked.

"Some guy that allegedly killed some people in Coyote Canyon. Jessica Yardley is friends with the PD and asked me to give her a call. The PD doesn't have any experience with capital cases, so she wanted me to take a look. I'm just going to have Roger up there call her."

Lily nodded. "Huh."

"What?" he said.

"I didn't say anything."

"Lil, come on."

She brushed some lint off her jet-black suit and wasn't looking at him when she said, "Well, Jessica could've called any attorney in the state."

"Yeah, and?"

"And she called you. It doesn't hurt to do favors for prosecutors. And this case will get a lot of media attention. Free publicity is the best publicity. If we want to grow and stop having to scrape by, we have to take cases like this."

He shifted uncomfortably in his chair. "It sounds like it's going to be a beast. Guy's got schizophrenia. No, can't do it with the caseload I have right now."

"You could continue your other cases if you wanted to. Are you too swamped, or is it because if you lose he's going to get the needle?"

He hated the way she could cut to the issue.

In Nevada, murder was charged as "open murder," meaning it included first- and second-degree murder and even manslaughter. The jury would decide which degree of murder fit the facts. In cases where the prosecution was seeking the death penalty, the jury almost always agreed with them because of the biased jury selection process to get a death penalty–qualified jury.

"That's not . . . it has nothing to do with that."

"You've never liked capital cases. Losing means your client's death, but that's just part of the job, Dylan."

He tapped his fingers against the desk a couple of times. "I can't do it."

"Why?"

Dylan wasn't about to tell her that clients with schizophrenia made him uncomfortable. He'd seen how the disease progressed and the utter ruin it created in people's lives, and he couldn't help but think of his mother.

"I just can't."

She nodded again and rose. "Okay, but just remember when we were fresh out of law school and what it felt like when some senior attorney would help us out. It felt like getting a life preserver in a storm, didn't it?"

She left with that, leaving him staring through his open door.

Damn it.

6

Dylan finished up his afternoon in court, a drug case where his client had been pulled over with a live snake stuffed with cocaine in his car. Snakes could, apparently, live for a while after they were surgically spliced open, stuffed, and then sewn back up.

He stepped out of the courthouse. The sun was bright, and there were no clouds. May was his favorite month, and he wondered if it was because when he was a kid, school ended in May and summer vacation began.

He thought of those months in the summer when his mother had been so medicated she could barely say hello to him in the mornings. Then there would be days when she was lucid and would spend time with him, and then the next day it would be like it had never happened. Schizophrenia was devastating to the families of the sufferers because their loved ones would still be there, under all that wreckage. Hope that they would go back to their former selves never faded, but it also never happened.

Arlo Ward had likely committed those murders during a psychotic break and might not even remember doing them now. If that was true, Dylan couldn't even imagine the shock of being told what he'd done for the first time.

He let out a long breath and called Madeline Ismera.

"Hello?"

"I'll take a quick—really quick—look and give you my thoughts. Email me over what you got."

"Wow, I cannot thank you enough. Thank you so much."

"Don't thank me yet; I might not tell you anything you don't already know."

"I don't care. Just having someone else look it over is a huge help. I'll send everything over right now."

Dylan realized he hadn't eaten lunch, since the court appearance today had taken longer than anticipated, so he walked to the Strip, which wasn't far. Though he loved May, one downside was that it occasionally came with the intense Las Vegas heat. He took off his suit coat, undid his tie, and rolled up his sleeves. His undershirt still became drenched with sweat.

The restaurant he chose, a steak place, was packed, and he had to wait for a table. When he was seated, he ordered a sandwich and soda and opened Madeline's email. It contained scanned copies of some of the preliminary police reports for Arlo Ward's case. Not much, as the case was fresh, but a few notes from the detectives that could potentially be helpful.

Dylan read the detective's narrative first. Written by Detective Hank Philips—and considering he only had the preliminary autopsy, forensics, and toxicology reports, it was stunningly detailed and absolutely devastating. There were four victims: April Fallows, Michael Turner, William Page, and Holly Fallows.

April Fallows had died of smoke inhalation and had third-degree burns over much of her face and torso. One of the boys had his skull crushed and then his throat slit, and the other had died from severe blunt force trauma to the head. The injuries were consistent, according to the coroner, with a thick wooden or aluminum baseball bat.

All three had been mutilated postmortem, and the bodies, or more accurately the body parts, had been staged in vulgar ways. The corpses had been made to look like they were engaged in sexual acts with each other. Whoever had killed them had enjoyed it, and enjoyed what they did after the victims were dead even more.

Holly Fallows had survived, but not without massive injuries. She had apparently run from the assailant and come to a cliff in Coyote Canyon, where she jumped and landed forty feet below before rolling down the rocky hillside. Dylan pictured her having to choose between the maniac and the jump and felt sorry for her.

She couldn't identify the assailant and had failed to pick Arlo out of a photo lineup, stating that it was too dark to see anything. She was sure he had worn something over his head. Possibly wrapped his face in black cloth.

The only physical evidence left by the perpetrator was two cigarette butts. Assumed to be his because none of the victims smoked. There wasn't enough saliva left on them for DNA testing.

One of the strangest parts of the entire narrative was how Arlo was arrested. He was pulled over for speeding three miles from Coyote Canyon and almost immediately confessed. He had been covered in blood, and when the officers asked him about it, he responded by saying, "Oh, I just killed four people."

The bat had not been found. Neither had the hunting knife suspected of being used to mutilate the bodies. Arlo stated he didn't remember where they were but had given a full confession to everything else.

The written confession, in his own handwriting and signed, went into gruesome detail about the murders. Arlo stated he had stumbled upon the four young adults at a gas station talking to the clerk about going camping. The campground they were going to was a spot Arlo frequently used when he wanted to be alone, so he knew the area well. Arlo said he had fantasized about killing someone since he was a teenager but never had the right opportunity. Here, nobody was around, the kids were unarmed, and the moon looked like it was bleeding from a crimson tint. That was when the demon came to him and said if he didn't do it, he would be destroyed.

Arlo lay in wait for a while. When Holly Fallows and her boyfriend, Michael Turner, wandered off from the campsite for a walk, he attacked.

William Page had gone into the woods to relieve himself. Arlo immediately leapt out at April Fallows, tied her up, and threw her into the campfire. The screaming drew William back, and while he was trying to get April out of the fire, he received the first blow to the back of his head. The blow caused him to fall and twitch, like, as Arlo wrote, "an insect that got stepped on."

Holly and Michael were on their way back to the campsite about half an hour later when Michael stepped on a bear trap that Arlo had covered with leaves and twigs. Arlo described how he'd laughed when he saw that Michael's calf had been torn in half. When Arlo ran at them from the darkness, Michael pushed Holly away, shouting for her to run. She did, and Arlo crushed Michael's skull. Arlo estimated he'd chased Holly a good ten minutes before cornering her, and she chose to jump rather than face him.

I thought she was dead for sure, he'd written. *Can't believe she survived that. Bet she's ugly now, isn't she?*

Dylan moved on to the autopsy and toxicology reports. They were only preliminary, as a full autopsy report would take several more weeks to prepare. He skipped the external and internal examination sections, the laboratory data section, and the evidence-collected sections and went straight to the opinion section. The autopsy had been performed by the local coroner for Jackson County.

The death report and death certificate were attached at the end, and Dylan quickly glanced at them before returning to Detective Philips's narrative and rereading it.

His food came, but he wasn't hungry anymore.

7

Dylan stepped into a small side room at the courthouse. Lily came here two afternoons a month to donate her time to victims of domestic abuse who needed legal advice. She and two domestic violence advocates handled the entire county. Sometimes there'd be so many people lined up for the two hours the court gave them for the room that they would have to turn people away. Though Lily rarely went through with it: she would tell the victims to meet her outside in her truck and would occasionally stay well into the night. She had never talked about it, but she was passionate enough about the work that Dylan knew someone had hurt her in the past.

He saw her sitting at a table, speaking to a young woman who held a baby in her arms.

Lily looked like the girl next door. A sweet, innocent look that belied how absolutely ruthless she could be in a courtroom. She had once flirted with a married prosecutor who had shown interest in her, even speaking with him late at night on the phone and having dinner together. Subtly, she'd gathered as much information from him as she could. When the case went to trial, Lily used every weakness she had learned from the prosecutor to secure a not-guilty verdict. Dylan had been in the courtroom and thought the guy wouldn't be able to pick his jaw off the floor.

He remembered the first time he'd met her in law school. She sat by herself at a table eating lunch, the rest of the class ignoring her. Dylan sat next to her, and the first thing she said was, "How'd you get the scar?"

Most people did everything they could not to mention the scar on Dylan's neck, but Lily simply said what she was thinking without deception. Probably, Dylan had thought, the rarest trait in a human being.

"It's a long story."

"We got time," she said.

They had been inseparable ever since.

The woman with the baby thanked Lily and left. Dylan strolled up to the table with his hands in his pockets. Lily stretched her arms above her head and yawned.

"Didn't sleep much?" he asked.

"So-so. Little insomnia. How was court?"

He shrugged. "Fine." He looked down at his shoes, some old penny loafers, and thought he should get some new ones. "So I looked at that case in Jackson."

"Oh yeah? And?"

He shook his head. "It's the worst I've ever seen, Lil."

"That bad?"

"He didn't just kill them, he made them suffer. They had organs missing, one of the victims' hands was cut off, there were limbs missing . . . and then he posed all of them postmortem."

"Posed?"

"Like in sexual positions after he cut limbs off. Really gruesome. A jury'll take one look at the crime scene photos and convict him."

"Wow. But how's the strength of the case?"

"For the prosecution? Airtight. Arlo Ward was pulled over three miles from the campsite covered in blood and gave a full confession. He said the blood moon called to him and made a demon appear that ordered him to kill. I don't have the video or audio, but the confession was also written out by him, and I mean, he gave them every detail and said like twenty times that he did it and it was fun. I've already seen an article about the case that called him the Werewolf of Coyote Canyon."

She leaned back in her seat. "So what are you going to tell Madeline?"

"I don't know. Maybe, *Say your prayers and eat your vitamins, because that dude is going to death row.*"

She grinned. "I'm sure she'll appreciate it."

"Yeah, well, I'm smooth like that." He sighed. "You coming back to the office?"

She checked her watch. "Yeah, I've got a motion to write. Are you going to call her?"

"The PD?"

"Yeah."

Dylan eyed her a second. "You don't seem too shocked about all this."

She shrugged. "I may have received a call from Jessica about whether you'd be willing to talk to Madeline before she called you."

"What?"

"Jess really wanted you to look at it and asked me if I thought you would do it."

He shook his head. "Scandalous."

"Yeah, it's all a big conspiracy by us girls." She thought a moment. "It isn't just that the case is complex. The real problem is that Madeline thinks he didn't do it."

"She thinks he's innocent?"

"That's what she told Jessica."

"How can she possibly think that?"

Lily shrugged. "I don't know, but that's what she said. She thinks he's taking credit for what someone else did, and she's freaking out that she's going to get an innocent man executed. That girl is lost, and they're going to screw her client, Dylan."

"Maybe he deserves to get screwed?"

She leaned forward. "Do you remember the first rape case I ever defended? I came back to the office crying after the prelim because I knew I was going to get the case dismissed. Do you remember what you told me?"

He let out a long breath. "That we're not defending people, we're defending the Constitution, and that without it, we're just a dictatorship."

She nodded. "I've never forgotten it. Ever. I'm not saying take the case, but maybe point her in the right direction. She's young and scared. Besides, the publicity is going to be massive. Our names would be in the news every day for months. We seriously can't buy advertising like that."

He glanced at the woman with the baby who was speaking to someone in the hallway. She was wiping tears away as they whispered to each other.

"I'll think about it."

8

The corner office at the Jackson County District Attorney's Office was spacious and had a lot of windows. The furniture was plush, something Kelly had upgraded, since the previous two DAs had never been in the office enough to care what it looked like.

The District Attorney's Office employed twelve prosecutors and nearly twice as many staff. If she'd wanted, her senior attorneys could handle every case, and she could be out campaigning and making connections. Ensuring she'd get reelected. But that didn't appeal to her. That wasn't why she was in this office.

She had started her career as a trial prosecutor after leaving the Sheriff's Office, and unlike other prosecutors, many of whom began in misdemeanors, she'd started out in violent felonies. She had told the then district attorney in her initial interview that prosecution was all she wanted to do. She wouldn't do criminal defense work, and fighting over money in civil litigation wasn't up for consideration, so it was either this or find some other profession. She'd been hired on the spot.

The morning newspaper was on her desk. On the front page were two photographs. One of her walking up the steps of the courthouse, next to a photo of Arlo Ward. The headline read "Werewolf of Jackson County Case Heats Up."

She hated the moniker the true-crime bloggers had given Arlo Ward. It made him seem mystical, with the allure of the nefarious.

There was nothing mystical about him: He was human garbage. The type of person that shouldn't have ever been born. Someone who was going to do nothing to make the world a better place but had taken the lives of people who would have.

She folded the newspaper in half and looked at the man sitting across her desk from her. James Halden was her chief deputy DA. He had bright-white hair, a prodigious belly, and freckles that looked almost comical. He was who she turned to for advice. James was inherently an administrator—a skill she lacked; he handled all her management and public relations duties so she could be in court.

"You really want to certify this as a capital case?" James said. He gestured to the Arlo Ward files spread out on her desk. "I mean, with schizophrenia, the jury will convict, but there's a chance they won't impose death."

"I don't care about that. I don't need him dead, just locked away for the rest of his life. Death penalty–qualified juries are more likely to convict."

James took out a piece of gum and put it in his mouth before saying, "This thing is going to be even bigger once all the details get out, Kelly. The media loves misery and no one's seen anything like this for a long time. Not just here, but anywhere. You sure you're ready for the scrutiny?"

"Why wouldn't I be?"

James thought a moment before saying, "When I was with Clark County, we had a few celebrity cases that got a lot of national media attention. Athletes and such. They weren't like other cases. Everything you do is picked apart, and everything in your life is laid out there for everyone to see. The case becomes about the players more than the facts. We may want to avoid death, offer a quick plea on insanity, and get him locked away in the state hospital before the media gets its hooks into it."

Kelly opened one of the files. She slid out a large color photo of April Fallows, her face charred from the fire, most of her hair burnt, her eyes—what remained of them—slick and red from the layers that had been seared away.

"He pushed her head down into the fire until she suffocated to death. The coroner thinks it took about three minutes for her to go unconscious before she died. Imagine her last three minutes, James . . . and now tell me again how I'm supposed to tuck Arlo Ward away in a hospital until he's ready to be a good boy and come out again."

There was more to it as well, but she wasn't ready to get into it with James. Only she and Hank Philips knew about the Angel Lake murders, and she intended to keep it that way for now.

Kelly stood. "I have to go—no comments to any media for now. Call the public defender and let them know to be ready to go forward to prelim unless she wants to plead her client to life without parole. We'll take death off the table if she does that."

James nodded, eyes still on the photo. "You got it."

She grabbed her bag and left the office. The DA's Office was buzzing with activity, and Kelly could see some of the staff gathered in small groups, whispering, and knew they were discussing the case. Scipio, the seat of Jackson County, was a town of sixty thousand. Large enough to occasionally get extremely brutal cases, and small enough that everybody would know every detail about them.

When she'd gone to the café this morning to grab a bagel, she'd heard a table of police officers discussing, almost relishing, the gruesome details of the murders. One officer cracked a joke about April Fallows roasting like a marshmallow. Kelly turned to him and said, "That girl's father had to go down to the morgue and look at his daughter pieced back together by the coroner. I hope you never have to see someone you love like that and then have some jackass joking about it over his omelet."

Kelly got into her truck now but didn't need to use her GPS. From her days as a sheriff's deputy on night duty, she knew this city inside and out. Knew where the prostitutes gathered, knew the major drug players, knew the homes that would have five or six calls of domestic violence every year. Occasionally, she thought about moving. The city held so many dark places for her that it felt overwhelming at times. Her only fear was that she would lose the fire she had. Like how some boxers moved into bare, run-down apartments before fights so they could stay hungry, she felt she had to stay in the city she was protecting.

Her ex-husband, Travis, called during the drive, and she put it on speakerphone.

"Hey," she said.

"Hey. Sorry for bugging you during the workday."

"It's fine. What do you need?"

"I just want to see the girls this weekend," he said.

"It's not your weekend."

"I know, but I miss them, and there's a show I wanna take them to up in Vegas. A magic show with animals. I think they'll get a big kick out of it."

"I'll think about it."

"Yeah," he said softly. "Okay." There was a pause in the conversation before he said, "So how are you?"

"Goodbye, Travis."

The home she'd been heading toward was in a nondescript neighborhood on the east side of Scipio. The city, it was widely known, was split along east and west. The upper east bench consisted of larger homes of the wealthier professionals in the city, and the west side consisted of the middle class. It created an odd atmosphere where the town felt split, and the two high schools in the city, one on the west side and one on the east, had a rivalry in sports that bordered on obsession.

Kelly parked at the curb and went to the front door. She knocked and had to wait a few moments before the door opened, but only just a crack. A young woman answered. Even after several weeks, her face was still deeply bruised, a crutch was under one arm, and the faded tan discoloration of scars covered her arms and face.

"Are you Holly Fallows?"

Her voice was barely audible. "Yes."

"May I come in? I'm your prosecutor, and we need to talk about the man that did this to you."

9

Holly Fallows's home was decorated how Kelly would have expected a young woman in her twenties to decorate. Exuberant, colorful energy permeated the space, though it was messy right now, and she had a feeling it usually wasn't. April had lived with her sister, and she wondered if Holly had put her items in storage or if they were still here.

Holly had a steel contraption around her wrist and a boot on her leg and had to rely entirely on the crutch as she made her way to the couch. Instead of sitting across from her on the love seat, Kelly sat next to her.

"How are you feeling?"

Holly looked away as she leaned the crutch against the coffee table. "I'm in pain a lot of times. I don't wanna take too many meds, but the ibuprofen and Tylenol don't help much. And I still need another surgery on my leg. I shattered this ankle and they have to put metal pins in it."

Kelly nodded as she stared at the boot, which went all the way up past the knee.

"You said you're my prosecutor," Holly said. "What does that mean?"

"It means I'm the one that's going to convict Arlo Ward. I wanted to meet with you and give you my number in case you needed anything. I wanted you to know, Holly, that you can always reach out to me personally. If something's not making sense, or anyone is treating you in a way you feel is unfair, I want you to call me."

Holly seemed to barely be holding it together. Tears welled in her eyes, and her hands were unsteady.

"I know what you're going through," Kelly said softly. "It—"

"Do you?" Holly snapped, the tears flowing now. "You know what it's like to have your boyfriend and sister murdered? You don't know anything."

Kelly swallowed and watched as the young woman wiped tears away. A box of tissues on the coffee table was nearly empty.

"Not my sister, no. My mother."

Holly looked at her but said nothing.

Kelly hesitated. She wasn't sure she wanted to do this now, but there would never be a good time for it. "I, um, wanted to give this to you." She reached into her bag, which she had set on the floor, and pulled out a black jewelry box. "It was found in Michael's pocket. I thought you should have it."

When Hank Philips had told her about the engagement ring, Kelly's stomach had dropped. The engagement ring represented an entire life that Holly should have had. A life that had disappeared like fog and would never return.

Holly opened the box and saw the ring. She began to sob. "Mikey . . . no . . . no, baby."

The two of them sat a long time while Holly cried. When she calmed, Holly said, "Do you know what Michael used to do with his spare time?" A small grin came to her. "He volunteered at the adult literacy center. He thought reading was the most important thing for an adult to know."

She was silent for a moment. "A modeling agency once approached my sister. April was always really pretty, even as a kid, but she turned them down. It was a lot of travel, good money and stuff, but her dream was to be a teacher because she loved kids so much." She wiped a few tears away. "They were good people. They didn't deserve this."

Holly took the ring out of the box and slid it on her finger. Kelly figured the purpose of the camping trip was Michael's proposal, and it broke her heart to watch Holly stare at the ring and imagine what could have been.

"My sister helped take care of my dad," Holly said, still looking at the ring. "He has MS. I don't know what I'm going to do now. I can barely move around. There's no way I can take care of him, and he doesn't have anybody else."

She looked up at Kelly.

"Why would he do this? We didn't have any money or anything. Why?"

Kelly had to bite down to relieve some of the anger she felt. "I don't know why these men do the things they do, Holly. In fact, I think this may not have even been the first time he did something like this."

"But, like, is he crazy?"

"We're not sure."

Holly wiped tears away and then stared down at the ring. "I have this nightmare where he comes after me in the hospital and kills me, too." She looked at Kelly, the tears still rolling down her cheeks, though she was no longer sobbing. "If he's crazy, is he going to get away with it and come after me?"

Kelly reached out and gently took the girl's hand. "No, he won't."

Holly's eyes were rimmed red. They told Kelly that Holly had seen too much for how young she was, and it had already aged her. Kelly knew that had she met her a few weeks before, she would have looked like a completely different person.

As Holly lightly touched the ring and tears flowed again, Kelly took her hand. "I promise you . . . I will make him pay for what he did."

When she was leaving, she called James's cell phone.

"I've changed my mind," she said. "I want the death penalty for Arlo Ward."

10

The drive to Scipio was scenic, and the air got cooler the farther they got from southern Nevada. Dylan sat in the passenger seat as Lily drove. They listened to country music, Lily's favorite, and Dylan reread the police reports in the case. The oddest thing about them was how little information there was about Arlo Ward. He was born in North Dakota and then bounced around the Pacific Northwest, but his rap sheet was clean, and there was no credit history, no major purchases, no voting record. Nothing that would put him in the system at all.

Dylan read the grisly details of the crimes again. He had emailed Madeline and asked for some photos. He studied the way the bodies were mutilated and then posed, pondered the time it took to pose them, and stared in bewilderment at the amount of blood that covered Arlo. The county's criminalist, Dr. Andrew Lang, had taken hundreds of photos of the scene and of Arlo. Because of the popularity of television shows like *CSI* and *NCIS*, juries had come to expect a lot of forensic evidence. A trend had developed where good cases were ending in acquittals because there wasn't a smoking gun of physical evidence, no matter how many eyewitnesses there were.

Many police departments now had specialists in every area of forensic science—blood spatter analysis, ballistics, DNA, prints, trace evidence—grouped into much larger scientific investigation sections. But Jackson County, like many smaller counties, couldn't afford a plethora of experts. So they hired general criminalists that wore all the hats.

Dylan closed the file and stared straight ahead at the road. They were surrounded now by trees, and the air smelled like pine.

Lily placed a call through the car's Bluetooth, and Dylan glanced at the caller ID on the dashboard display. It was her sister. He had met her once when she'd come out to Las Vegas to visit, and she and Lily couldn't have been more different. Lily was physically strong and muscular, while her sister was squat and plump. Her sister never went to college, and Lily had degrees in economics and history. Even the way they spoke—Lily taciturn and straight to the point, her sister rambling on and on with various stories—couldn't be more different.

Lily left a voice mail asking her sister to call back, then said, "So? What are your thoughts about Arlo?"

Dylan placed the file down by his feet. "The confession's detailed," he said, "and the blood on his clothing was matched to two of the victims. If he didn't do it, the best explanation would be he found the scene and then purposely dipped himself in the blood. But if he wanted to get caught, why not alert the police? Why try to go home? If he really wanted to take credit for this, he would've called the cops and waited around."

"Unless he planned on calling the police but had to get farther from the canyon. That area is hit or miss with cell reception."

Dylan glanced out the passenger window at the entrance to a ranch with a rusted gate. Several men in cowboy hats were standing by it and gave him dirty looks. "I don't think so. I think he would've done it as soon as he got reception off the mountain, not three miles away. This doesn't add up. I think he killed those people and manipulated Madeline into believing he didn't."

"So what do you want to do?"

"Just give her some advice and move on."

A silence passed between them.

Lily glanced at him. "You haven't talked about the offer from LA much. You still thinking about it?"

Almost every minute, he thought. "Three hundred grand a year, Lil. How can I turn that down?"

"Yeah, three hundred grand, but for a giant firm where you have to keep track of every minute and take criticism from partners that know less than you. You'll hate it. What's the point of working if you hate what you do?"

He stared out the window awhile before replying. "I've been poor long enough. I'd like to try being rich now." He looked at her. "Are you trying to get me to take the Arlo Ward case so it blows up all over the news and convinces me to stay?"

She grinned but didn't reply.

He leaned his head back on the headrest and smiled.

Scipio was the next exit. The town was relatively large because of how it had been spread out over the valley, but it had the feel of a small town. Not that many restaurants or stores, one government building for all their municipal services, and a handful of churches. Dylan liked it. He had always lived in small towns and enjoyed the open space.

The Jackson County Jail was in a gray brick building that resembled a massive box. No windows. Lily parked in a guest spot, and they went up a ramp to get inside. The front desk clerk logged them in after checking their Nevada State Bar cards and then sent them through the metal detectors.

Madeline Ismera was already waiting for them. She was thin, with bright-green eyes and hair that came down to her shoulders. She smiled widely and shook their hands. She wore a small pin on her lapel: a flag of another country Dylan didn't recognize below an American flag.

"Haiti," she said, noticing Dylan looking. "So, seriously, I cannot tell you how thankful I am for this. You guys are doing me such a huge favor."

"No worries," Dylan said.

Madeline led them down the hall to the visiting area. They sat at a steel table in a room with concrete walls painted white.

Lily said, "What do you know about Arlo? There wasn't much in the file."

Madeline shook her head. "Not much. He has no real history, and when I ask him about it, he's vague. I think it's because he doesn't remember, not because he's being manipulative. Some of his medications affect memory. He also has a wife and young daughter, but the wife's not talking to anybody. Even me."

Dylan asked, "Have you had any psych evals?"

"Not yet." She sighed. "That's kinda the problem. He won't let me."

"What do you mean?" Lily asked.

"He refuses to plead not guilty, and he doesn't want me to challenge competence. He insists he did this and wants to take credit."

"Maybe because he did do it?" Dylan said.

Madeline shook her head. "I haven't been doing this long, but I know human behavior. I was a social worker before law school. I can't be a hundred percent certain, obviously, but I don't think he did this. I think he *wants* to believe he did this. He wants the attention. The first thing he asks me when I visit him is if the news has picked up the case yet."

Lily said, "A lot of people with antisocial personality disorder are narcissistic."

"I know, but I don't think that's what this is."

The door opened just then, and Arlo Ward stepped into the room.

11

Dylan noticed his hands first. Arlo's hands were tiny and pale. The hands of, almost, a teenager. Arlo didn't have much muscle; he was more stringy than anything and looked entirely plain and unnoticeable. Dylan was surprised, considering how long he'd done this and how many clients he'd defended. He'd expected someone else. Someone that looked like they could butcher people with joy.

Arlo had large brown eyes the color of dark chocolate and walked with a limp.

Dylan knew schizophrenics ran the mental health gamut. Many were perfectly healthy and could lead productive lives, but some couldn't function enough to complete even minor daily tasks. At first glance, he couldn't tell which camp Arlo fell into.

"Hi, Madeline," Arlo said as he sat. He turned to the guard and said, "Thanks, Eddie."

"Sure thing. I'll give you guys some privacy, but I'll be right out there if you need me, Ms. Ismera."

"Thank you."

Arlo brought his hands together on the table and smiled at Dylan and Lily. Madeline said, "These are the attorneys I told you about, Arlo. This is Dylan Aster and Lily Ricci."

"Hello," he said.

Arlo smiled wider. His teeth were white and well taken care of. His hands had thick calluses on the palms just underneath each finger but were otherwise unscarred. No large cracks in the skin, no dirt under overgrown fingernails, no hair falling out from malnutrition. He didn't look different from anyone Dylan would see at a hotel or mall.

"So since I got three lawyers here, can I ask something?" Arlo said.

Dylan glanced at Lily. "Sure."

"I'm writing a book about my killings, but some of the inmates here said I can't because there's laws against us making money off our stories. That true?"

Nine times out of ten, when visiting an incarcerated client, the first question they asked their lawyer was, *How long am I gonna be in here?* As far back as Dylan could remember, he had never once been asked what Arlo asked him.

"There was a law," Dylan said, "called the Son of Sam law that barred people from making money off their crimes. But the Supreme Court eventually overturned it, so yeah, you can write a book if you want to. But I don't recommend it."

"Why?"

"Because you'd be admitting you did this."

"I did do it."

There was a silence in the room before Lily said, "You killed those three people?"

He nodded and flashed a slight grin. "Yup. Two of 'em with a bat and the third one burned in the fire. I tied her up good so she couldn't move and roasted her on it."

Madeline sensed the discomfort in the room and quickly said, "Arlo, why don't you tell them about your condition?"

He shrugged. "Not much to tell. I got schizophrenia. I hear things and see things sometimes, but a lot of other p-p-people got it worse."

Arlo closed his eyes and let out a long breath.

"Sorry. I have a stutter that sometimes comes out when I'm n-nervous."

"It's all right," Dylan said. "Take your time."

Arlo inhaled and then let out another long breath. "I graduated high school, worked all sorts of jobs, and my favorite games are Go and *Call of Duty*, both really hard games. I'm not smart, I know that, but I'm not like those people talking to themselves under bridges either."

Dylan glanced at Madeline and then said, "Arlo, why did you kill those people?"

He shrugged. "The demon told me to."

"That's it?"

"Well, no. I'd been fantasizing about it since I was a kid. When I saw them at the gas station, they were lost and had a lot of alcohol with them. So I knew they wouldn't be hard to follow and pick off."

Dylan tapped his finger softly on the table, watching Arlo as he sneezed and apologized. "That's a pretty secluded area. Why were you even up there?"

"I go up there s-s-sometimes. It's quiet, and nobody bothers me."

Lily said, "And you followed them up there?"

He nodded. "They camped really close to some abandoned cabins I sleep in sometimes. Then they got drunk. Wasn't hard after that to pick 'em off."

Dylan leaned back in the chair and stared at him. The softness of his voice and the sadness in his eyes gave him a sympathetic appearance. Many murderers relied on the instinct human beings had to help one another and could seem warm and kindhearted.

"Did you speak to them at all?"

"Nope."

"You just managed to pick them off one by one?"

"Yup."

Lily said, "I saw pictures of the victims. The boys were muscular. Both played football, and one of them was a champion wrestler, but you didn't have any injuries. They didn't fight back?"

"Didn't really have time to. I caught them by surprise. People just aren't c-c-cautious anymore. They think the world is a safe place until it decides to show them it isn't."

Dylan felt a small chill at Arlo's words. He looked to Lily, who cleared her throat and asked a few questions about his mental illness. He spoke without inflection, but there was excitement in his voice when he talked about the crimes. Too much excitement, as though he were describing a trip to an amusement park.

"What type of bat was it?" Dylan interrupted.

"What?" Arlo said.

"The bat. They never found it. Wood or aluminum?"

He hesitated. "Wood."

"What brand was it?"

He shrugged. "I don't know. Just a bat."

"How long was it?"

"Long?"

"Yeah. The length. What was it? There's different lengths."

"I don't know. I ignore stuff like that."

"What type of wood?"

"I don't know."

Lily said, "What type of knife did you use?"

"Hunting knife. Bowie."

"What size?"

He glanced at Madeline and said, "I don't know. I bought it from the store 'cause it was big."

"How long did it take for April Fallows to die?"

"I don't know. Not long."

Lily said, "Where'd you get the bear trap?"

"I found it in one of the cabins up there and kept it in my trunk."

Dylan sat forward. "Arlo, you know they might be seeking the death penalty in this case, right? If you're convicted, you might die for this."

Arlo inhaled deeply and said, "If the Lord wants to take me, the Lord wants to take me. But that book might make enough money for Leena and Amy to be all right after I'm gone."

"Your wife and daughter, I'm guessing?"

He smiled. "Yessir."

Lily said, "What if the Son of Sam law was still in place and you couldn't make any money from your book? Would you still be taking responsibility for these crimes?"

He was silent a moment. "I guess."

"You guess?" Dylan said incredulously. "You *guess* you'd take credit for something that could get you executed?"

"I mean, I would. You're confusing me on purpose, Mr. Aster, and I don't appreciate it."

Dylan grabbed his cell phone off the table and slipped it into his pocket before standing. "It was nice meeting you, Arlo. We're going to let you get back."

"You sure you don't got any other questions?"

"Not right now."

"Okay." He held out his hand. Dylan shook. Then Arlo shook Lily's and Madeline's hands and said, "I'm sorry you had to come out here just for that."

They watched him as he shouted for the guard. Eddie came back in and said, "Ready?"

"Yup. Thanks again, Eddie."

The guard didn't even hold his arm. He had a casual demeanor with him, and Dylan knew, though the guard would probably never admit it, that he liked Arlo Ward. There was, Dylan had to admit, something likable about him.

When Arlo had left, Madeline said, "So?"

Dylan shook his head. "I was sure when I came here, but I don't know. There's something about him copping to this that doesn't sit right."

"It feels like he's lying, doesn't it?"

"Maybe. How far away is the crime scene?"

12

It was afternoon by the time Dylan, Lily, and Madeline trudged up the trail to where the victims had been killed. Coyote Canyon was an hour-and-a-half drive outside Scipio and then a hike of a few miles. The air was muggy and hot, and Dylan's collar was soaked with sweat. Lily had changed into shorts and sneakers from her truck and looked entirely comfortable, while he felt like he was sitting in a sauna fully clothed. The paper file for Arlo's case was tucked under his arm.

Surrounded by thick forest on all sides, Dylan couldn't see much. When they got high enough, they found a viewing spot with a wooden bench. They rested for a minute and looked out over the valley—green trees surrounded by small mountains and hills.

After another half hour of hiking, Madeline said, "It's right here."

There was a grassy open clearing surrounded by trees on three sides. The trail cut through it and headed higher up. Another smaller path led down into a thicket of pines. Dylan put his hands on his hips and looked out over the space. The trees were tall and provided shade. Even on a night with a full moon, there would be little light after sundown—much less beneath a blood moon with dim crimson light.

Nothing was left indicating anything horrific had happened here. As if the earth itself had washed it all away.

Lily said, "Where's the cabin?"

Madeline pointed. "Down this other trail over here."

They took a path that splintered off from the main trail and came to a hill. Down the side of the hill was a cabin with old, chipping wood and two broken-out windows. It looked like it could collapse at any second.

They made their way down to the front door, and Madeline said, "He told me he's been coming up here for two years. I guess when his hallucinations get really bad. The police found a lot of old food containers and wrappers, so someone's definitely been staying here."

A grouping of trees, more densely packed than the rest of the forest, loomed about twenty yards away. Dylan took the file from under his arm and flipped to Arlo's confession. Arlo had written that he'd hidden in the darkness near a dense grouping of pines north of the cabin and watched as the bear trap caught Michael. Then he rushed at them.

Dylan flipped to Holly's statement. She'd told the police she and Michael were exploring the cabin and heard the door slam. It spooked them enough that they decided to head back to camp. About a hundred feet up the trail, she heard something metal snap, and Michael Turner fell to the ground next to her, screaming.

"I noticed Arlo had a limp, but they didn't find any injuries," he said to Madeline, still skimming Holly's statement.

"I asked him about it. He got injured years ago. Hit by a car. Says he can still run just fine, though."

Dylan looked up to the grouping of trees. "So that's the cluster of trees he and Holly agree he was hiding behind, yeah? So he sprints from there, kills Michael, and is fast enough to catch up to Holly, even though she got a head start."

He handed the file to Lily. "Time me."

She took out her phone and opened a timer app.

Dylan went over to the grouping of trees. Lily held up her hand and then dropped it. He flew into a full sprint.

His dress shoes didn't grip well, and he slipped twice before running past them and then bending down to gulp large breaths.

"Man, I am out of shape. I blame McDonald's. Let's sue."

"You also run like a six-year-old," Lily said. "Ten seconds."

"Okay, so Arlo hears the trap go off, and he runs for them as soon as he sees Michael's not getting out of it. Ten seconds. Then he has to kill Michael. With the number of blows it takes with a bat, we have to assume at least twenty to thirty seconds. So after thirty seconds, he looks up and sees Holly gone. Now he has to catch up with her."

Lily nodded and slipped her phone back into her pocket. "Even if she did make wrong turns down the trail, she had a huge head start. Arlo would have to be much faster than you to catch up to her in the dark."

"That limp," Dylan asked Madeline. "Do we have verification it's real?"

She shrugged. "I don't know, I haven't gotten any of his medical reports yet. But he says he was hit by a car and it shattered his femur, which never healed right. So who knows?"

Dylan looked back to the trees and then ran his eyes along the path to the cabin. "He couldn't have made that run. Not fast enough to still catch up with Holly."

Lily said, "Well, congratulations, Madeline. You may very well have an innocent client on your hands."

Dylan let out a long breath through pressed lips and said, "Damn."

13

Lily Ricci sat at Harry's Bar and Grill and nursed her second drink of the night. She kept staring into the glass, lost in thought, before being brought back to where she was by music on the jukebox or the sound of laughter from a group at a nearby table.

Dylan had asked her to go out for a drink again tonight. The visit to the crime scene that afternoon had been rough on both of them, she could tell. But that wasn't why she'd said no. She'd tried hard for the past two weeks to stay neutral with him. She'd never want to be the reason he turned down the job in LA, and yet that was exactly what she wanted him to do. Was she jealous? She'd asked herself that. Was she scared? They'd been partners practically since they'd met in law school; there'd really never been any question about if they'd go into practice together. But it wasn't that either. So what was it?

She thought about the secluded cabin in the woods they'd visited that afternoon and Holly Fallows. What would it feel like to lose the man you loved and your sister at the same time, in about the most horrific way you could lose them?

Lily had left her family when she turned eighteen and wasn't particularly close to them anymore. It made her wonder if she'd be as devastated as Holly.

"A Heineken for me," a man said as he sidled up to the bar next to her, "and another of whatever the young lady's drinking."

Lily smirked as she finished the last of her whiskey. "Now there's something I haven't been called in a long time."

"Really? I would think men would be stumbling over themselves to call you young lady and court your affections."

She looked up at him. The turtleneck and jeans he wore were stylish, but an elastic tied around his prodigious beard made it appear like a tail coming down off his chin. "*Court my affections?* Did you just step out of a time machine?"

He grinned as his drink arrived and he took a sip. "English teacher." He held out his hand. "Nicolas."

She shook. "Lilith."

"Ah, the first woman. The one that rebelled against God and refused to be second to man. Did your parents know that when they named you, or is it just a coincidence?"

"I was actually named after my father's favorite horse."

"Even better." He squinted and turned fully to her. "I'm good at guessing people's backgrounds. So let me take a stab at it: rebellious preacher's daughter strikes out to Las Vegas to get revenge on Mom and Dad and needs a rough exterior to keep the vultures away. Am I close?"

"I'm no rougher than anyone else. We've all got pretty much the same story, don't we?"

He held his bottle of beer up to give a toast, but before a single word came out of his mouth, Lily shot her whiskey down her throat and set the glass upside down on the bar. Then she took his bottle and guzzled the entire thing.

"Wow. I have never seen a woman able to do that. I'm impressed."

She rose and got her bag. "You're impressed because men will always believe two things about a woman: that she's weak, and that she's attracted to him. I'm neither." She patted his arm on her way out. "Thanks for the drink, Teach."

She felt buzzed and thought it better to call an Uber than risk driving, but she didn't feel like going home yet. She asked to be taken to a popular bar on the Strip, then checked her watch. Jake had asked her to come over tonight. He hated when she was late if they had agreed on a time to meet. Why, then, she wondered, was she always late on purpose?

"Visiting or live here?" the driver said.

Lily stared out the window. "Live here."

"What part?"

She checked the time on her phone to make sure her watch was accurate. It would be almost ten in Kansas, where her sister lived.

"I'm sorry," she said. "What did you ask?"

"Where you live?"

"Suncrest."

"Oh yeah? I got friends live up there. Nice place."

She bit her lip, her eyes glued to her phone, and then finally tapped call. The phone rang three times before her sister's groggy voice said, "Lil?"

"Hey, sorry, I don't want to wake you. Did I?"

"You know you did. I have work in the morning."

"I'm sorry, Lucy, I just—"

"The answer is no, and you can't call here this late. Good night, Lily."

"I know, but I won't get a chance for a couple days, since you guys are going to Mom and Dad's."

"No, Lil. Go to bed."

Her sister hung up. Lily watched the screen a moment, then slipped the phone into her bag.

She rested her elbow on the door and stared through the window at the passing casinos and hotels. Glittering neon lighting up the darkness like fire. Some nights the Las Vegas Strip appeared like burning stars in a galactic cauldron, and other nights it appeared like glittering garbage in a dumpster. Tonight it fell somewhere in between.

"I've changed my mind," she said to the driver. "Just take me home."

14

Dylan was sitting in court, waiting for the bailiff to call his case, when he got an email from Madeline. He had started her on the right track but was still hesitant to file an appearance on the Arlo Ward case.

Popular culture portrayed defense attorneys as loving to defend the innocent. After all, who wanted to defend the guilty and help them get away with their crimes? But in reality, innocent clients were nightmares. If the attorney lost the case, an innocent person was going to get locked away. Or worst-case scenario, like in Arlo Ward's case, they might be executed. It produced an atmosphere of obsessive workaholism, with Dylan routinely pulling eighteen-hour days and sleeping at the office. He couldn't get involved with something like that right now, he told himself. It would take him away from Markie too much. And then there was the decision he needed to make about LA.

No, he'd ask his friend Roger to get involved and cocounsel. Madeline could handle it with Roger's help.

Still, gnawing anxiety wouldn't leave him. Arlo was severely mentally ill and clearly didn't understand the implications of what was happening. He only thought about the money he would give to his wife and seeing his face on the news. It was the reasoning a child would have.

Dylan opened Madeline's email. Attached to it was a notice from the prosecution of intent to seek the death penalty.

Dylan thought a moment. *I'll call you in an hour.*

After handling his hearing, a car theft case that he just needed to continue for a month, Dylan went out to the courthouse steps and sat down. The sun was harsh, and he had to put on his sunglasses. The courthouse was busy, so he tucked himself on the far edge of the stairs for some privacy.

"Jackson County District Attorney's Office," the receptionist said.

"Hi. I'm calling about the Arlo Ward case and need to speak to Ms. Whitewolf."

"One moment."

The line clicked, and some downbeat jazz music played. Then a woman's voice on speakerphone said, "This is Kelly."

"Hey, Kelly, I don't know if you remember me, this is Dylan Aster. We've had a couple cases together the past few years."

"I remember. What can I do for you?"

No chitchat. Not a good sign.

"Well, I'm looking into this Arlo Ward case as a favor to a friend. I just saw your notice to seek the death penalty, so I'm assuming there's no offer on the table."

"Yes, that's correct."

"He's severely mentally ill, you know that, right?"

"Mr. Aster, let me stop you right there. I remember you better than you think. You filed thirty-one motions on a burglary case we had a few years ago."

"Thirty-one. You remember the exact number, huh?"

"You strike me as one of those attorneys that will do anything to win, regardless of what actually happened. I don't play by those rules. Arlo Ward brutally murdered three people and nearly murdered a fourth. If I offered anything, I would not be representing the people of the state of Nevada adequately."

Dylan let out a sigh. "Risking a trial with a severely mentally ill defendant isn't the smart play."

"Are you done? I have a lot of work to do."

"I think we're getting off on the wrong foot. I'm calling because I think there's some serious problems with your case. I'm sure after further digging, even more issues are going to surface that'll help us get to reasonable doubt. Madeline just doesn't have the experience to get the jury there yet. I think taking an insanity plea right now is a good resolution for everybody."

Kelly laughed. "So that some third-rate psychiatrist can let him out to do this to someone else? I'll pass."

"Are you seriously saying you're going to execute a man who might have no idea what he's done or why?"

"Yes."

Dylan was stunned into silence. He'd come across prosecutors like this before—stubborn—but rarely on a capital case. The stakes were too high, and any error by either side would be looked at more closely on appeal, so prosecutors were typically more cautious than they might otherwise be.

"It's not right. I don't think he understands what's going on."

"I have a lot of work to do, Mr. Aster, and you're not even on this case. File an appearance and I'm happy to talk as much as you like. Until then, please don't call me."

She hung up. He lowered the phone and tapped it against his palm a few times. This was always the dilemma of any attorney: *Do I do good for those that can't help themselves, or do I do financially well?* Dylan was experienced enough to know you could typically only do one at the exclusion of the other.

Damn it.

He texted his receptionist.

Please file an appearance of counsel on the Arlo Ward case. And continue all my court appearances for the next few months.

15

Dylan drove to the Jackson County Jail by himself and signed in to see Arlo Ward. He had to wait twenty minutes, as it was lunchtime and no guards were available to take him back. When a guard finally came out, he was curt and searched him twice before ordering him not to touch the prisoners.

This time, Dylan was sat in an attorney-client room, and Arlo came in wearing an orange jumpsuit with white slippers. His hands were cuffed, along with his ankles, and the guard led him over to the table. A metal lock was on the floor, and he fastened the ankle cuffs around a metal ring, holding Arlo in place. Then he left.

"Sorry to interrupt lunch," Dylan said.

"It's all right. Wasn't very good anyway." Arlo's chain rattled as he put his forearms on the table. "What can I do for you, Mr. Aster?"

"Madeline and I spoke, and I'm going to be working on your case, Arlo. I'm going to be your lawyer."

A smile appeared on his face, and he said, "Really? That's great. I read that you get a lot of attention in the news. You think we'll get on the news? Not the local news, I've already been on that, I mean the national news?"

"Once the case heads to trial, they'll likely pick it up. They love these types of cases."

The smile didn't leave Arlo's face as he leaned back in his chair. "I started my book. I should send you some of the pages."

"Arlo, do me a favor, take notes if you want, but don't write the book just yet, okay? Anything you write, the jail can confiscate and introduce in court as an admission."

He lost his smile. "I can't do that. I don't r-r-remember things too well. I have to write it now or I'll forget a lot."

"Well, do this then: on every page, write 'To my attorney Dylan Aster.' If you do that, it's a communication to your attorney and it's protected by attorney-client privilege. It can't be introduced against you in court. Can you do that?"

"Yeah, I can do that."

Dylan leaned back in the uncomfortable metal chair and folded his arms. Arlo's grin returned as he said, "You wanna know about them, don't you?"

"Them?"

"Every severe schizophrenic has a 'them.' The CIA, aliens, monsters under the b-bed, ghosts . . . a 'them.'"

Dylan watched him a moment. "Do you have a 'them'?"

He nodded. "Yeah, I do. I was fifteen when I first saw them. It was in a cemetery near my house. An old cemetery that used to be a gallows. So it had a lotta bad people. People that killed women and children. The worst people."

Dylan didn't point out what the implications to him were for that statement and instead said, "What happened?"

"I was walking home from my job at a movie theater and it was late. I was staring out at the cemetery and saw s-s-something move. Real fast and right across the graves." He stopped and stared down at the table. "I looked around but didn't see anything."

Arlo ran a finger over the tabletop. He didn't speak for a long time, and Dylan didn't interrupt his thoughts. It was clearly painful for him, and Dylan saw something across his face he hadn't expected: fear.

"I started walking again, away from the cemetery, and standing right there in front of me was this . . . thing. It looked kinda like a m-man but its flesh was falling off its face. It had really bright-red eyes. It roared at me like an animal would roar. I fell over, and when I looked up, it was gone." He swallowed. "I swear I never ran so fast in my life. But the next day, I took my brother and we went over to the graves and looked around. Then I felt something hit me from behind. It was so strong. Like a w-wave hitting you in the ocean. It knocked me down. The thing was standing there, and I got a real good look at it."

Dylan watched the fear in his face turn to terror. "What was it?"

"A demon. That's the only way I can describe it." He licked his dry lips and wouldn't lift his eyes from the table. "I yelled for my brother, but the demon was gone by the time he came over. There was nothing. No footprints, nothing. That's when I knew something was wrong with me. It started getting worse, I was seeing the demon everywhere, so my school sent me for a psychiatric evaluation. I was told I had schizophrenia with auditory and v-visual hallucinations." He sniffed and wiped his nose with the back of his wrist. "They said it would only get worse."

"Do you still see the demon?"

He nodded.

"Did you see it on the night you think you killed those people?"

"Why'd you say it like that? I *think* I killed them? I did kill them."

Dylan watched Arlo fidget. The pads on his fingers seemed to be worn down. Like he had been rubbing them nonstop for too long.

"Arlo, I know you've been resistant to this, but I'd like a psychiatrist to come here and talk with you for a little bit. I think it would really help me understand what's going on. And we don't have to release his findings to anybody if we don't want to. Would that be all right if I sent him here?"

Arlo shrugged. "Why not? I got all the time in the world. Until they kill me, at least."

———

On the way out of the jail, Dylan called Dr. Leyton Simmons, a psychiatrist he had used on multiple cases. Leyton answered on the third ring and sounded out of breath.

"Working out?" Dylan asked.

"Elliptical. Best exercise for you. What's up?"

"I need you to evaluate a client. He doesn't have any money, but I think I can get the county to pay your fee."

"What's the issue?"

"He says he was diagnosed with schizophrenia at fifteen, and I need to see if that's the right diagnosis."

"What's he charged with?"

"Triple homicide. He insists he did it, had the victims' blood all over him, and gave a full confession, but he's not fitting the mold. I need to know if he's making this all up for the attention."

Dylan heard the elliptical machine stop. "Well, I need a minimum of forty hours with him. Bit booked right now, but in two months I can—"

"Can't wait that long. Trial will probably be going by then. I need you to start today."

"There's no way I can do that, Dylan."

"Then I have no choice. I'm calling in my favor."

He chuckled. "You would do that, wouldn't you?"

Dylan had once defended Leyton's sixteen-year-old son after he was caught selling pot to his buddies at school. He'd gotten the kid community service—and a sealed record when he turned eighteen. Dylan had done the case pro bono for this exact reason: he wanted Leyton to owe him a favor.

"All right, I'll move some stuff around. Text me his information."

"I really appreciate this."

"Well, don't get too excited. In most cases like these, defendants are found competent, and I have to testify that they understood the consequences of their actions. What I find might really hurt your case."

16

Over the next few days, Dylan and Lily focused on nothing but Arlo Ward's case. Madeline assured them she could get the fees for investigators and experts covered by the county and that she would give them half the payment she was receiving: $15,000. Which meant the firm of Aster & Ricci was defending a triple homicide for a little above minimum wage once they put in their several hundred hours.

"The publicity will make up for the low fee," Lily said, sitting in his office.

"What's with you and publicity lately?"

She was silent a moment. "I have some things that are going to require higher income. So I've got marketing plans to make sure our firm sees growth every year. And big cases that get a lot of attention are an important part of that plan."

A week after meeting with Arlo, they were in Madeline's cramped office in Scipio. The office was near the courthouse, and the entire floor had a single shared receptionist. There was one bathroom for the whole building.

The view from the fourth-floor office would have looked out over the courthouse across the street, but stacks of papers were piled up on the windowsill. Only two decorations personalized the office: a Ruth Bader Ginsburg bobblehead figurine and a series of historical flags from Madeline's native Haiti.

A scheduling conference to set the preliminary hearing date was slated for half an hour from now.

"So," Madeline said with a sigh, "what's next?"

Lily said, "Depends on Arlo. He's tying our hands with his refusal to plead not guilty."

"I know, I wish I could get him to change his mind."

Dylan said, "Doesn't matter for now. Right now, we fight everything. Every single thing the prosecution does, we have to fight. If they say the sky is blue, we have to object and file a motion saying it isn't. Complain, challenge, yell, and argue every single issue to try to create chaos for the prosecution. It might get Kelly to soften on offering an insanity plea and sending Arlo to the state hospital."

"Good luck with that," Madeline said. "I've worked with her a lot. She's one of the most stubborn people I've ever met."

"This is different. She's taking a huge risk by not offering anything, since she could lose a trial. She's got some personal thing with this she's not telling us about."

"Like what?"

He shrugged. "No idea. But we need to find out."

———

The assigned judge in Arlo Ward's case was Timothy V. Hamilton. Dylan knew him from multiple cases, as Hamilton used to be a deputy district attorney in Clark County.

There was, in legal jurisprudence, a school of thought known as the Truther's school, expounded on and made famous by a law professor at Yale University.

The basic premise was that a jury and judge should be given all the facts in a case, and nothing should be suppressed. If the police violated someone's constitutional rights, then they should be administratively punished, but the evidence in the case should still come in. "The truth," one of Dylan's Truther law professors had said, "is more important than any violations of the Fourth Amendment, and trials are a search for truth."

Dylan couldn't have disagreed more. Once the police saw that basically nothing would happen to them for violating someone's rights, why wouldn't they do it in every case? The Truther philosophy, he believed, if actually applied in the American legal system, would effectively rip up the Constitution and make it worthless.

Judge Hamilton was a Truther.

The one thing Dylan and Lily had going for them was that Hamilton loved media attention. On one famous case they'd had together when he was still a prosecutor, Hamilton had gone to the media before Dylan could and given interviews to anyone who wanted them. It was something prosecutors rarely did, as they would be accused of trying to taint the jury pool, and the potential for it to backfire was huge. Everyone thought Hamilton had done it to increase the likelihood of a conviction, but Dylan recognized the truth: he had done it because he couldn't help himself. He loved the cameras more than the practice of law. It was difficult to turn down a judgeship when your father and grandfather had both been judges, though. Dylan suspected Timothy Hamilton hated being a judge, since judges almost never got media attention.

Judge Hamilton's courtroom wasn't huge. It could probably hold fifty people, and Dylan had a feeling it would be packed every day if this case went to trial. There was nothing the media liked more than tragic, bloody stories with sympathetic victims and defendants people could hate.

Dylan sat at the defense table next to Lily, and Madeline sat at the end of the table.

Arlo was brought out. He gave a broad smile and shook their hands before sitting. The prosecutors came in a moment later. There were two of them, James Halden and Kelly Whitewolf. James was calm and logical, and Dylan had always liked him. He wondered if he could convince

James that an insanity plea was the best resolution and if James could then convince Kelly.

"All rise," the bailiff said. "Tenth Judicial District for the State of Nevada is now in session. The Honorable Timothy Hamilton presiding."

Judge Hamilton came out and sat down at the bench before saying, "Please be seated." He booted up his computer. "Okay, we're here for the matter of *State v. Arlo W. Ward*. Will Counsel please state their appearances?"

"Kelly Whitewolf and James Halden for the State."

Lily stood and said, "Lily Ricci, Madeline Ismera, and Dylan Aster for Mr. Ward."

The judge looked over to Dylan. "Good to see you again, Mr. Aster."

"You as well, Judge."

"Haven't seen you up here much."

"I prefer home games, Your Honor. Why give up home-court advantage?"

The judge gave a slight grin as he glanced at his computer screen. "So it looks like we're here for a roll call. I'm looking at two weeks from today for a preliminary hearing, Thursday the seventeenth. That work for everybody?"

"It does, Judge," Lily said.

"That's perfect," Kelly said.

"Then we'll get that scheduled. Any other matters to address at this time?"

"Just a minor one, Your Honor," Kelly said, rising to address the court. "Our criminalist, Dr. Lang, found two eyelashes on the body of one of the victims in this case, possibly from the perpetrator, as it did not match any of the victims. We would ask that Mr. Ward be ordered to provide eyelashes for comparative analysis. We could have someone over at the jail today to get it done."

"I would object," Dylan said, rising. "They had ample opportunity to take my client's eyelashes and chose not to do so. It would be inappropriate at this time to force my client to go through such an invasive procedure as pulling his eyelashes."

Kelly chuckled. "That's absurd, Your Honor. The Court does this as a matter of course for nail clippings, blood, hair, urine, and everything else. And there is nothing invasive about providing eyelashes."

"I disagree, Your Honor. Pulling eyelashes is aggressive and could potentially be traumatizing and doesn't provide anything useful to the prosecution. Study after study of cases across the world show that forensic technicians cannot successfully match hair to a suspect at rates higher than random chance would allow. As such, we would be willing to provide one eyelash to the State as a courtesy, but no more."

"This is ridiculous. We would ask the Court to order the defendant to provide the samples immediately."

Judge Hamilton stayed quiet a moment and thought. Kelly was right; this was a routine request that nine times out of ten would be granted without hesitation. The fact that the judge was considering it meant only one thing: he knew as well as Dylan did that this case would be popular and widely televised. Every decision he made would be scrutinized by a national audience of media legal scholars and professors, as well as voters who had the power to remove him in a retention election.

Hamilton would want to appear the consummate thoughtful judge. He couldn't do that by immediately granting prosecution requests without any thought.

"How many eyelashes would the State need to perform a comparison?"

Kelly's jaw might as well have hit the floor with the shock that Dylan saw on her face. She couldn't answer for a moment, then folded her arms and said, "We need an eyelash from every portion of the eye to make a match since we don't know what portion these lashes came from. I would say we need twenty."

"Twenty!" Dylan nearly shouted, feigning outrage. "Your Honor, they might as well shave his entire head. We will agree to one. That is the least invasive number that still provides the State with what they want. Before the Court decides, we would request a hearing on the eyelashes."

"What?" she said, looking at him now. "We don't need a hearing on this."

"I disagree."

"Your Honor, this is an obvious attempt by the defense to stall this case in the hopes that—"

"Judge, that is offensive, and I don't appreciate Ms. Whitewolf's implication. I'm simply trying to preserve my client's dignity and his right to be—"

"Dignity? Are you kidding me? He lost any dignity he had when he held that girl's face into a fire."

"Your Honor! I don't appreciate the State's tone and would ask for the Court to censure Ms. Whitewolf for her—"

"Censure *me*! You can kiss my a—"

"All right," Judge Hamilton quickly interjected, "both of you calm down." He tapped the pen in his hand against his bench a few times. "I'm going to set a hearing on the matter of the eyelashes for the same day and time as the preliminary hearing, and we will address it then. Please, both of you, file briefs on the matter at least one day before that time. Anything else from either party?"

"One thing, Your Honor," Dylan said. "We would ask that Mr. Ward be granted bail."

Kelly yelled, "That's insane! He murdered three people and tried to kill a fourth, and I have no doubt he would attempt to finish the job if he's let out."

"Apparently, Ms. Whitewolf has forgotten the use of the word *allegedly*. This is America, and we're still presumed innocent until proven guilty. I would ask the Court to remind Ms. Whitewolf of this fact."

"Your Honor," she said, calming her voice, "you cannot risk this man getting out. We already addressed bail at the bail hearing and it was denied. There's no reason to renew this issue."

"Judge, Mr. Ward was fully cooperative with the police and is ready to go to trial on this matter. He has no history of criminal behavior, not even a traffic ticket, other than the speeding he allegedly did here. He's got a wife and young daughter, as well as ties to the community through his church. He should be granted bail."

Judge Hamilton, Dylan could tell, wanted to tell him how ludicrous that argument was on a triple homicide, but he didn't. Instead, he simply said, "I am denying bail at this time. Thank you, Counselors, and I'll be looking forward to reading your briefs."

Kelly gave Dylan a hard stare as she left the courtroom, but James gave him a quick nod, acknowledging that he understood this was just part of the job.

Dylan looked at Arlo. He was staring out the windows, and Dylan could tell he hadn't paid attention, maybe hadn't even heard what had just happened.

A scene entered his mind: Arlo Ward, a potentially innocent, severely mentally ill man, strapped to a table while receiving a lethal injection. The machine humming its electric buzz as the first medication paralyzed him, the second anesthetized him, and the third caused his heart to stop. It would take him six minutes to die, and during those six minutes, he would still not understand what was happening to him or why.

If that occurred, Dylan knew he would never forgive himself.

"Well, that was just a straight-up brawl," Madeline said.

"If you thought this was a fight, wait until the trial."

17

Of the two of them, Lily was the legal writer. She was meticulous and nearly unemotional, whereas Dylan was passionate and disorganized and liked the anarchy of being so. In law school, she basically wrote the final paper for him in his legal writing class, and he had taught her tricks for cross-examination so she could get a good grade in trial advocacy.

Dylan read through her brief on the eyelashes a week before the hearing.

"This is way more than I thought we needed," he said. "I only objected because I wanted to see how Hamilton would react. This brief might actually convince him we're right."

She leaned back in her office chair. "I can't do things half-assed. Want me to argue it?"

"Yes," he said, tossing the brief back on her desk.

They were waiting for Dr. Simmons to arrive with his evaluation of Arlo Ward, and Dylan, sitting across the desk from her, decided to ask, "So how's old Jake?"

"Good. He just bought a Bentley."

"I didn't think you cared about stuff like that."

She grinned. "I don't, but I love the look on your face."

Her office phone beeped, and the receptionist said, "Leyton's here."

"Send him back."

Leyton Simmons came in wearing a gray button-up shirt and jeans. He didn't fit the image Dylan had of a psychiatrist. He pictured Freud, and Leyton was more like a haggard basketball coach. He tossed a thick stack of papers held together by a clip on Lily's desk and then sat down on the couch and said, "You want the long version or the short version?"

Dylan said, "How about we split the difference and do the medium version?"

Leyton watched as Lily flipped through his report. "I've spent a total of forty hours with him now and feel comfortable enough giving the Court my opinion. I think schizophrenia is a spot-on diagnosis. The hallucinations, the time of the onset, and the daily struggles he describes are consistent with that diagnosis. We'll have to get an MRI, CT, and some blood work to rule out any physical causes, but I think the original diagnosis is correct."

"The big question, Leyton: Is he lying?"

"First impression? Yes, he's probably lying."

Lily's brows rose. "You really think there's a chance he didn't kill those people?"

Leyton nodded. "I think he's a man who has never had any affection or attention. His father himself was mentally ill and violent. The father became so abusive to him that Arlo was taken from his parents by the State and bounced around foster families for years before his parents regained custody. His mother was never able to give him any type of attention, since she was a victim herself and just trying to survive.

"At school, he was bullied for his excessive thinness and his stutter, probably from kindergarten until he graduated high school. He can't recall having a single friend his entire life; all he did was play video and board games, sometimes for ten or twelve hours a day. It was his escape from the world, which is what the brain attempts to do when suffering from this disorder."

Dylan thought about the damage parents could do even in the absence of abuse. "If we put you on the stand," he said, "what would you testify caused this disorder in Arlo?"

"We don't truly understand the origins of the illness, but it seems to be a combination of predisposition through genetics and massive childhood trauma. The brain attempts to protect itself from trauma as best it can, but if it gets to the point where the trauma is unbearable, the brain can simply schism, and that's what severe schizophrenia is."

"So why do you think he's lying?"

"Despite having a wife and daughter, I think this man has lived in isolation his entire life. I don't believe he can connect with another person in any meaningful way. When I asked him why he got married, he replied that 'it's what you're supposed to do.' For someone that's been so cut off from society and other people, the attraction of taking credit for an incident like this would be massive."

Leyton's cell phone vibrated, and he checked it and sent the call to voice mail.

"There's also the fact that he doesn't have any criminal history. None. Someone capable of butchering three people, mutilating the corpses, and then posing them would very likely have a record of abnormal behavior. Probably several convictions for violent crimes and a history of being unable to complete probation or parole. As far as the juvenile record, a person like this would have a string of incidents displaying cruelty to animals, friends, and siblings, but there's nothing there. The guy's a mouse."

Leyton's phone rang again, and he said, "Excuse me a sec," before typing a quick text in response. "By the way, I tried to talk to his wife and she hung up on me."

Dylan said, "She's refused to talk to anybody. She's probably scared she's going to make the case against him worse."

Lily said, "How would you explain all the evidence against him if you think he's just taking credit for this?"

Leyton slipped his phone into his pocket. "My guess? I think he stumbled on the scene after the murders had taken place and covered himself with the blood. That's why he's not in possession of the bat or the knife and doesn't have any injuries. He also becomes confused about details quickly, and the story changes slightly every time he tells it. In one iteration, Holly Fallows was wearing a T-shirt. In another, a sweater. The beer cans by the fire were Budweiser, and later on he says they were Coors. He told the detectives he hit Michael in the back of the head with the bat when he was caught in the trap, but the coroner determined that all the blows were to the frontal lobe region. Everything he's stated is very detailed and at first glance convincing, but if you look at all his statements from the time of arrest until now, you don't get the impression that there's one coherent story. Don't get me wrong; there's a lot of evidence against him, but gut feeling? I think he's taking credit for something he didn't do."

Dylan said, "And you're willing to testify to all this?"

"I can't say any of this to a medical certainty, but it is my opinion. A guess. If you want to bolster that guess, I do have a suggestion."

"What?"

"Regression hypnosis. It's worked with dozens of patients to bring out details of an event they didn't recall. It's proved accurate in the past and might be worth a shot. There's a risk, though."

Dylan leaned his head back against the chair and stared at the ceiling. "If he admits to it and the prosecution finds out, they can introduce it in court and reinforce the confession."

"Exactly. Up to you, though. I'm not the lawyer. What do you want to do?"

Dylan looked at Lily. "I say we go for it. The case couldn't get any worse for us."

"I agree. I think we should be there, too."

Leyton said, "It needs to be just him and me so he can focus."

"We can get him transported to the sheriff's station and use their interview room with the one-way glass."

Leyton yawned. "All right. Set it up and I'll be there. Remember, though, if this backfires, this was your decision, not mine."

18

Holly couldn't turn around to look at him.

He was dressed in a T-shirt and jeans and had a thick leather brace-let. She'd parked in front of the medical offices building in handicap parking, and he was smoking when their eyes met. He watched her as she got out of her car. When she got to the glass doors, she saw the reflection in the glass of him tossing his cigarette and following her into the building.

At the elevators, he stood behind her. It made the hairs on her neck stand up, and she had to swallow because her throat went dry. She gripped her crutch tighter and wished someone else would come out of an office.

It was just the two of them on the elevator, and she could feel his eyes on her. She leaned against the elevator wall as far away from him as she could.

"What happened?" he said.

She had to swallow again and felt her heart pound. "Car accident," she managed to say without her voice cracking.

He smiled, and a shock of fear went through her. It felt as if a scream was building inside of her and trying to force its way out.

The elevator dinged on the fourth floor, and he got out.

Holly's hands trembled as the doors closed.

She was still fighting back tears when the receptionist led her into the therapist's office. The space was lavishly decorated with beautiful art: African masks, Japanese paintings, classical busts, and carpets from the Middle East. Holly sat in the soft chair and stared at one of the masks. A white mask with red paint running down the cheeks as though it were crying blood. Michael had once worn a mask similar to it for Halloween when they'd first met at a party. He'd commented on her costume, a character named Miranda from a video game Holly used to play with her sister when they were younger. After an hour of talking in the kitchen, they took a walk around the block to be alone and kissed after exchanging numbers.

She had to push Michael out of her thoughts, because she knew she wouldn't be able to function if she fell too deep into that well.

Dr. Mane sat in a chair with his legs crossed and a legal pad in his lap.

"What about your dreams?" he said. "What's been going on there this past week?"

"I still have nightmares. I had a new one last night."

"What was it?"

Holly picked at a hangnail, trying to distract herself with the minor pain it caused. "I was caught in a trap and a shadow was running at me. I couldn't get out. I had to sit there until it got to me."

"What did it do when it got to you?"

She swallowed. "It engulfed me."

"Engulfed you?"

She nodded. "It swallowed me, and all I could see was black." She gave a slight chuckle that held no mirth. "It's funny—when I woke up, I really did think I died. And you know what I thought? *Good.* Why is it fair that April and Mike and Will are dead, but I'm still alive? They were better than me. They would've—"

"We've been through this many times, Holly. Survivor's guilt is part of your posttraumatic stress. It clouds your thinking and makes you believe things that are simply not true."

"But I could've done something," she said, trying to hold back tears. "I could've tried harder to get him out, or maybe . . . maybe April was still alive and if I had just gone back . . . if I'd just gone back . . ."

The tears came now, and she buried her face in her hands. Dr. Mane set a box of tissues on the table in front of her.

"I can't even breathe sometimes," she sobbed. "I don't know who I am or what I'm even doing anymore."

He looked at her sympathetically, and Holly wondered if it was genuine or if therapists were trained to seem like they cared.

"You're surviving. That's what you're doing. And I promise as time passes, things will get better. It will never go away, but it will get better."

She wiped at her tears. "Doesn't feel like it."

19

Kelly sat in her office, talking to one of her daughters on the phone.

"She ate the last pizza slice, Mommy, and that was mine and I told her it was mine. And then she told me she wished I was never born."

Bella shouted from somewhere in the house, "She told me I was adopted!"

"Bethany, listen to me, you girls are sisters and need to be able to work out your own problems. I won't always be there to do it. So you two sit down and figure out how to fix this. I have to go, I'll see you tonight. Love you."

Bethany sighed and grumbled, "Love you, too."

The receptionist knocked on Kelly's door, Holly Fallows trailing behind her. Kelly smiled and motioned for Holly to sit down in the chair across the desk. Holly appeared extraordinarily nervous, holding her purse so tightly in front of her that the tips of her fingers were turning white. Her other arm worked the crutch.

"I appreciate you coming down."

Holly kept glancing at the floor and said, "It's okay."

Her bruises had faded since Kelly's visit to her house last month, but there were dark shadows around her eyes. "How are you feeling?" Kelly asked.

"Okay, I guess. I had the other surgery on my leg." She glanced up shyly, then turned her eyes to the floor again. "It still hurts a lot. I'm scared it won't get better."

"You don't need to be. I've had surgery on my leg, and it just takes time. I had an old soccer injury I was ignoring until I couldn't ignore it anymore."

"You played soccer?"

"I did. All through college. It was brutal, far more violent than the men's division. One girl, a big Polynesian girl twice my size, rushed me and decided to put me out of commission. She hit me like an NFL linebacker and broke my leg in two places."

Holly, for the first time since coming in, looked Kelly in the eyes. "I played three years in high school."

"It's a great sport. It's a shame it's not more popular here."

Holly didn't say anything and returned her gaze to the floor. The melancholy in her eyes was pronounced. Kelly pictured her crying herself to sleep every night.

"Holly, I wanted to go through something with you, and it's not something I like to do over the phone. I know you couldn't identify the man who did this, but I'm hoping now that you've had some time to process it, you can recall some facts that help us make sure Arlo Ward can never hurt anyone again. Do you feel up to talking about it?"

Holly nodded but didn't look up from the floor. "It's April's birthday next week. She would've been twenty-two."

Kelly looked at her sympathetically but said nothing. The full impact of a murdered family member didn't hit someone right away. It developed over time, as the loved ones saw that the victim really was gone. It left a gap in their lives, a vast open space that rarely filled again.

When her mother had been murdered, for weeks afterward Kelly would wake up and rush down to her parents' bedroom, expecting to see her there. She remembered that the day she stopped running down in the mornings was the saddest day of her life.

"I'm so sorry. You're too young to have to see this side of life."

Holly had tears in her eyes but didn't look up for a long time. When she did, the tears streamed down her cheeks, though she didn't speak until Kelly offered her some tissues.

"Thanks," she said, wiping away the tears. "I'm ready."

Kelly picked up a pen and brought out a fresh legal pad from a drawer. "Tell me about the gas station attendant, Henry Dykes."

Holly shrugged. "We stopped and asked for directions because the GPS wasn't working up there. He gave us directions and joked around with us."

"I looked up Mr. Dykes's history. He's been to prison before."

Holly nodded. "I don't doubt it. He had really faded tattoos on his hands and said he'd gotten them 'inside.' I didn't know what that meant until Mike told me when we'd left. Why are you asking about him?"

Kelly let out a breath. "Well, we can't find him. He didn't show up for work the next morning."

"You think it was him?"

"No, but we need to talk to him. I'm sure he'll turn up down the line."

"He said he likes to camp up where we were going, if that helps. That's why he knew the area so well."

Kelly nodded. "Well, let's forget about Mr. Dykes for a second. I want to ask you about what happened at the cabin. When you were inside, you heard the door slam, and that's the first time you realized someone else was there, right?"

She nodded. "Yeah, I think so. It was windy, too, though. So I don't know."

"How long was it after the door slammed that you left the cabin?"

"Right then."

"How long did it take to get outside?"

Holly took some tissues and dabbed at her eyes. "Like maybe ten seconds. Mike just thought it was a cool old cabin and wanted to look around. When the door slammed, we both knew we should leave. We started walking back to camp, and I heard this, like . . . loud sound. Like a metal pipe hitting another metal pipe or something. I thought maybe it was Will or April trying to scare us, but then Mike . . ." She paused a moment as more tears came. "Then Mike screamed in a way I've never heard anybody scream before. He fell down and I saw that thing on his leg. It had ripped his calf apart. I could see the bones in his leg." She sniffled and said, "I thought it was an accident at first, but then I realized that the trap wasn't there when we walked to the cabin."

Kelly scribbled a few notes. "Tell me exactly what you saw when you looked at those trees and saw the man there. Describe him."

Holly looked up to the ceiling as though recalling a memory she didn't want to remember. "Mike saw him first and told me to run. The man was already running at us by the time I saw him. I wouldn't leave Mike, but . . . he pushed me away and kept screaming for me to run . . . so I did."

"Was this man tall, short, wide?"

"Normal height, I guess. And his face was completely dark. That's why I think he was wearing, like, a mask or something. I couldn't see any part of his face."

"What about his hands? Was he wearing gloves?"

"I didn't see any gloves."

"What kind of pants?"

"I don't know for sure, but they looked like jeans."

"Shirt?"

"I think white, but in my dreams it's sometimes black, so I don't know. Maybe it was black and I just can't remember it that way when I'm awake." She wiped some more tears away and crumpled the tissues in her hand. "My therapist says trauma affects our memories."

"Was he limping?"

Holly shrugged. "I don't know. He was moving fast, though."

"When he started chasing you, how far behind you was he?"

"I don't know, I wasn't looking back. I got lost because the trail went three different ways. I didn't look back until I got to the cliff." She swallowed. "Then I saw him on the trail behind me. I could see he was holding something, and it looked like a baseball bat. I knew he was going to kill me. So I closed my eyes and jumped."

"When you came to a stop below after jumping, did you look up to see him?"

"No, I blacked out from a concussion. When I woke up, I had to crawl out to the road. I don't know how long it took me. I just knew I didn't want to die there, and that he was probably coming down to find me. But someone eventually pulled over and called 911."

"Do you remember anything else about what he looked like? Beard, tattoos, scars, anything that stands out about him? Anything we can use to identify him?"

Holly wiped the remaining tears away. "No, I told the police everything I remember."

Kelly exhaled. This was all information she already had. She was hoping Holly would remember bits and pieces she had blocked out. Close to a traumatic event, memories were hazy and fragmented. In many victims, they solidified only after enough time had passed. She would have to try again in another couple of weeks with Holly to see if she remembered anything else.

"Is there anything you remember, Holly, that you didn't tell the detectives?"

Holly thought for a few moments, staring at the floor. "He was breathing really heavy."

"When?"

"When he was running at me. He wasn't that close, but his breathing was loud enough that I could hear it. He was out of breath. That's the only thing I think I didn't tell the police." She looked into Kelly's eyes. "Can I ask you something now?"

Kelly crossed her legs and put the pen down. "Of course."

"Did my . . . did my sister really die in the fire like the news says?"

Kelly hesitated. "We think William was away from the camp, maybe relieving himself or getting some more wood for the fire, when Arlo Ward tied your sister up and put her on the fire. Her screaming probably drew William back, and Arlo Ward hit him at that point. It took several blows to render him unconscious, and then Arlo Ward slit his throat and William died from blood loss."

"What about April?"

Kelly glanced away. She didn't want to be honest here but knew Holly would find out the truth regardless. "He held her face in the fire for three to five minutes. That's how long the coroner thinks it took for her to suffocate to death."

"And then that's when he . . . when he cut them up?"

Kelly nodded. "Yes."

Holly swallowed. "I can still hear him breathing. I'll be in the shower and hear him breathing behind me, but there's no one there. Does that ever go away?"

Kelly didn't answer for a bit but flexed her jaw muscles to have some type of motion. The thought of this young woman suffering decades from now because of one piece of human garbage filled her with nothing but pure, hot rage.

"I don't know. I'm sorry."

Holly nodded and then used her crutch to stand herself up before Kelly could help her. "I'm sorry, too," she said bashfully. "It must be hard that I don't remember anything."

"You have nothing to be sorry about. And it doesn't matter anyway. He confessed. It would just be nice if you could point a finger at him during the trial and say it was him."

"Trial?" Holly said, her eyes widening. "I have to see him again?"

"We will likely have to go to trial and have you testify, Holly. I know it's hard that you have to see him again, but most victims in cases like these tell me afterward they were so, so glad they did it. You get to tell him to his face he's not going to beat you. And I'll be there the entire time protecting you. Nothing is going to happen, I promise."

Holly didn't say anything, just seemed to zone out a moment before saying, "I better go. I need to take some pain meds, and I won't be able to drive after."

Kelly followed her to the door, and before Holly could leave, Kelly gave her a hug. After a short time—seconds—Holly trembled and started sobbing.

Kelly let her cry as long as she wanted. It brought up a memory she hadn't thought about in years: a young girl crying in the arms of a police officer who had just informed her that her mother was dead. Later that night, Kelly had heard two officers talking about how a man had tackled her mother off her bike, raped her, and stabbed her to death. It was years before Kelly could even remember that she'd heard the officers discussing it. Her mind had simply shut that memory out.

She felt the emotion like a stone in her throat but refused to give it release. She would use it instead. The anger and disgust and sadness would fuel her work on this case, and she needed it. Because the first hearing with Ward's attorneys had taught her something: this case was going to be one of the toughest fights she'd ever have.

20

It was that Friday when Dylan and Lily were led back to the one-way glass in the Jackson County Sheriff's Office interview room. Kelly Whitewolf was already there in the hallway with a clove cigarette dangling between her fingers. She didn't acknowledge either attorney with a greeting and instead said, "I'm recording this."

It was a warning, Dylan knew: *You go through with this and it blows up in your face, I'm showing it to the jury.*

"That's fine," he said.

Seated in the room was Leyton with Arlo across from him. A detective poked his head in and said they could begin.

"Look at me and only me, Arlo . . . now, I'd like you to look into this penlight I'm going to hold near my eyes. I'm going to move very slowly from left to right and back. I want you to focus only on the light and count each time I move it from one direction to the next. Do it quietly. You ready?"

"Yeah."

This was the attention phase, and it took Leyton a good four minutes before Arlo's eyes appeared to glaze over, and he didn't blink. Then Arlo closed his eyes.

"Arlo, I would like you to relax. Relax every muscle, starting with your calves, then your thighs . . . now your stomach and back . . . now your arms, all the way from the shoulder to the tips of your fingers. As you feel yourself relaxing, I want you to picture yourself lying down on a fluffy, soft, white cloud . . ."

The words carried on for a long time, and Leyton spoke progressively more slowly and quietly until he was almost whispering a word every few seconds.

"You will now feel my hand softly touch your shoulder. And when it does, you will drift inside the cloud. The rest of the world doesn't exist. It's only you and your cloud in the sky, above the world. You breathe the fresh air and it relaxes you more. You couldn't move your muscles even if you wanted to because they are so relaxed . . ."

Within another three or four minutes, Arlo's body swayed in a slow, circular motion. Leyton leaned forward and said, "Arlo, I want you to picture something for me. It's a warm night in May, and you're in Coyote Canyon. There are four campers there, and you're there with them. Do you see them?"

"Yes."

"Where do you see them?"

Arlo murmured, "I see them at their campsite near a fire."

"Tell me what you see."

Arlo didn't speak for a moment. "There's two tents and a buncha beer cans on the ground near the fire. I'm hiding behind the trees."

"Who do you see first?"

"I see the girl first. She's in the fire. There's a man there, too. Both of them are dead. There's something else there moving around."

"Thing?"

"Yes."

"What do you mean by 'thing'? What else is there besides the man and the girl, Arlo?"

He swallowed, though his eyes stayed closed. "A demon."

"What's the demon doing?"

"He's cutting their bodies with something."

"With what?"

"A knife or a saw. He has hands like a man."

"Can you see what the demon looks like besides his hands?"

"No, it's too dark and I'm scared. I stay quiet."

"What else do you see?"

"The moon is red. The demon stops and looks at it. Then he looks right at me."

"What do you do when he looks at you?"

Arlo continued to sway, but his movements grew slower. "I don't move. He starts cutting the bodies again."

"What happens then?"

"He leaves, and I hear screaming. A man and a woman. I wait a long time. Then I come out and go to the bodies."

"Do you smell or hear anything?"

"I smell something really strong."

"What is it?"

"It smells like lighter fluid. The girl has it on her."

"What do you do now?"

"I hike down to the cabin I was staying at because my phone is there. There's another man on the way. His leg is caught in a trap and his head is crushed into a mess."

Leyton leaned across the table and lightly touched Arlo's shoulder. "What do you do then?"

"I get my phone out of the cabin. I'm going to call the police."

"Do you?"

"No."

"Why not?"

"Because the demon already killed all of them."

"So what do you do instead?"

Arlo was silent a long time, his lips curling and uncurling. He was fighting whatever thoughts he was having right then.

Leyton softly touched his other shoulder now.

"Tell me what you're doing, Arlo. You are perfectly safe and relaxed. You want to talk about what's happening. Tell me what you're doing."

"I'm g-g-going . . . ," he finally stuttered. "I'm going to the girl's body and the other man's at the campsite. The . . . the demon cut them really bad. Cut their arms and legs off and did really bad things with them. I don't want to look at them, but I need to. I get their blood in my hands. It's still warm."

"What do you do with their blood?"

"I put it all over me. I didn't like touching the girl's body parts."

"Why not?"

"Because I felt bad for her."

Leyton let him sit a moment quietly. "Why did you take their blood and put it over yourself?"

"I thought if people knew it was me and not the demon I might become famous. Like the Night Stalker. You see him on TV shows. I want to be famous like the Night Stalker."

"Why do you want to be famous?"

"Everybody loves famous people."

Leyton touched his shoulder again. "Where's the demon right now? Can you see him?"

"He's watching me. He laughs at me. I don't know why he laughs at me. It makes me really angry, and I want to yell at him to shut up, but he stops laughing and leaves."

"Where does he go?"

"Down the t-trail."

"Does he look like a man, Arlo?"

"Yes. He took the shape of a man."

"Do you recognize him?"

"I don't know."

"If you saw a picture of him, would you recognize him?"

"Maybe."

"What are you doing now that the demon has left?"

Arlo swallowed. "The demon yells at me from the forest. He tells me I deserve to be famous. So I have to make sure there's a lot of blood. I get more of it. I get some in my mouth and throw up. I get scared and run back to my car and start driving."

"Where are you going?"

"I'm going home. I'm so scared. I'm driving really fast because I'm so scared."

Arlo's face contorted in fear.

"What's happening now, Arlo?"

"Police lights are on behind me. I'm so scared. But I want to be famous. The demon said I should be famous."

Leyton glanced back, as though saying, *I told you,* and then turned back around. "Is it the same demon you've seen since you were a child?"

"Yes. He tells me I want to be famous."

"So what do you do when the police pull you over?"

"One of them shines his flashlight in my car and sees the blood. He's telling me to get out of the car. I'm telling the police I did it. I'm telling them what I saw, but I'm telling them it's me, and they believe me."

Arlo was clearly agitated and had started to sweat. Leyton softly touched his shoulder and said a few words about relaxation.

"Arlo, did you kill those people?"

"No."

"Did you see who did?"

"Yes."

"Are you telling the truth?"

"Yes."

Leyton asked him the same questions again, and Arlo answered the same.

Kelly put out her clove cigarette in an ashtray on top of the garbage can in the hallway. "He's full of shit. See you in court."

21

Dylan sat at his desk and read the official offer letter from the law firm in Los Angeles. He kept looking at the compensation package: $300,000 per year, full benefits, a leased car, and a condo near the courts paid for by the firm. It was more than he had ever dreamed he could get.

To get that, he would have to leave Lily, the freedom of his own practice, and the ability to make his own schedule. Not to mention leaving Mama and Markie if they didn't want to go with him. He told himself he'd come back every chance he got, that he'd stay involved, make sure both of them were getting the support they needed, but how long would it be before those promises proved as empty as they sounded to him now?

His phone dinged, indicating the email he was waiting for had arrived—a psychological profile of the murderer of April Fallows, William Page, and Michael Turner. An ex–FBI agent Dylan knew would write them up for paying clients, mostly prosecutors, but occasionally defense attorneys.

Profiling, though a pseudoscience at best in Dylan's estimation, could occasionally provide insights into potential suspects. But it wasn't based on some magical psychological inevitability like the FBI wanted portrayed to the public. It relied on basic deductive reasoning. If a crime had occurred in the middle of the day during the workweek, it was a good guess that the perpetrator was unemployed. Assumptions like that could be used to whittle down a list of suspects. Those were the types of logical deductions Dylan looked for in the reports.

He skipped the description of the crime, the victimological traits, and the crime scene dynamics and went directly to the summary.

Murder is typically ancillary to the primary intent of the perpetrator, and not the main goal in and of itself. The primary intent underlying murder falls into three categories: sexual motivation, emotional or "cause-specific" murder, and criminal enterprise. The particular set of murders in State of Nevada v. Arlo W. Ward *has all the hallmarks of a sexual slaying without a sexual act. No semen or signs of forced sexual intercourse were observed in any of the deceased victims, according to the coroner. The SAFE kit administered to the living female victim by a forensic nurse at Roosevelt Hospital found no signs of bruising, tearing, or other injuries that would indicate sexual assault.*

The killings show extreme inefficiency and lack of planning, indicating an inability to think in rational terms. The killer simply saw an opportunity and acted, which indicates he lacks control, and this type of disorganization is concomitant with severe mental illness. Potential disorders include schizoaffective disorder or schizophrenia, or an organic origin such as frontal lobe injury or lesions on the brain.

Dylan skipped to the paragraphs about Arlo.

Mr. Ward has given a detailed confession to the murders. However, there are discrepancies in his account. Law enforcement will sometimes ask about false information in order to ferret out an actual perpetrator from one just wishing to take credit. In this case, law enforcement told Mr. Ward several false details about the crimes, which Mr. Ward agreed had occurred.

While Mr. Ward certainly meets the criteria for a perpetrator of this sort—bullied, shy, insecure, unusually attached to a distant and cold mother, harboring hatred and rage toward a violent father, and suffering from severe mental illness—many inconsistencies and the fact that he admitted to incorrect details of the killings potentially hint at his taking credit for these murders in an attempt to gain notoriety. For this analysis, the recording of the regression hypnosis session with Dr. Leyton Simmons was viewed, and we cannot rule out the possibility that Mr. Ward was telling the truth under hypnosis. It is possible, though not highly probable, that he simply came upon the scene, saw a man who he perceived as a demon, and is attempting to take credit for killings he had no part in perpetrating.

It is this profiler's opinion that Mr. Ward is possibly not the perpetrator of these crimes. A real chance exists that they were committed by another male in the manner Mr. Ward describes.

Dylan let out a long breath and put his phone down before swiveling in his chair and staring out of the windows at the courthouse across the street. Mondays were always the busiest days, and now that lunchtime was over, lines had formed again to get to the afternoon court sessions.

As he was watching a young mother pull her stroller up the stairs and wondering why no one was helping her, his phone rang. It was his investigator, Brody.

"I was just thinking about calling you," Dylan said. He hadn't spoken to Brody since giving him the files on Arlo Ward and asking him to dig up whatever he could.

"Yeah, well, it must've been your Spidey-sense, because I need your help."

"What's up?"

"I'm going to text you an address, and you need to drop whatever you're doing and get down here. Bring Lil, too. You're gonna need to tag team it."

"You're making me nervous now, Brody."

"You should be nervous. I'm at the cabin up at the crime scene."

22

Lily drove, and Dylan sat staring out the window at the passing land-scape. He had asked Brody to search the cabin Arlo claimed to have stayed in. The police had searched the area in the dark after they already had a suspect who'd confessed, and in situations like that they usually only did a once-over and had a tendency to miss things.

It didn't help his anxiety that Brody wouldn't tell him what he had found. Never a good sign when your own investigator says you better see it in person.

"Bet it never gets this gray in LA," Lily said, looking up at the darkening sky.

Dylan watched some boys in a field throwing around a football. "Wouldn't you take an offer like theirs? Don't you want to be rich?"

"I just want security, Dylan. I grew up as poor as you did on a farm that was barely scraping by. I don't want to be poor again, but I know money's not the measure of being rich either."

"I know that."

"Says the guy abandoning something he loves for something he hates in exchange for money."

"I'm not exchanging something I love for something I hate."

"Seriously?" she said as she turned up a dirt road leading to the canyon entrance. "You think they're paying you three hundred grand to defend the innocent? You're going to be doing business litigation.

Defending big companies when they've wronged some poor soul and want to get away with it. You'll be the big guy crushing the little guy, Dylan."

The annoyance he felt with her words dug into him, and it dug deeper that she would bring all this up now when he had enough to think about. Lily had, from the first moment they'd met, always been honest with him, and he in turn was always honest with her. Most of the time, it made their partnership stronger, but occasionally tempers would flare when something was said that cut a little too deep. Truth seemed to always hurt more than lies.

"Well, someone's gotta be the bad guy," he said, shocking her enough that he knew she wouldn't bring it up again for a while.

They parked and hiked up to the cabin. Dylan was drenched in sweat by the time they arrived, but Lily, like the last time, seemed unaffected, which annoyed him even more.

Brody stood near the cabin with Paul, a nephew who worked as his assistant while he was trying to break into the private investigation business. Paul looked and dressed like he was still in high school. Brody wore black dress pants and a yellow button-up shirt with Gucci glasses, even though he'd known a hike was involved. His bald head glistened with sweat, and he took a small handkerchief out and wiped it away.

"Can't you just wear shorts and sneakers once in a while, man?" Dylan said.

"*Pfff*, that is straight-grandpa-Fourth-of-July-barbecue uniform. I ain't about that. You need to get yourself some style, Dylan. This 'humble kid from the Podunks' look is played." Brody saw Lily and smiled. "You're still running around with this miscreant?"

"What can I say?" Dylan heard the forced smile in her voice. "He needs someone to look after him."

"Fair enough. Y'all know Paul."

They greeted each other, and then Dylan said, "So what's the big secret?"

"See for yourself."

Brody turned toward the cabin and led them past it. Down the trail, through a thicket of trees, was another cabin much like the first. Dylan guessed it was a couple hundred feet away, and it wasn't visible from the trail because of the trees.

Brody opened the door and went inside with Paul and Lily beside him. As Dylan followed them, he noticed that cardboard covered the windows, blocking the view of the interior.

"Was this open when you got here?" Lily asked.

"On the record, yes. Off the record, every former cop knows how to break into a home without damage."

Brody hadn't spoken much about his time at the Las Vegas Police Department. Other than saying he rose in the ranks quickly, all the way to detective sergeant in only a handful of years, and then was mysteriously fired. Not really fired, but fired in that they made his life miserable and hoped he would quit.

The cabin was the cluttered disaster Dylan was expecting. Garbage and abandoned junk everywhere. Profanity was spray-painted on the walls; the stink of mold filled the air.

Brody led them to the bedroom. The closet was open. Inside, Dylan saw something that made his stomach drop. For the first time in a long time, he was at a complete loss for words.

It was a baseball bat.

23

Paul and Lily stood in front of the closet, while Brody sat on the edge of the dilapidated bed, which had no mattress. Dylan paced as he bit his fingernails. Lily said, "Dylan, your fingernails."

She always reminded him when he did it, and they had an agreement that he would stop when she mentioned it. In exchange, he would tell her when she ground her teeth, something that had caused her trips to the dentist.

"Crap," Dylan said.

The bat was hidden underneath some garbage Brody had kicked aside. Paul reached out to touch it, and Lily and Dylan both shouted, "Don't touch it!"

He startled and pulled his hand back as though he'd touched a boiling pot of water.

"The second you touch that," Dylan said, "the four of us become witnesses in this case, and we could be forced to testify against Arlo."

Paul took a step back. "Did the police search the cabin?" he asked his uncle.

Brody nodded. "Probably. I didn't see it in any of the reports, though. If they did search it, they must've just done a quick run-through. Or somebody put it here after, hoping the police would find it."

Lily turned away from the closet and looked over the bedroom as she thought. "Okay, so he leaves the murder scene, stashes the bat, then drives home. Why? Why not toss the bat over a cliff where the police aren't likely to find it?"

Dylan shook his head. "I don't know."

Brody said, "Maybe it's just a random bat someone left up here?"

Dylan took a few steps closer to the bat. The wood was light in color, almost white, and clean. "I don't see any blood. He could've cleaned it, but it also might not be the murder weapon." Dylan put his hands on his hips. "We got a bigger problem. Do we have an obligation to turn this over?"

Brody said, "Yes," and Lily said, "Maybe," simultaneously.

"Of course we do," Brody said. "It's possibly the murder weapon."

"It's also evidence against our client that *we* found after speaking with him. That's protected by attorney-client privilege if we don't intend to use it in court."

Brody's brow furrowed, and he stared at the bat. The four of them were silent for a moment before Brody said, "Well, this here is a lawyer problem, and I got somewhere to be. Good luck with this circus."

Dylan watched him and Paul leave and then turned back to the closet and let out a long breath. "Why? Why would Arlo hide the bat but take credit for everything else? If it's the murder weapon, he'd want it on him as more proof he did it. None of this makes sense."

"Let's ask him about it," Lily said.

Dylan nodded and said, "Should we keep this between us for now?"

She shook her head. "If it turns out to be the murder weapon and we concealed it, we'll get more than thrown off the case. The judge would file bar complaints and ask for sanctions. He might even hold us in contempt. I say we be honest up front."

"Okay, I'll call the court and schedule an emergency meeting." Dylan sighed. "And I guess we better let Kelly Whitewolf know about the meeting, too."

Dylan stared at Judge Hamilton's photos on the walls of his chambers. There was an autographed photo of him with Ed Sheeran, and one with him shaking hands with Jay Leno at a restaurant. Several more with local politicians and a few senators and congressmen. Dylan scanned his bookshelf and noticed among the lawbooks and treatises were a few books on filmmaking and the history of Hollywood.

Kelly Whitewolf came in by herself and didn't say hello to either of them as she sat in one of the chairs before the judge's desk. He only had two chairs, and Lily sat in the other while Dylan leaned against the wall.

Hamilton came in a second later wearing his robe. He removed it, revealing a white button-up shirt and black slacks, and hung the robe on a coatrack. He loosened his tie and sat down and said, "All right, Mr. Aster, I've taken a fifteen-minute recess, but I've got thirty people waiting to have their cases called. Make it quick, please."

"No worries, Judge. I just have a hypothetical I need to run by the Court."

"A hypothetical?"

"Yeah," Dylan said, glancing at Lily. "Suppose there's this lawyer that's working a murder case. And suppose further that he goes somewhere the defendant might have gone. He has no particular agenda in going there, but he stumbles upon something the police might have missed."

Hamilton leaned back in his seat. "Uh-huh. And what does this hypothetical attorney find there?"

"Hypothetically, maybe he, again hypothetically . . . maybe finds one of the murder weapons the police have been unable to locate."

"What!" Kelly shouted, nearly jumping out of her chair.

"I said hypothetically."

"Get me that weapon *now*," Kelly said.

"Your Honor," Lily said calmly, "the problem is that informing the State about this hypothetical murder weapon would be a violation of the duty to the attorney's client. So this hypothetical attorney is in a catch-22. They have an obligation to hand the evidence over, but by doing so they violate their duty and attorney-client privilege. I would remind the Court of *Michigan v. Stetson*, in which a suspect in a kidnapping had told his attorney where the victim was, and the State attempted to force the attorney to tell them. On emergency appeal, the Sixth Circuit Court of Appeals stated the attorney was under no obligation to violate privilege, which is the most protected facet of our legal system. Even to save a life."

Kelly didn't waste a moment. "The reasoning in *Stetson* and its progeny has been rejected in three circuits and will no doubt be rejected in the Tenth soon, Judge. And the attorney in *Stetson* did the right thing and told them where the victim was. I would ask that Mr. Aster and Ms. Ricci hand the weapon over to the State immediately. And if they have handled it in any way, I will be calling them to the stand, so I ask that they be removed from this case."

"Hypothetically," Dylan said with a twinge of anger in his voice, "this attorney wouldn't be stupid enough to touch anything. I had a friend who was a criminal defense attorney, Your Honor. A client of his called him on the phone and said, 'I just robbed a bank and have the money and gun in my car. What do I do?' My friend said he had the wrong number and hung up. The hypothetical attorney in the matter before you could have done what my friend did and never mentioned this to the Court, and no one would have been the wiser. If said attorney did bring it up to the Court, it would be in good faith, and it would be a miscarriage of justice to punish their client for the attorney attempting to do the right thing. Hypothetically, of course."

"Bullshit," Kelly said. "They need to hand the weapon over and be withdrawn from this case, Your Honor."

Hamilton laid his head on the back of the chair. He stared at the ceiling for what seemed like a long time while he tapped a pen against his desk. "Here's what I'm going to do," he finally said. "Ms. Whitewolf, draft a search warrant for me to sign, and then you are free to send your detectives to have another look wherever the weapon is located to see if they can find anything. As far as I'm concerned, these hypothetical attorneys' search and your detectives' search are two unrelated incidents and hence do not violate privilege."

"That's entirely improper," Kelly said. "I want to call them to the stand to testify about what they—"

"No one has touched the weapon, it was simply seen. Your detectives, should they find the weapon, can offer the exact same testimony either attorney could offer. I'm not ordering them off the case. Is there anything else?"

Kelly's jaw muscles clenched, and she stood. "No." She turned and left.

Hamilton watched her leave and then went to the coatrack to get his robe. Lily had followed her out, and Dylan was near the door when Hamilton said, "Mr. Aster?"

"Yeah, Judge?"

"I appreciate you not saying *wrong number* on this."

24

The night before a preliminary hearing was usually a rush of poring over evidence and lining up arguments, but Dylan and Lily had spent so much time doing that, they felt they were getting diminishing returns at this point. So instead, they picked up dinner and drove out to his house, where Jake, Lily's boyfriend, joined them.

She had met Jake while browsing at a bookstore. Lily was a sapiophile, and chitchat bored her immediately, so Dylan wondered what Jake had said to capture her attention enough to go out with him. Despite Lily's joke about the Bentley and the fact that he did something for work involving trading derivatives on Wall Street, he seemed down to earth enough.

Dylan sat with his mama, Markie, and Jake at the table. Lily got water for everyone before sitting down to eat. Burritos from a nearby Mexican grill.

"Dylan, guess what?" Markie said with a mouthful of burrito.

"What?"

"I got second in my spelling bee today."

"No way! That's awesome."

"Yeah, the word I lost on was *inchoate*. I thought it had a *k* in it, but it don't. But it wasn't fair because Mr. Miller gave Tommy Preston the word *blanket* right after me and he won. Why would they give him *blanket* and me *inchoate*?"

Lily said, "Some men are intimidated by really smart girls because they know men can get by pretending to know things, while women have to actually know them."

Markie nodded as though she already knew that and took another bite of burrito. "All the judges were boys. That was unfair, too, but I didn't say anything."

"Well, now you know. Next time say something. Don't let them get away with it."

"Or," Dylan said, "it was just unlucky that she got a harder word. Not everything's a conspiracy."

Lily rolled her eyes. "You couldn't understand unless you've been through it, Dylan. Isn't that right, Mama?"

"Sure as hell is. Your papa, Dylan, Lord rest his soul, didn't understand, either, until he saw how all the men at my work were getting pushed up and I didn't get nothing, even though I worked twice as hard."

The conversation brought up a memory Dylan didn't want to think about: the last words his father had said to him.

Take care of your mama and Markie, Dylan. You the man of the house now.

Take care of them. Dylan had done the best he could to make ends meet but always felt guilty that he couldn't give his mother and sister the life they deserved. And he had spoken with his mother's social worker, who told him her schizophrenic delusions would only get worse with time. At some point, she would need to be put into a facility, and that would run upward of four grand a month.

Dylan wondered how much of his temptation to move to Los Angeles was because of his mother's condition, and how much was his own desire for wealth. Was he just trying to convince himself LA was what he wanted—like Lily thought—or did he actually want it?

Dylan excused himself to go to the bathroom. He splashed water on his face and took a few deep breaths before going back out. He said, "We should go through things one more time, Lil."

The files were in his car, so Dylan retrieved them. When he came back in, Jake was kissing Lily good night and saying his goodbyes to Mama and Markie. Lily waved to him from the front door as he left.

While Mama cleaned up and got Markie ready for bed, Dylan spread the files on the coffee table in the living room.

Lily sat down without a word and picked up the first few reports.

———

After several hours of going through documents, Dylan's vision became blurry, so he and Lily took a break for beer.

Tomorrow, he fully expected Kelly Whitewolf to lose her mind in court. Dylan had had Brody serve a subpoena to every single witness even tangentially related to the case. From the officer taking Arlo's photo when he was booked, to Kelly's receptionist on the day they filed the case. Oddly enough, the only one Brody couldn't find was the gas station attendant that was the last person to see the victims alive. He hadn't shown up to work the day after the murders. Dylan had asked Brody to dig deeper into him.

He had also used an old trial lawyer's trick where he served the subpoenas at the last minute so Kelly wouldn't have time to prepare, or a lot of witnesses wouldn't be able to show up and Dylan could ask that they be held in contempt. He'd had more than one case where someone arrested for contempt no longer cooperated with the prosecution.

If she'd had the time, Kelly would have filed motions to quash the subpoenas, stating that he shouldn't be allowed to call most of the witnesses, but Dylan had deprived her of that. On one occasion when he'd pulled that little trick, a prosecutor shouted so long at him that his high blood pressure caused him to faint and he had to be taken out of court on a stretcher.

Dylan and Lily sat on the swinging bench on the porch.

Crickets filled the night, and the stars were bright in a jet-black sky. They sipped good beer without speaking for a long time.

Dylan finished one bottle and opened another. "I wanted to ask you something, but I thought it might be weird."

"That sounds mysterious. What did you want to ask?"

"You've been acting kinda . . . distant lately. I'm wondering if it has anything to do with your time overseas? You never talk about the war."

She shrugged as she stared at the fizzing bubbles in her bottle of beer. "Not my most pleasant memories."

"What happened over there?"

"Exactly what you think. War's always been old people arguing and young people dying."

Dylan didn't know how to respond, so he kept his gaze on the fields in front of his home. The moon gave everything a pale glow, and a breeze sent ripples through the long grass. "My dad fought in Vietnam. Never talked about it either."

"He sounded like a good guy from what your mother was saying."

"He wasn't a bad person. Had a long rap sheet, but it was all drug stuff. He was actually trying to stop the guy that was robbing the gas station when the cops shot him. He was the one with the prison tattoos and the haggard look, so he caught the first rounds."

"Did they charge the officers?"

He shook his head. "Different time back then. Cops said he pointed the gun at them and that was it. Everybody knew it was a lie, but they still let them get away with it." He suddenly didn't feel like drinking and set the beer down. "He told me once that if the government wants to get you, they'll get you."

"Ain't that the damn truth." She finished her beer in a few swallows. "I think we're all set for tomorrow. Better go."

"Jakey-boy going to get worried about you?"

"You're adorable when you're jealous."

He watched her drive away, then decided to keep drinking.

25

Holly had never been inside a courtroom before. She saw Will's and Mike's parents in the audience. They looked at her and whispered hushed greetings and asked how she was, all of them except Mike's mother. She blamed Holly for her son's death, and Holly thought she was right. If only she'd been stronger or smarter, maybe Mike would still be alive.

She sat down in the first row. Ms. Whitewolf and the other prosecutor were already there. She turned around and gave Holly a warm smile.

"Do you need anything?" she asked.

Holly thought she might cry again if she spoke, so she just shook her head and looked down at the floor.

Two women attorneys came in, followed later by the young man. The defense attorneys were younger than she would have thought, and they didn't look at her. She tried not to feel animosity toward them—she understood they had jobs to do—but she couldn't help it. They were helping the man that had turned her life inside out. Anger flooded her, and she was glad for it. Anger was better than helplessness.

The bailiff said to rise, and she did as the judge came in, before being told to be seated again. Then another bailiff brought out a man that made her feel like she might collapse.

He wasn't large or tall or muscular. He was the type of man she could walk by on the street and not notice. Arlo Ward didn't look at her, but he said hello to Ms. Whitewolf, and she was glad that Ms. Whitewolf didn't acknowledge him.

Holly's hands were trembling, her vision narrowing to a tunnel, as the judge asked the attorneys if they were ready to proceed. She looked over to Arlo Ward, trying to remember if that was really who she'd seen that night. Was he the shadow that haunted her?

He glanced around the courtroom, and as his eyes passed over her, she felt a chill.

She dug into her memories, desperate for any detail that would tell her whether the man that killed her sister and Michael was sitting ten feet away from her, but there was nothing. No recognition, no anger, no despair.

Nothing.

While everyone's attention was on him, she got up and left the courtroom.

26

For the first time, there was real media at the courthouse. Two reporters from national stations with just two staff, but it was the trickle that would start the tsunami, Dylan knew. He walked by the reporters and said, "No comment right now, guys."

The hallways were crowded with all the people Dylan had subpoenaed. Almost every single one stared at him in silence as he went by, except when he passed two uniformed officers and one of them let loose a string of profanities.

Kelly and James were already at the prosecution table, Lily seated at the defense table. In the spectator benches was a group of about fifteen people. The victims' families, along with Holly Fallows, who Dylan recognized from the photographs taken at the hospital. Madeline sat quietly at the end of the defense table.

Victims sitting in the courtroom had never much bothered him, except for one.

Dylan had defended a man accused of killing someone in a bar fight. The father of the victim came to every single hearing. After the case ended in a decent plea bargain, the father kept coming to all Dylan's hearings. He never said a word. He would just sit in the spectator benches and watch quietly. One day he stopped coming, and Dylan had always thought it was because he had died and not because he forgave him.

"All rise, Tenth District Court is now in session. The Honorable Timothy Hamilton presiding."

The judge came out and said, "Please be seated." He looked to his bailiff and nodded. The bailiff went to a back holding cell and brought Arlo out. As he walked by the prosecution table, Arlo said, "Hi, Ms. Whitewolf," with a pleasant smile. Kelly didn't respond, and for a moment, Dylan thought he looked hurt. Like a child who said hello to a teacher they liked and wasn't acknowledged.

Arlo's wife, Leena, wasn't in the courtroom.

Arlo sat in between Dylan and Lily.

"Hi, Dylan, you look really nice."

"Thanks. How'd you sleep?"

"Good. I was reading *Charlie and the Chocolate Factory* before bed. Have you r-r-read it?"

"I have. It's a good book."

He nodded. "I read it as a kid and it always was an escape f-for me."

Dylan watched him a moment. Sometimes he seemed intelligent and aware of what was going on around him, and sometimes he seemed like a child in the body of a man.

Judge Hamilton said, "We ready to proceed?"

Dylan heard a noise behind him and turned to see Holly Fallows hurrying out of the courtroom.

He turned his attention back to Arlo. "We found something at a cabin two days ago in Coyote Canyon I need to speak to you about, Arlo."

"What?"

"We shouldn't talk here. I'll come visit you."

Kelly said, "The State is ready, Your Honor."

"Defense as well, Your Honor," Lily said.

"Excellent. Then we're here for the matter of *State v. Arlo W. Ward*, case number 2014765. Counselors, please state your appearances."

"Kelly Whitewolf and James Halden for the State."

"Dylan Aster, Madeline Ismera, and Lilith Ricci for the defendant."

Judge Hamilton said, "The first issue we should address is the matter of the eyelashes. I have reviewed the briefs submitted by both parties and do not find the defense's argument persuasive that twenty eyelashes impose an undue burden. Oral argument will therefore not be required. I will sign the State's order for the collection of the samples now and incorporate it into the record."

Dylan gave Lily a glance, and she shrugged; they had both expected this.

He glanced at the camera before signing the order and then leaning back in his chair. "Ms. Whitewolf, the floor is yours."

27

"Your Honor," Kelly said as she rose, "I have here fourteen 1102 statements the State wishes to introduce in lieu of live testimony. They are marked plaintiff's exhibit one through fourteen." She put a stack on the defense table and then said, "May I approach the bench?"

Dylan had anticipated she would try to introduce the affidavits in lieu of the witnesses testifying, to rob him of the opportunity of cross-examining them.

Before the judge could say anything, Dylan was on his feet. "Your Honor, we would object to the introduction of these statements in lieu of live testimony. This is an attempt by the State to prevent us from cross-examining the witnesses and ensuring the State has probable cause to move forward."

"*State v. Gesler* is binding law in this jurisdiction, Your Honor, and makes clear the State can introduce 1102 statements at preliminary hearing. Mr. Aster's objection is unwarranted, and we would ask the Court to censure him for—"

"The State is acting in bad faith, and *we* would ask for censure in—"

"Counselors, approach, please."

Hamilton hit a button that sent static through the speakers, and Dylan and Kelly went up to the bench. It was set high, and they had to stare up at the judge as though they were looking up at a giant statue.

"This is not how this case is going to be conducted in my court. I understand the passion from both sides, this is an emotional case, but I expect proper decorum while inside the courtroom. If either of you can't abide by that, please remove yourselves from the case, because I will start holding contempt hearings if this continues unabated."

Kelly shot a venomous look at Dylan, then said, "My apologies, Your Honor."

"Sorry, Judge," Dylan said.

"I appreciate that from both of you. Now let's get back on the record."

Dylan went back to the defense table and Kelly to the prosecution. Dylan looked at Arlo, who was drawing landscapes on a legal pad.

"We're back on the record, and the Court is finding that the 1102 statements from the State will be introduced as per *State v. Gesler*. I will now read plaintiff's exhibit one into the record."

This part of a preliminary hearing, where the judge read the statements into the court record, happened only occasionally, as most judges simply read them in private and made their findings. Judge Hamilton was doing it for the benefit of the cameras.

Before the judge could start, Dylan said, "Your Honor, may we approach again?"

Hamilton looked bothered but said, "Certainly."

Once the judge had turned on the static again to conceal their voices, Dylan said, "Your Honor, I believe the reading of these statements with the media present will be prejudicial to my client. The most graphic highlights will be the sound bites on tonight's news and will taint the jury pool. I would ask that the Court read them in private and make its ruling."

Kelly scowled. "They'll be part of the public record anyway."

"A journalist summarizing them and you reading them verbatim in front of the camera is a whole different ball game. You're an authority figure, Judge. The potential jurors will give greater weight to a detective's statement if they see you read it than if they read a blurb on some website."

Hamilton thought a moment, tapping the pile of pages against the bench. "I think it's important to have a full record. I'm going to read it. But I'll note your objection on the record for any appeals."

———

After the reading, which put Arlo to sleep and forced Dylan to grab his arm to wake him up, Judge Hamilton asked if there was anything else from the State. Kelly said there wasn't, and Lily rose and said, "Your Honor, the defense would call Holly Fallows to the stand."

Kelly shot to her feet. "Your Honor, we would object to the defense's calling of this witness, and every witness they have subpoenaed. We filed some motions to quash but were of course not given enough time to file all of them, as Mr. Aster decided to sandbag us with—"

"I object to the use of the term *sandbag*," Lily said.

"Oh, sit down," Kelly said, turning her gaze to her.

Hamilton bristled. "Ms. Whitewolf, how about I tell people in my courtroom when to sit?"

"Of course," she said, glancing down at the table. "My apologies."

She was angry, and the anger was causing her to act recklessly. Dylan wondered how far he could push her when a jury was present. Every trial attorney acted differently in front of a jury. Mostly, as if their parents were watching them. But if angered or frustrated, many of them couldn't keep the act up.

Kelly cleared her throat. "We've provided the Court with Ms. Fallows's statement and the statements of all the relevant witnesses, and their testifying today would add nothing new for the Court to consider. I would also note, again, that the defense sent the subpoenas the day before this hearing, preventing the State from adequately responding with motions to quash in violation of Rules 4 and 7. It was done in bad faith and needs to be addressed."

Lily said, "*Gesler* hasn't taken away our right to subpoena witnesses, Your Honor. And the code simply says the subpoenas must be sent within five days or a 'reasonable time' as determined by the Court."

"You think the night before is reasonable?" Kelly protested. "You did it on purpose to upset our witnesses."

Hamilton looked at his computer screen and said, "Ms. Ricci, you have subpoenaed every guard who has brought Mr. Ward a meal while in custody, the detective sergeants of the entire Sheriff's Office, the custodians who were present in any building Mr. Ward was held in, and the list goes on and on to eighty-four. Eighty-four witnesses to an incident where there was only one witness present. There were also only nine law enforcement officers directly involved in the entire case. There couldn't possibly be eighty-four people that have relevant testimony."

"Frankly, Judge, that's not your determination to make. This hearing affords us a chance to prod the prosecution's case and ensure they have the necessary evidence to move forward. Those eighty-four witnesses will determine exactly what the prosecution has and whether probable cause will be met."

"That's nonsense," Kelly said. "This is an attempt to burden the State and conduct a fishing expedition. If they want to talk to these witnesses, they can interview them themselves. Preliminary hearings aren't the venue to do that."

Judge Hamilton took a moment to read the names on the list, then said, "Ms. Ricci, I am not going to allow you to call eighty-four witnesses, of which seventy of them or more are immaterial. And I agree with the State that one day is not a reasonable amount of time to allow the State to respond to this many subpoenas."

"We would note that is erroneous on the record for appeal, Judge."

Hamilton, for the first time, looked flustered. Dylan guessed this was probably not how he wanted the first media appearance on this case to go. "So noted. Do you have any other evidence to present?"

"We would again call Ms. Holly Fallows to the stand, as is our right per Rule 7 in the Nevada Code of Criminal Procedure."

"Request to call the victim is denied. Will Mr. Ward be testifying?"

"He will not."

"Then I am finding probable cause in this matter to bind the case over for trial on counts one through thirty-three. Counsel, would you prefer to come back for arraignment or handle it today?"

"Today, please," Lily said.

"Then having found probable cause in the matter of *State v. Ward*, and having bound over for trial, how does your client plead to counts one through thirty-three in the information?"

"Not guilty."

Arlo jumped to his feet. "Your Honor, that's n-not right."

Dylan's stomach dropped.

"Arlo," Dylan said, "sit down."

"No, it's not right. I'm guilty."

The sudden realization hit Dylan that he hadn't prepared Arlo for court well enough. Arlo was so quiet and nonconfrontational that Dylan had assumed he would continue to be so.

"Arlo! Stop talking and sit down."

Madeline put a hand on his arm. "Arlo, please don't say anything else."

The judge glanced at Kelly, who had a grin on her face, then said, "Mr. Ward, you have counsel for a reason. Everything you say on the record right now can be introduced against you in trial. I suggest you follow the advice of your counsel."

"N-no, Your Honor. It wouldn't be right to lie. I did it and won't say I didn't."

Dylan, for a few seconds, sat frozen in his seat. Arlo had just confessed on the record in front of the judge and the media. There was only one thing he could think to do.

He shot to his feet. "We enter not-guilty pleas by reason of insanity." He turned to Arlo and whispered, "It means you did it, but you shouldn't be held accountable for it."

Arlo thought a moment and said, "That's fine."

"Okay," Judge Hamilton said, "we will enter not-guilty pleas by reason of insanity on counts one through thirty-three. I will set this matter for a scheduling conference for next Tuesday. Thank you for your time, Counselors. We stand in recess."

The journalists in the courtroom scurried out, no doubt to get the jump on everybody else about Arlo confessing in open court and then pleading insanity. Kelly lifted her satchel and came over to the defense table.

"That defense works in less than one percent of cases and has never worked in this county. Idiotic move," she said before leaving.

Dylan looked over to Lily, who shrugged.

The bailiff came to get Arlo, and he asked, "Can I take the pad and p-pencil to my cell? I'm not done with my drawings."

28

The bathroom used to be clean. April had always insisted that it be spotless and scrubbed with antibacterial cleaner every day. Holly smiled faintly as she thought about how she would purposely leave clothes on the floor or toothpaste caked to the counter, and April would yell at her while she ran to the pantry to get cleaning supplies. April had been diagnosed with obsessive-compulsive disorder as a child, and there had been nothing more terrifying to her than messiness.

It wasn't clean now. Clothes were everywhere, and the bathtub and sink had stains encircling the cheap porcelain. Pictures of Mike and April were taped to the mirror, and written across the top in pink marker were the words *IT WILL GET BETTER.*

Holly hadn't slept well for days. Since she had seen Arlo in court. Nightmares woke her up constantly, and she couldn't get back to sleep.

She had dark half moons under her eyes, and her hair looked frazzled and unkempt. She wore a tank top with a pair of Mike's boxers and stared at herself in the mirror.

"He can't hurt you now," she whispered to her image, not fully believing the words.

The doorbell rang, and she debated not answering it but knew there was only one person it could be. She got her crutch and hobbled to the front door. She looked out the peephole.

Her father, a large man with silver hair and massive hands calloused from a lifetime of manual labor, stood there with a bag of bagels. She let him in, and they went to the dining table. Her father took out the bagels while Holly put her hand underneath her chin and rested her elbow on the table, mostly because she wasn't sure she could keep her head up.

"You don't look good, honey. You need to eat."

She lifted her bagel and took a small bite.

"Do you wanna go out today?" her father asked. "I thought we could go to the park and take a walk."

"I don't feel like it."

He looked down at his food, which he hadn't touched, and said, "I miss her, too—every day. A parent shouldn't have to outlive their child. I'm just glad your mother isn't here to see it." He looked at her and then put his hand over hers. "You know they're together, right? Waiting for the day when we join them?"

She pushed her bagel away. "Yeah, sure."

"Holly, we have to keep faith that—"

"What kind of God would let this happen, Dad? Why would he sit there and watch while the people I love are torn apart?" She inhaled deeply and slouched in her chair. "He isn't there."

"Don't say that. Life is hard for everyone, you hear me? Not a single person has an easy life. But God gives us challenges when we have to find strength we can't find any other way." He slipped a finger beneath her chin, raising her eyes to meet his. "The world is a tough place. Real tough. But you gotta be tougher. You *gotta* be tougher. Do you understand?"

She looked out the window to the small apple tree she and April had planted when they moved in. They couldn't possibly have guessed that the tree would outlive one of them.

"Yeah," she said. "I understand."

29

The jail was loud and buzzing with activity when Dylan signed in to visit Arlo.

Arlo was sitting in the visitation room, staring down at the floor. His eyes had glazed over, and he wasn't blinking. He didn't move or acknowledge that anyone else was in the room. Not until Dylan sat across from him and said something. Arlo blinked once and looked up.

"You okay, Arlo?"

"I'm fine. I haven't had my m-medication for two days. The nurse is sick and hasn't come in to work."

"I'll make sure you get it." Dylan put his arms on the table as he watched Arlo. He reminded Dylan of a boy he'd known in his youth. A sickly child who had gotten a fever and, inexplicably, died. They both looked fragile. As though they should be sheltered in a bubble and not out among everybody else.

"Can you guess what we found at a cabin near the crime scene?" Dylan asked.

"W-what?"

"Arlo, I need you to be honest with me. What do you think we found?"

Arlo shook his head. "I don't know."

Dylan watched for facial movements and fidgeting but didn't see any and couldn't tell if Arlo was lying. He looked perfectly still, almost like he couldn't move even if he wanted to. "We found a baseball bat. One of the really heavy wood ones. The police are testing it for blood right now. Even cleaned, they can potentially still find traces of blood in the wood."

Arlo looked back down to the table. "Yeah, I put the bat there." He began slowly rocking back and forth.

"When?"

"Right after."

"Why leave the bat and the trap behind?"

"I didn't want them in my car."

"I don't believe you."

Arlo didn't protest.

"Is that the bat that killed those people, Arlo?"

He nodded. "Yes."

"You sure?"

"Yes. I cleaned it, that's why there's no blood."

"So you took the time to clean it but then left it in a cabin where anyone could find it?"

Arlo shrugged.

Dylan exhaled and glanced at the square window on the door to see if the guard was listening. "That doesn't make any sense. I don't believe you, Arlo. You need to tell me the truth."

Arlo said, "I am," but couldn't look him in the eyes.

"I don't think you are."

Arlo said nothing.

"Look at me, Arlo. Please."

He raised his eyes.

"You didn't kill those people, did you?"

Arlo's eyes went back to the table. "I want to go back to my cell."

30

Dylan paced the office as Lily sat at her desk, mindlessly scrolling Instagram on her phone. Night had fallen, and there was no moon or stars, since clouds hung heavy in the sky. He stopped at the windows and put his hands on his head as he stared outside.

Lily put her phone down and said, "So Arlo's up there like he always is, sees this man murder three people, and then the man convinces him to take the blame, or he wants to take the blame and concocts this entire story about a demon." She shook her head. "Too many contingencies. No way a jury buys it."

Dylan let out a long breath. "There's a simpler explanation. Arlo cares about this person, so he's covering for them."

"Maybe," Lily said. "If we can find the right person to accuse."

"Where was Leena the night these killings happened? She has no alibi."

"His wife? No jury's going to buy that a young mother butchered three people."

"Maybe she had help." Dylan shook his head. "None of that matters because we have a bigger problem: How do we defend someone that insists they're guilty and won't let us argue they're not?"

"It might be time to push for a deal, Dylan. See if we can wear Kelly down."

"Even if we got life, how long you think Arlo can last in prison? He's, what, a buck sixty soaking wet? And if he doesn't get his meds every day, he's completely helpless. He's not going to survive. And there's no way Kelly offers commitment instead of prison. We had that conversation already, remember?"

Dylan moved from the window and lay down on the couch against the wall. The ceiling was made of wood to look like an old industrial building, and he stared at the black nails protruding in spots that had worn down over time.

"It all comes down to one thing," he said. "Motive. I've never seen anything even close to the brutality of this. There is no way the jury is just going to say, *Oh well, guess we don't know why.* They'll want a reason."

"Kelly will say it was because he's insane."

"That's tricky because our entire defense right now is that he *is* insane and shouldn't be held responsible. If she says he's insane and that's why he did it, she risks the jury finding him not guilty by reason of insanity. I don't think she'll risk it. She *has* to find a motive to tell a story. And if our story isn't better, Arlo's going to die."

31

The next few days were spent knocking on doors with Brody and his nephew, who were charging $200 per hour to do so.

Arlo rented an apartment in a crowded building, so Dylan went with them on a Saturday morning to interview the neighbors. Had they seen anyone the night of the murders? Were there any cars parked or driving by that they didn't recognize? Did they know anything about Arlo, or had he mentioned anything to them that seemed unusual?

No one remembered seeing anything out of the ordinary. As one elderly neighbor put it, "You forget Arlo's even there. He's as quiet as a mouse."

The neighbor in the apartment right next door to the Wards' told them that Arlo sometimes went to the local playground and brought sodas for the kids playing baseball. "He doesn't sit or talk with them or nothin'," the man said. "Just brings the sodas in an icebox and then goes into the bleachers and watches 'em play. Saddest damn thing I seen."

"Why's that?" Dylan asked.

"Well . . . he's . . . you know. Retarded or disabled or whatever they call it now. Kid probably never played a day of sports in his life. I feel for him. And they live off his and Leena's disability checks. It's not enough for a new family. Sometimes my wife'll make 'em dinner and drop it off. They're always so grateful. I gotta tell ya, it's hard for me to swallow that he could do something like this."

It was past noon, and Dylan was going to call it quits when Brody texted him and told him to come up to the top floor of the building.

The apartment was plain, with potted plants throughout. Standing at the open front door was Brody with a middle-aged woman in a pink T-shirt. Dylan came up with a smile and said, "Hi. Dylan Aster."

"Stephanie, nice to meet you."

Brody said, "Stephanie told me something interesting."

"What was that?" he said, looking at her.

"I was just saying you may want to ask Evan about it."

"Who's Evan?"

"Arlo's brother."

———

By Monday, Brody had been looking for Evan Ward for two days and had found almost nothing about his whereabouts. He had told Dylan the guy didn't seem to want to be found, and this would take a while.

Dylan went through all the police reports again and saw that the detective had mentioned a brother who lived locally. Why, he wondered, had he not focused more on that? Was he getting too emotionally attached to this case, and things were beginning to slip past him? The thought made him uncomfortable.

On Tuesday, after the scheduling conference, Dylan and Lily had filed a 110-page motion. They'd asked the judge to suppress everything from Arlo's statements to the blood found on his clothing and the search of his car. The judge ordered further briefing, and they amended the motion to add coercion by the detectives to garner a confession, violation of Arlo's Miranda rights, and everything else they could think of. By Dylan's estimation, they had less than a 10 percent shot of actually winning on any of the major issues, since the police had done a decent investigation, but that wasn't the point of the motion. The point was to wear Kelly down before the work wore them down.

Dylan hadn't slept well for several nights before the morning of oral arguments. Fatigue made him feel like he had to pull his thoughts out of sludge to be able to speak.

At the end of four days of arguments, he'd slept maybe ten hours total, and Kelly didn't look like she'd fared much better.

Hamilton made his ruling in an hour-long soliloquy in which he allowed practically everything in and denied almost all the defense motions. The only things suppressed were evidence that didn't matter, and Dylan knew he did it to throw them a few bones in front of the cameras to seem objective.

When Dylan turned around to leave, he now saw several cameras instead of one or two, and the bailiff had set up a portion of the spectator benches as a press box.

Over the following days, they filed several more motions. This round, they filed them one at a time, arguing each before submitting the next one. They didn't have to win any, just show Kelly that she had the fight of her life on her hands. At some point, offering indefinite commitment at the state hospital might seem the better option.

Dylan coughed one day as he took out his documents from his satchel in court, and Madeline said, "This probably isn't my place, but are you okay?"

He coughed again. "Fine. Why?"

"You look thinner and pale, Dylan. And you've had that cough for a week. Are you sure you're doing okay?"

"I'm fine. Just tired."

He didn't tell her how little he actually slept. Some nights, he passed out fully dressed, and other nights he pounded energy drinks to grind through until the sun came up.

Mama and Markie were understanding, but Dylan still tried to make time for them, especially for Markie. One Thursday afternoon, at an arcade, he passed out on a bench and woke up two hours later with Markie shaking him and asking for more money to play Skee-Ball.

That Monday morning, on the brink of running out of motions to file and submitting to the idea that Kelly Whitewolf could outpace him, he received a call from Brody. Brody asked if Dylan wanted to go with him to meet Evan Ward, who, it turned out, lived not half an hour from the Strip.

"I'll be right there," Dylan said. He guzzled an energy drink and then rushed out the door.

32

Kelly Whitewolf tried to sleep. The coffee no longer had any effect on her, so she slept on her office couch. The only sleep she had gotten in the past twenty hours. When she opened her eyes, the lids felt heavy, and she wanted nothing more than to close them again. The moonlight glinted off the dream catcher in the corner her aunt Noya had made for her a long time ago.

When she awoke, she got some coffee from a vending machine and sipped it while looking out of a window in the hallway at a busy intersection.

Last night, her aunt had made her a concoction of jam that she spread on a warm piece of flatbread. The jam, whatever it was made of, calmed and relaxed her and helped her sleep for a little while. Noya assured her it was all herbs gathered from the nearby desert, nothing synthetic. She told Kelly how their family had been using the jam—which they called Ashki's Jam after the great-grandmother who had first made it—for generations.

"Good luck, Kel," a detective said as he passed her in the hall. "Hear it's gonna be a long one."

The longest trial she had ever experienced was twelve weeks. She knew the trial of Arlo Ward might last much longer and didn't know if she had the stamina to do it. She was the district attorney and still had to have meetings with the mayor and county council, not to mention campaigning, fundraising, and meetings with the public. How could she possibly fit all of it in when she was putting in eighteen-hour days for Arlo Ward?

"It'll be no different from anything else," she said, heading to her office.

She knew that was false. This was most certainly *not* going to be like anything else. This wasn't a criminal case anymore but a war of attrition, and she was no longer confident she would be the one to come out on top.

The door to her office opened, and James poked his head in.

"You're not going to believe this."

"Dylan Aster has decided to make all our lives easier and retire?"

"No. Arlo Ward's mother-in-law is here."

Her brow furrowed. "Why?"

"I don't know. She walked in and said she wanted to talk to the attorney 'trying to kill her son.' Said she won't leave until she talks to you."

"Bring her up."

James left, and Kelly took out a digital recorder from her desk. She placed it next to a stapler and turned it on, then put on her suit jacket before sitting back down. She hadn't brushed her teeth this morning, and she quickly took out some mint gum and shoved it in her mouth.

A couple of minutes later, an elderly woman with faded tattoos on both forearms came in, led by James.

"Kelly, this is Patricia Iden. Arlo Ward's mother-in-law."

Kelly rose and held out her hand. Though she felt nothing but contempt for Arlo Ward, his family members were his victims, too.

Patricia Iden shook her hand. The woman's hand was cold and slightly trembling.

"Please, have a seat," Kelly said.

She sat, and James took a seat behind her on the couch. Patricia had a tic, and Kelly wondered if it was from medication. Some of the antipsychotics could cause facial tics.

"What can I do for you, Mrs. Iden?"

"Ms. My husband died years ago."

"I'm sorry to hear that."

"Don't be, he was a son of a bitch." Her back was hunched, and she tried to straighten up. Kelly could tell it gave her pain.

"I came to talk to you about Arlo because I don't want my daughter to go through all this."

Kelly leaned back and folded her hands in her lap. "Okay, I'm listening. What did you want to tell me?"

She took a moment to compose herself. "His father had the same sickness he did. When Arlo was born, it got real bad, and his father started thinking the government was after them. Made him and Evan live in a cabin with no electricity, no phones, nothing that would make life easier."

She lost her thoughts a moment and said, "Now where was I?"

"His father."

"Well, anyway," she said with a dismissive wave of her hand, "that's neither here nor there. I came to see if I can talk you outta killing that poor boy."

"You know what he did, correct?"

"I do."

"Then you know there's no punishment that can make up for what he did, so we have to give him the most severe punishment the law allows."

Patricia watched Kelly in silence and clutched her bag tighter. "That boy has suffered more than you can imagine. His father used to think all sortsa crazy thoughts. He thought leeches could get rid of the tracking gadgets the government put in blood and would bleed his boys. He'd lock them in the dark for days at a time to cleanse their bodies of the rays in the air. He thought beatings could cure the brainwashing the government was doing through the schools. That boy has suffered as much as a boy can suffer and still be walkin' and talkin'."

"Not for nothing, Ms. Iden, but I'd take Arlo's self-reported history with a grain of salt. The records are too sparse for us to really know anything." Kelly picked up her pen to take a few notes. "How did your daughter and Arlo end up together?"

"They were in a therapy group together, for addiction, I think. They just got to know each other and got pregnant, so I told her she needs to get married. That it's a sin to have a child out of wedlock." Patricia sighed. "My daughter and granddaughter are prisoners right now. There's people with cameras in their faces everywhere they go. I just want this to be over."

Kelly placed the pen down. "There's another case from about six years ago that has some interesting similarities. Arlo has an attorney, so I can't speak to your son-in-law, but you or your daughter can. Talk to him about it, and maybe I'll see what I can do."

"Talk about what?"

"Arlo will know. Just bring up Angel Lake."

Patricia looked down to the strap of her bag and ran her thumbs along the strip of leather. "He's sick. He shouldn't die for this."

"When did he tell you he began showing signs of mental illness?"

"He was young, fourteen or fifteen." She looked behind her to James and then sat a little straighter in her chair. "My heart breaks for those kids and their mamas. But more death ain't gonna bring them back. I'm askin' you to spare the life of a sick man. I understand you'd want him in prison the rest of his life, but could you find it in your heart to spare his life? Are you Christian?"

Kelly glanced at James, who sat stone faced. "No."

"But you believe in God?"

"Ms. Iden, what I do or do not believe—"

"I'm just sayin', if you believe in God, then you know forgiveness is the most godlike thing we could do. Killin' a sick man who hears voices telling him to do things ain't gonna help nobody, and I promise you this, you won't forget it. It'll keep you up at night. It's not worth it for no one."

Kelly inhaled deeply and said, "I'm sorry. I want to help you, but my job is to get vengeance for the victims. That's what the entire system is to me. There is nothing I can do that will even come close to avenging what he did to those kids except give him the death penalty."

Patricia was silent a long time and then stood. "I understand, but it's a mistake. You will regret this one day, Ms. Whitewolf. Karma is real, and whatever you put out into the world is what you get back."

33

Dylan pulled up to the apartment complex and parked. The buildings were gray with red doors, and two dumpsters overflowed with trash on either side of the complex. The pavement was cracked, and the railings on the second floor had rusted in splotches.

Brody pulled up a few minutes later, and Dylan met him on the sidewalk.

"Evan Ralph Ward," Brody said, handing him a color printout of a booking photo. "Arlo's older brother by four years."

The man was muscular with a bald head and dark-brown eyes. His neck looked thicker than Dylan's thigh, and a tattoo poked out of the neckline of his shirt.

"Thought you might wanna be there in person when I interview him," Brody said.

"Do I? He looks like a pro wrestler that ate another pro wrestler."

Brody laughed. "Must be half brothers or something, because Arlo could be this guy's walking stick."

They headed farther into the apartment complex. A car with five kids stuffed inside drove by. The mom was yelling at them and tossed a cigarette out of her window that hit Dylan's shoe.

"You look like a zombie, man," Brody said. "You been sleeping at all?"

"Not really."

"This case working you, huh? How much you getting paid?"

"Probably a little more than minimum wage by the time the trial's done."

Brody shook his head. "Brother, I work for a lotta attorneys, and if you wanna get ahead, you spend time on the cases that pay big money. Not on low-rent public defender contracts. Why would you think this was a good idea?"

Dylan looked through the windows into some apartments. They were oddly recognizable: before his father built their house, Dylan had grown up in cheap apartments. "My daddy was in and out of prison. I ever tell you that?"

"No," Brody said, his eyes to the pavement as they walked.

"We never had money for lawyers, so it was the public defenders that always tried to help him. There was this one he always got, Sean Clay. He was really old and an alcoholic, so you'd expect him to be cranky, but I'd never once seen him raise his voice. When court was done, every time, he would come out to the benches and sit with me and my mama and explain to us what happened.

"One time, she was crying because my daddy got a two-to-five sentence, and Sean took me out so she could have some time alone. Got me ice cream and told me stories about being a lawyer. The lawyer helped my family when no one else would."

"Well, that's cool and all, but Lily said you got a real offer from LA?"

"Yeah, three hundred a year with a condo and car thrown in."

He whistled. "That's what I'm talkin' about. Hope you're not thinking something stupid like turning them down." They reached apartment 10A. "This is him."

"You sure he's home?"

"Called his PO, and he said he works nights." Brody knocked and took a step back. Then he knocked again and rang the doorbell several times. No one answered.

Brody tried looking through the front room windows, but the curtains were too thick to see through.

"You sure the PO said this exact time?"

Brody was trying to unlatch one of the windows. "He should be here." The latch wouldn't budge. He put his hands on his hips and looked around the complex. "No one out here, man."

"I know what you're thinking, and no."

"You said yourself you think someone else did this and Arlo's covering for them. Could be a lot in this apartment. Maybe even pics or vids of him committing the crimes your guy's gonna fry for."

Dylan took a moment to think about it. "No, can't do it, man."

"D, there could literally be evidence in there that proves your guy didn't kill those people, and you're worried about breaking a window?"

Dylan turned around and put his hands on the railing, looking out at the parking lot. He fought aggressively for his clients—some judges and prosecutors even said unnecessarily aggressively—but this was something else. This was clearly illegal. Though most lawyers had, at some point in their career, committed minor unlawful or unethical acts—like billing hours when they were on a beach somewhere and calling it *case analysis*—this wasn't that. They were about to break into someone's home like common burglars.

"Yo, Dylan," Brody whispered. "Wake your ass up."

"Why are you whispering?"

"Eleven o'clock," he said as he motioned with his head toward the entrance of the complex.

A large man in a T-shirt and shorts with a bald head was walking through the parking lot, a phone to his ear as he spoke and a bag of groceries under his arm. His shirtsleeves looked like they were about to tear from his biceps. Thick veins snaked around underneath his forearms and tree-trunk legs.

"Brody, you sure about this? He could turn us into pretzels without even getting off his phone."

Brody kept his eyes on Evan and said, "I'ma go talk to him. He might think we're cops and take off. If he does, you take him down."

"What?"

"Take him down."

"*Take him down?* Dude, I've been in one fistfight and that was in sixth grade. And that kid beat the hell outta me. I can't take him down."

"Pretend you have a gun or something."

In a flash, before Dylan could protest, Brody was gone and heading toward Evan.

"Damn it, Brody," Dylan mumbled as he ran around the other way to get behind them.

34

Dylan felt warm sweat on his palms, and his heart beat furiously against his ribs. He crouched down a little and then stood straight, then tried to act casual. He guessed Evan Ward outweighed him by at least 120 pounds.

Okay, take him down, take him down. Trip. I'll trip him. Unless he just swings and crushes my head, and then my corpse will trip him.

He could hear the two men speaking. Brody said, "Hey, man, how are you? Had a quick question, I'm looking for the manager. You know where they at?"

Evan didn't say anything. He was already suspicious, an instinct probably bred by prison life. Dylan ran his eyes over the tattoos on his left arm, which covered every inch of skin. It was a scene of death and misery: skulls littering the ground, the sky on fire, someone's boot crunching bones to pieces. If Dylan could see that much detail, he was too close. But before he could turn to get some distance, Evan saw him.

Their eyes met, and for a second, neither of them moved. And then Evan dropped the bag of groceries he had with him and bolted.

"Go around!" Brody shouted as he ran after him.

"Around what!"

Evan sprinted in between dumpsters and was over a chain-link fence in a flash, with Brody close behind him. Brody had played college football and was lean and muscular. Dylan felt like the Pillsbury Doughboy huffing and puffing his way after him.

He ran around the chain-link fence but had lost them. He doubled back and went the other way. An empty field was nearby, and Dylan jogged over and found himself in the back of a vacant parking lot. The asphalt had holes the size of soccer balls, and fissures ran the entire length.

He made his way across, gingerly dodging the holes and avoiding the cracks that looked like they could widen at any second and swallow him whole. As he hit the sidewalk, relief washing over him, he looked over to see Evan Ward rushing right for him, Brody just behind him.

Oh shi—

He held out his hands and bent his knees but immediately flew off his feet as Evan slammed into him shoulder first. The world spun as he hit the sidewalk with Evan's weight crashing down on top of him. A groan escaped like he'd been kicked by a horse.

Brody grabbed Evan by the arms and lifted him off. He pinned him to the pavement, all three men breathing heavily, and slapped cuffs on him before Evan could fight. Evan struggled at first but quickly realized there was no point. So instead, he rested his face on the pavement.

"I ain't done nothing," he said.

"I'm not a cop, you stupid bastard," Brody said, out of breath.

"Then get the hell off me."

Dylan sat up, resting his forearms on his knees and noticing the scrapes on his elbows where the cloth had torn. Every muscle felt like it'd been pulled and then snapped back into place.

"I'm Dylan Aster," he said, puffing for breath. "So glad to make your acquaintance."

Evan spit on his shoes.

———

When the three of them had calmed, Brody lifted Evan, and they led him back to his apartment. They explained to him that they were only there to talk about his brother to see if Evan could help his case. Dylan gathered the fallen groceries and said he'd pay for the broken bottle of spaghetti sauce.

"I'ma let you go," Brody said, "but don't run, my man. I ain't a cop now, but I used to be. One call, and I get your parole violated."

"Yeah, whatever. Uncuff me."

Brody did, and Evan rubbed his wrists and then took out his keys. He unlocked the door, and they went inside.

The apartment had a futon, a television, a kitchen table with two chairs, and almost nothing else. The blinds were drawn, and the place smelled like burnt marijuana.

"Shut the door behind you," Evan said.

He went to the kitchen and took down a cereal box. He opened it up, dug around inside, and came up with a baggie of pot and pills. He got a pipe and sat down at the kitchen table and packed it before crushing two of the pills and sprinkling them on the pot. Brody and Dylan sat opposite him. Brody slid his hand down to his pocket and turned on his digital recorder, a cutting-edge one he had ordered from Israel that was the size of a lighter.

Evan lit the pipe and inhaled deeply. He let it soak his lungs and then leaned his head back and blew out the sweet-smelling smoke.

"You wanna know if my brother killed them people, don't you?"

"Yes," Brody said.

Evan took another pull off the pipe and grinned as he let the smoke escape his lips.

35

Dylan watched as Evan Ward quickly finished off the marijuana and whatever the contents of the pills were. His eyes became wet and red, and he looked much more relaxed, almost sedated. He even offered them strawberry Fantas.

"I don't know if he did it or not," he said as he loaded another pipe.

"You know your brother confessed, right?" Dylan said.

"Yeah, I'm sure he did. He's always been strange as hell. I used to tease him that Josie dropped him on his head when he was a baby. He's got mental sickness. Really bad kind."

"Josie?" Brody asked.

"His mom. We got different moms and the same dad."

Dylan noticed photos up on a shelf, mostly Evan hunting and fishing with friends. "What we're trying to figure out is what's going through his head."

"I don't know what's goin' through his head. But I'll tell ya one thing, I ain't never seen him hurt even an ant when we was kids."

"That was a long time ago," Brody said. "People change."

"Sure, yeah, I guess. But you askin' me if I think he did it and I'm telling you I don't know. And it ain't like we close or nothing for me to lie. I would say he doesn't have the balls, but I've seen him when he thinks demons are talkin' to him, and he just ain't there when that happens."

Brody said, "He moved out here five years ago. Why'd you move with him?"

"I didn't. I came out here a few months before with my girlfriend. Then one day, Arlo shows up at my door and says, 'Can I stay with you?' And I'm like, 'Hell no, you can't stay with me.'"

"You didn't help him?" Dylan asked.

"Nah. He followed me up to Portland before that, too, and did the same thing. Showed up at my apartment and asked if he could stay with me. Boy was starting to get like a stalker."

"When was the last time you talked to him before these killings?"

"Shoot, I dunno. He called me to come to his wedding, but I didn't feel like it. I told you we weren't close."

Brody asked, "Did you talk to him after his arrest at all?"

Evan took a sip of his Fanta. "Nah. We don't have nothin' to do with each other."

"You guys have a falling-out?" Dylan said.

"Something like that."

Dylan watched as he took another pull of smoke and stared off into space. He would probably pass out soon if he kept smoking like that. "You remember where you were later in the day on May ninth?"

"Why?"

"Just curious."

Evan held Dylan's gaze as he took another hit off the pipe. "What day was it?"

"Friday."

"I'da been getting off work, probably."

"What time does your shift start?"

"None of your damn business, that's when. And if you boys don't mind, I'd like to eat somethin' and watch some shows before going to bed."

Evan led them out, and once the door was shut, Brody said, "Well, that was a waste'a time. Sorry you ruined your suit for it."

"It's cool, I'll put patches on it. But it did help, actually."

"How?"

"We can give the jury one helluva story with Evan. Look at him, the guy looks like a killer. Arlo looks like a sick teenager. Out of the two, who would you believe killed a group of people? We can point to Evan and say Arlo is covering for him and avoid using a losing insanity defense."

Brody shrugged. "Your call, man. Let's get the hell outta here, though. That behemoth is all sortsa scary."

36

Kelly Whitewolf sat in her office and listened to the two men in suits explain their success rates with juries. Peter Deluge and Mark something or other. Peter was slim with black curly hair and glasses, while Mark was chubby with a belly that hung over his belt.

They were the owners of Delphi Consultants, a company that did nothing but run focus groups and handle data collection for attorneys, politicians, and big-name corporations.

Peter had read about the upcoming Arlo Ward trial in the *Las Vegas Sun* and wanted to offer their company's services for free. Services, he said, that usually ran upward of a quarter-million dollars.

"So we would begin," Peter said, "simply by showing some of the arguments you've made in the motion hearings, as well as Mr. Aster's, and get the focus groups' reactions."

Mark added, "And it's not one focus group. We've found we need a minimum of three groups to gather good data to be able to make recommendations."

Kelly nodded politely but said nothing. The two men grew uncomfortable and glanced at each other. She was amazed at how many people couldn't stand silence. They would rather fill the silence with nonsensical rambling than tolerate it for more than a few seconds.

"Um," Peter said, clearly uncomfortable, "so you can see how valuable a service it is. The last trial we consulted on was a medical malpractice case where the plaintiff obtained a twenty-million-dollar verdict, one of the highest for the state at the time."

"And what fee did you guys collect on that case?"

Mark said, "Eight hundred thousand."

"Eight hundred thousand," she said with a raise of her eyebrows. "Going from that to free seems like quite a drop, doesn't it?"

Peter glanced at Mark again and said, "Um, this is different. We want to do this."

Kelly leaned back in her chair. "And why would you want to do this?"

Her cell phone rang before they could respond. It was her ex-husband, Travis. He'd been bothering her lately about getting more time with the girls. She sent it to voice mail.

She took out a package of cloves and lit one, inhaling the smoke deeply. It had a pine taste, and she let it out slowly as she ran her eyes from one man to the next. Peter coughed.

"Just get to the point. What do you think you can do for me?" Kelly asked.

Peter swallowed. He was clearly intimidated by her.

"Um, we think we can help you select a jury that will convict Arlo Ward. A lot of cases, the data shows, are won or lost in jury selection."

Mark said, "And juries are all a product of their communities. You can't try a case to a Manhattan jury the same way you would try a case to a Peck, Idaho, jury. They wouldn't know what the hell you're talking about. So what we want to do is nail down exactly who a Jackson County jury is, and the most likely traits in prospective jurors that will lead to a conviction."

"Mm-hmm. You know I haven't lost a murder trial in my entire career, right? What makes you think I need you at all?"

"Well, frankly, this case is, based on our opinion anyway, going to be massive. The news cycle is really slow right now . . . I mean, they're going to eat this up because not much else is going on. It's gory and sexy in just the right way."

"Sexy?" she said with disgust.

"I just mean they're already starting to show images of Holly and April Fallows every time they air the story because of how beautiful they are. They'll tie that beauty to the gory scenes for clicks and viewers, and this thing will hit a tipping point and explode on the national stage."

"So that's why you want to do this? Fame? Get on all the cable news shows and drum up business for yourselves? Eight hundred thousand isn't enough for you?"

They glanced at each other, and Mark said, "Frankly, Mrs. Whitewolf—"

"Ms."

"Oh, sorry. Ms. Whitewolf. But what I was saying was if you asked us to remain anonymous, we would. We're not doing it for that."

"Then why are you doing it?"

Peter looked down to the floor a moment before looking back up at her. "I had a niece I was very close to. Her name was Cathy. My sister's daughter. When she was seventeen, she went camping at Yosemite with her friend Heather and no one ever heard from them again. They found Heather's skeleton three years later in the bed of a stream that had dried out during a hot summer. They never found Cathy's." His eyes glistened, and he coughed, pretending to clear his throat. "I know exactly what the Fallowses feel, and I want to help."

Kelly looked from one to the other. "You should know then that I don't think this is Arlo Ward's first rodeo. I think he's been killing a long time. And if we lose, he will kill a lot more. We can't lose."

They glanced at each other. "Then you're accepting our help?"

She blew out a puff of smoke. "My mother was murdered by a sick piece of garbage a lot like Arlo Ward. So if you two can help me put the needle in a man like that, I won't say no."

37

Dylan had called Leena Ward three times, been hung up on once, and gotten voice mail twice. He asked Brody for Leena's mother's address, where she was staying, but he didn't expect any better reception in person. Even Arlo had been unable to say why his wife wouldn't talk to them.

Dylan and Lily sat at the defense table and whispered about how long jury selection was going to take. The longest selection Dylan had ever been involved in took two months. Lily had one last three months.

"No way Hamilton lets it go on for months," Lily whispered.

"You don't know him as well as I do," Dylan said. "He loves the press it's getting. He'll want this to take as long as possible so he can become a commentator on CNN."

The bailiff bellowed for them to rise as the judge came in. Hamilton sat and asked if they were ready to proceed and then said, "Bring in the panel."

Sixty potential jurors came in. They were a good mix of races and ethnicities. Dylan had used jury consultants before but found them unimpressive. Selecting a jury seemed like random chance either way. People were simply too complicated an animal to predict how they thought.

He opened his binder, which held information on all sixty potential jurors. They'd filled out questionnaires through the mail weeks ago, and he began going through them again as the judge explained the process.

After an hour of explanations, Hamilton began questioning the panel. *Have you ever been convicted of a crime? Are any family members employed by law enforcement? Do you have any beliefs that would make you incapable of rendering a just verdict?*

This wasn't the meat of jury selection, however. These were questions meant to exclude the jurors that would most likely have a bias in favor of or against the defendant. These were the easy pitches.

After a couple of hours, there was a bathroom break. Then Judge Hamilton let the attorneys begin their grilling of the panel.

Kelly was allowed to go first. She went through massive lists of questions, most of them about the jurors' stances on the death penalty. The questioning went into the evening and continued the next morning.

Before lunch, they all took a break with the judge to discuss some of the potential jurors and whether to exclude them. When they were back in the courtroom that afternoon, Dylan noticed two men in the benches. They were taking copious notes and paying careful attention to each potential juror's answers. Jury consultants. He had never seen the prosecution on a case hire consultants before. Most of the good ones charged over a hundred grand, and counties just didn't have the budgets for them. He wondered how Kelly was affording them.

"You ever seen those guys before?" Dylan whispered to Arlo.

"No."

Dylan took a picture of them as subtly as he could and sent it to Brody with a text saying, Jury consultants. Can you find out who they are?

When they broke that night for dinner, Brody texted him. Those men were not just jury consultants but the most high-profile consultants in the state.

At the prosecution table the next morning, Kelly sat with James and went over a thick folder of notes. Dylan leaned toward Kelly as the judge was speaking to the jury panel and said, "How'd you manage to afford them?"

Kelly grinned. "Why? Nervous?"

"It's just unusually aggressive for a prosecutor to do that."

She looked him in the eyes and said, "Get used to it."

———

Jury selection dragged on for thirty-two days. Arlo, as far as Dylan could remember, didn't ask a single question about what was happening. He had filled eight legal pads with drawings of everything from flowers to jets to galaxies.

Lily conducted jury selection for the defense, something she far surpassed Dylan at. She could build rapport quickly and somehow elicit honest answers that Dylan knew he could never get.

Every so often, one of the two jury consultants in the room would text something, and Kelly's phone would vibrate. She would then ask a new question to a juror or ask to go back in chambers and discuss a juror that needed to be cut. It happened often enough that Dylan grew frustrated, but Lily kept her calm and just pushed through.

On the last day of jury selection, the panel had been whittled down to eighteen people—twelve jurors and six alternates. An even split of six men and six women, excluding the alternates; nine white jurors, one Asian, and two African Americans. A generally educated group that had all stated they would have no issue imposing death on a defendant if that was what the law required.

"Your Honor," Dylan said when it was all over, rising on feet that ached from twelve-hour days in dress shoes. "I would like to make an objection."

"One moment then." Hamilton told the jury the lawyers needed to discuss something outside their presence, and they would reconvene momentarily. Once the bailiff cleared the courtroom, he said, "What is it, Mr. Aster?"

"Your Honor, the prosecution has certified this as a death penalty case, and we'll have to go into the death qualification process. I would object to that process."

Kelly chuckled.

Dylan glanced at her and then continued. "Your Honor, study after study has shown that the death qualification process excludes disproportionate numbers of those who are against the death penalty. It creates a subgroup of jurors that no longer represent the community from which they're selected. Support for the death penalty in this country has declined, and yet the vast majority of death-qualified juries still impose death. Why? Because they're artificially created to be predisposed to death by this process. Just as Mr. Ward's jury is in this instance. It is a fundamental violation of my client's due process rights to have a jury selected that is this favorable to imposing death."

Kelly rose. "Defense attorneys have tried this trick for decades, and the Supreme Court has always upheld the process. Imagine the opposite scenario, where people who are against the death penalty are deciding whether it's fair to impose it. Would there be any doubt that we wouldn't have a single execution in this country?"

"Better to err on the side of life, isn't it, Your Honor? I would like to file a brief and have a hearing on the matter."

"That's absurd," Kelly said.

"You think getting a fair trial is absurd?" Dylan said angrily.

"Your Honor, he could have objected before voir dire began but waited purposely until after we've put in the work of selecting a jury. This is just another attempt by the defense to delay and aggravate, hoping to get—"

"You're abusing the process to get a jury that's more likely to convict. This should be delayed, and—"

"You're the one fighting for a monster that—"

Judge Hamilton bellowed, "All right, enough, both of you." He gave a quick glance to the cameras and took a few seconds to regain his composure. "Mr. Aster, this matter is untimely, as the jury has been chosen, while—"

"Your Honor, I needed to wait until an actual jury was selected before—"

"Please don't interrupt me when I'm speaking." The judge stared at Dylan to see if there would be any pushback, and when there wasn't, he continued. "I find it untimely and am denying the defense's motion."

"Then the defense will be filing an emergency interlocutory appeal."

Hamilton got a look on his face like he wanted to shout. An interlocutory appeal sent the case directly to a higher court, freezing the case in the lower court. It could take months to settle, and if the appeals ran all the way to the Supreme Court, even years. Judge Hamilton would lose his press time, maybe even the case entirely.

Arlo lightly touched Dylan's elbow. "I don't want that. I want my trial."

Dylan was stunned into silence for a moment. He hadn't even thought Arlo had been paying attention, much less had an opinion about the process.

Dylan leaned down and whispered, "Arlo, this process is unfair, and we need to fight it."

"I want my trial, Dylan. I'm the client, and I don't want this."

Lily said, "Arlo, I think we should fight this."

"I agree," Madeline added.

"No. I don't want to. I don't want to sit in jail and be forgotten w-w-while you do that. I want my trial now."

Dylan and Lily exchanged a glance before she said, "Call in the jury, Dylan."

"Lil—"

"He's the client. We work for him. Call in the jury."

"We have a duty to protect clients that may not—"

"Arlo, are you clear and lucid right now? Do you understand what's happening?"

"Yes."

"What?"

"Dylan wants to take a long time to appeal the jury selection. But I don't want that. I don't want to sit in jail while you two do that. I just want my trial."

Lily exchanged a look with Dylan.

Dylan didn't budge at first but finally accepted that Lily was right. A lawyer was there to tell the client something was a bad idea, but if the client wanted to do it, it wasn't the lawyer's job to force them not to. If Arlo was so confused as to not be able to make decisions in his own interest, Dylan could act against his wishes. But Lily had shown he was lucid and knew what was going on.

Dylan looked to the judge and said, "I would like my objection noted for later appeal."

"So noted. Now let's get the jury back in here."

When the jury took their seats, all of them glancing quickly at the media and spectators, Judge Hamilton said, "Ms. Whitewolf, is this the jury the State has selected?"

"It is, Your Honor."

"Ms. Ricci, is this the jury the defense has selected?"

"It is, Your Honor."

"Then, ladies and gentlemen of the jury, my bailiff will take you to your hotel. Please keep in mind that there will be no television or internet usage allowed, including cell phones. And I'd like to thank you again for bearing the imposition to seek justice in this case." He turned to the lawyers. "We will begin with opening statements tomorrow. Court is in recess until then."

38

It was late afternoon when Kelly arrived with James at the offices of Delphi Consultants. They were located in a flashy office building with valets hanging out in front and several floors dedicated to an investment bank.

"Wow," James said as they got out of Kelly's truck and she gave her keys to the valet. "We went into the wrong business."

The elevators were plush with crimson carpets and mirrors for walls. Delphi Consultants was on the tenth floor. The front facade of the office was glass, and a receptionist told them that Peter and Mark would be with them soon.

When they were seated and waiting, James said, "How do you think we did with the jury?"

"It's a good group."

"I'm worried about juror six. Sigourney something."

"Sigourney Temples."

He nodded. "She said she'd convinced a prior jury to convict who initially wanted to acquit. I think they'll select her as the foreperson."

"I thought she was great for us—so did Mark and Peter."

"Yeah, but what if she wants to acquit and the others don't? She might have the power to persuade them."

"It was a good bet. She was married to a state rep who was pro–capital punishment and grew up in an affluent community with little crime . . . I don't know. I don't think we're going to get better odds than that."

He began fidgeting, touching the tip of each finger with his thumb and then working backward. "I get nervous about powerful personalities on juries."

Peter said, "You don't need to be," as he and Mark strolled up to them. "You have to play to those jurors, and they'll convince the others for you."

Mark agreed with a nod and said, "But before we start, you guys want anything to eat or drink? I know it's dinnertime. I'm happy to order in if you like."

"I'm good," James said.

"I'm fine, thank you," Kelly added.

"Then let's check out what we got. It's good stuff."

The conference room was massive and held a long glass table with at least twenty black leather chairs. A digital projector was aimed at a large screen, and they all took seats facing it. There was a video still on the screen of twelve people in a room with Peter at the front.

"So we'd just shown them roughly half an hour of arguments from both you and Mr. Aster and asked their general impressions of Mr. Aster."

He hit a button on the table, and the video came to life. One of the participants said, "I liked him. He seemed genuine to me."

Peter said, "Genuine how?"

"He had one of those faces where you trust him. I mean, his client should burn in hell, but I think he's genuine in the way he's defending him."

"I didn't like him," a man in a blue T-shirt said. "The way he was throwing around the people dying like it's the most normal thing in the world. He didn't have respect for 'em."

"What do you want him to do?" a woman in a flower-print dress said. "He has to defend him, that's his job."

A man in a baseball cap said, "Don't know why he's doing this anyway. Guy said he did it. I read it in the news just a couple days ago."

Peter asked, "Did you find any of his arguments persuasive?"

The man shook his head. "No, not at all. Who cares if the guy is crazy? He still needs to pay for what he done."

Another woman in a black top said, "My brother suffers from mental illness. We can't just execute mentally sick people, they're not responsible for what they do."

Most of the group groaned.

"That's exactly what's wrong with this generation," the man in the baseball cap said. "Everybody needs to be coddled, and everything's not their fault."

"So you'd rather kill someone who's mentally sick and has no idea what they're doing?"

"I'd rather we get back to punishing the people that need to be punished."

The banter went on like this for a while, and then Peter paused the video and said, "This held across all three focus groups. The majority found Aster likable, but his client's crimes are so heinous it taints him personally. The effectiveness of his arguments is hurt just by the fact that these crimes were so cruel."

Peter glanced at Mark in a way that seemed like he was nervous about going on. "This is what they had to say about you."

The video started again a good half hour from where it had stopped. Peter asked the focus group, "What were your general impressions of the prosecution?"

The woman in the black top said, "She seemed mean."

"Mean how?"

"Just, like . . . I dunno, kinda bitchy."

The group gave a quiet laugh.

"Can you be more specific?" Peter said.

"Like, why she getting so worked up? Just say what you gonna say without getting all emotional about it."

The man in the cap said, "Not knocking women or anything, but she coulda looked a little nicer, too."

"Elaborate on that."

"Her clothes were all worn out. You gotta wear nicer clothes if you're gonna do something like this on TV."

Kelly could feel the men in the room trying not to look at her, and she hoped she wasn't blushing. She glanced down at her clothing, an old suit she'd had for seven or eight years. The color had faded.

"And her hair," the woman with the black top said. "She needs a serious visit to the salon."

Kelly folded her arms.

The woman in the flower print said, "Mean and plain don't make for good TV."

Another chuckle from the group. Peter paused the video. "This, um, held across the focus groups."

"What the hell does my hair have to do with Arlo Ward killing those kids?"

Mark said, "Appearance, we've found, makes a bigger first impression on a jury than what an attorney says. We like to believe it doesn't matter, but it does."

Peter added, "You may want to . . ." He cleared his throat. "Do something different with your hair and maybe pick up a couple of new suits. Jurors particularly like skirts rather than pants on women."

The anger bubbled out of her. She couldn't take it anymore. Kelly rose and said, "I didn't hear them say shit about *his* appearance or *his* hair. And I don't need two men around that think me wearing a skirt is going to get a conviction. Consider yourselves fired."

She left the office and James followed her. When they were on the elevator, surrounded by mirrors, Kelly kept her eyes to the floor.

39

A reporter had shown up at Dylan's home, Mama said, and offered to pay her for an interview.

"Don't know what the hell he gonna get outta me, but I said I'd talk to you first."

Dylan took off his suit jacket and tossed it onto a chair before collapsing on the couch. Every muscle ached, and a fog seeped into his consciousness, attempting to lull him to sleep.

"You can't talk to them, Mama. I need to use them, and the fewer people talk to them, the more desperate they'll get to talk to me."

Markie ran up and jumped on him, making him groan.

"Can we fly your drone?"

"I'm *so* tired, Markie."

"Pleeeease. Please. Please. Ple—"

"Okay, okay. I swear you should be the lawyer."

She got a wide smile as Dylan retrieved his small drone and remote from his bedroom. They went outside as the sun was setting and flew the drone over the trees. Markie liked making it go high enough that she couldn't see it and thought it had reached outer space.

"Are you famous, Dylan?"

"What makes you think that?"

"My friend saw you on TV and told me at school. He said you're friends with a werewolf."

Dylan grinned as he watched the drone reappear far up in the sky. He sat down on the front steps of the porch. "I'm helping a man accused of doing some terrible things. They just call him a werewolf because they're so bad."

"So are you?"

"Famous? No."

She flew the drone over the house. "I wanna be famous when I grow up. Really, really famous. You think I'll be famous, Dylan?"

"Markie, listen to me, being famous or rich or beautiful—none of that matters if you're a bad person. So always try to be a good person, and the other stuff will come along."

She thought this over a long time. "No, I just wanna be famous."

———

Dylan arrived at the jail and was seated in the attorney-client room. Lily had texted and asked if he and his mother and sister wanted to join her and Jake at dinner tonight. He made up some excuse and declined.

Arlo limped in chained, and Dylan said, "Mind taking those off?"

The guard did it without a word and then left them alone. Arlo rubbed his wrists where the cuffs had been and said, "You look tired. It's important to get sleep. That's one of the reasons the doctors thought my disability got worse, is because I had really bad insomnia. I didn't sleep for days at a time."

"Why?"

He shook his head as he stared down at the table. "The demon would come to me a lot at night," he said in a hushed tone.

Dylan wondered if this little man that sat in front of him could really be responsible for the worst crimes he'd ever seen.

"Arlo, I wanted to talk to you again about what's going to happen tomorrow. I know you've said you only want us to defend you with an insanity defense, but I want to plead not guilty. I think there's a lot of inconsistencies in the prosecution's case, and it might get us to reasonable doubt. Do you know what reasonable doubt is?"

"No."

"It's where the jury doesn't fully believe you committed this crime and can't convict you of it. I think we might have enough to get there."

"How?"

"There's three things I'd argue. First is demeanor evidence. That means we would try to find anyone that saw you before and after these crimes were committed and could say you were calm and happy. That's not at all what a mass murderer would act like before and after a massacre like this. Then we'd argue timeline evidence. That you couldn't possibly have caught up to Holly Fallows in the time she says you did, especially with your limp. And then motive. There's no reason for you to do this, and the murders are so violent that a jury will *need* a reason to convict you. But by claiming insanity, we're admitting you did it, and I can't tell them you didn't."

"I did do it."

"That's not what you said under hypnosis."

He hesitated and made the ankle shackles rattle as he shuffled his feet. "Whatever I said there wasn't real. Doctors just mess with your head and get ya to say things you don't wanna say."

"Even if you did do it, and I don't think you did, but even if you did, I think we should say you didn't."

Arlo considered this while rocking slowly back and forth. His nose crinkled as he thought. "No, I don't want to do that."

"Why, Arlo?" Dylan said with a hint of anger in his voice. "You're looking at the death penalty. They might kill you over this. How many times do I have to tell you that?"

Arlo ran his fingers along a carving in the table. "You know what's worse than being seen as a wicked man, Dylan? Not being seen at all."

"I'm sorry, Arlo. I know that sucks. But what does that have to do with a jury ordering your execution?"

"Nobody ignores me now."

Dylan was used to statements like that from clients, but if the jury had just heard Arlo say that, they would've been frightened. "You could still get attention after this case without dying for it."

Arlo shook his head. "I made up my mind."

Dylan let out a slow breath to calm himself. "Arlo," he said in a somber voice, "today's the day. If you have anything to tell me, today's the day to do it. You won't get another chance . . . did you kill those people?"

Arlo watched him a second and said, "I'm tired, Dylan. I'll see you in court tomorrow."

He called the guard and didn't look back as he was led to his cell.

40

Lily pulled up to her condominium and parked in the underground parking. It was more than she probably should have spent on a mortgage, but she liked living someplace plush. Because in moments of solitude and silence, she imagined herself back in that damn small town where nothing ever happened and everyone accepted the fate of quiet mundanity. No one from Rock Hill, Kansas, ever imagined themselves daring to be anything but average.

The condo was on the seventh floor. She smelled cooking food when she came in, a pleasant scent of heated butter and frying vegetables. Lily tossed her keys in a glass bowl on the counter and saw Jake hovering over two pans on the stove.

She'd given him a key a few weeks ago but was surprised every time she came home and found him there. Jake had an amiable disposition, sometimes whistling when he didn't notice anyone watching him, and always cracking jokes. He was the polar opposite of Lily. She had always been austere and found men more like puzzles that needed to be solved than objects of love and affection. She didn't know what it meant that she wasn't excited to see him right now.

He had earbuds in and was humming to some song. Lily slipped off her heels and slowly approached him. When she was close enough, she jabbed her fingers into his ribs and said, "Boo!"

He screeched like a child, and the long wooden spoon in his hand went flying. Lily broke out into a laugh.

"What the hell? I could've been holding a knife, Lil."

"I saw you weren't," she said, making her way to one of the pans and taking out a sliver of tomato. She blew on it and then slipped it into her mouth. "Are you seriously mad right now?"

He picked up the wooden spoon from the floor. "A little."

"Oh, come on, Jake. We're not dead yet. Have some fun." She leaned against the counter and looked at him with her large brown eyes.

"Do I smell alcohol on your breath?" he said.

"I had a couple beers on the way home."

"You've been doing that a lot lately."

She playfully threw her arms around his neck, a broad smile on her face as she said, "What are you gonna do, spank me?"

"Not funny."

"Should I get a paddle?"

He couldn't suppress a grin. "It's not funny. Stop it."

They looked in each other's eyes a few seconds before he relented and kissed her. Then he went back to his cooking. Mixing in cut onions that sizzled when they hit the pan. "How's the case going?"

She sighed and practically fell into a chair at the dining table. She never felt the full extent of her fatigue until she was home. "I can't say the jury seems favorable. They're all fans of the death penalty."

He put the spoon down and picked up a dish towel, wiping his hands as he leaned back against the counter. "So you're going to lose?"

"Looks like it. Though Dylan will probably kill himself trying not to."

"He seems like that type of guy."

"Like what type of guy?"

"The type to bash his head against a brick wall."

She shrugged. "I guess. But sometimes it breaks because nobody else tried it."

He threw the towel on the counter near the sink and said, "Oh, almost forgot, your nephew called your landline. Guess your cell was off."

"I turn it off for court. When did he call?"

"Few hours ago. He had something to tell you about a game or something."

She retrieved her phone from her bag on the floor. "He had his Little League game today. He promised he'd call me after." She dialed her sister's number. When no one answered, she left a voice mail and then sighed and put the phone on the table.

"You sure you're all right?" Jake asked.

"Why do you keep asking me that?"

"I don't know if you've noticed, but you've been drinking almost every night for a couple of weeks. That's unusual for you."

Before she could respond, her phone buzzed with a text, and she read it. "I have to go."

"What? Dinner's almost ready."

"I'm not hungry," she said as she put her heels back on.

"Where do you need to be right now?"

"Dylan wants me to meet him somewhere."

"Oh, of course. We have to jump when he says jump, don't we?"

Lily stopped and looked at him. "What's that supposed to mean?"

"You know what it means."

"No, I really don't."

Jake folded his arms. "I don't wanna fight. I had a night planned for us, and you're just leaving like it means nothing. How would you feel if I ran out on you?"

"Crappy. And I'm sorry, but he wouldn't ask me to come if it wasn't important."

Jake shook his head and went back to the food, turning the stovetop off. "You told me when we started this that you weren't interested in flings. That you wanted a serious relationship. The way it works is if you're having problems, we discuss it. Not keep it bottled up. If we can't do that, this relationship won't work."

Lily shook her head as she grabbed her bag. "Does everything have to be some big thing with you?"

"Big thing?"

"Yeah. Can't you just, I don't know, go with it and have fun? You're trying to plan the future and it's nonsense. Nobody can plan for it."

"Lily, I just want to be here for you. You never talk to me and I want you to know you can. That's all. I don't think I'm asking a lot."

She slung her bag over one shoulder and said, "I have to go."

She got to the door but didn't open it. Jake dumped the food in the garbage and cleaned off the pans. She wanted to say something but knew no matter what she said, it would only make him feel worse. So instead, she opened the door and left.

41

It was late, and darkness had fallen when Dylan saw the text from Brody telling him where to go.

Scipio at night didn't look like most cities. There were no sparkling clusters of lights that appeared like bright stars in the inky black of space, no colorful store signs announcing they were still open . . . no people.

The city was predominantly older residents, and it shut down around nine o'clock. Even the bars closed at ten or eleven.

Dylan grabbed a glass of beer at one while he still could. He watched the bartender, a surly man with a red cap and dirty jeans, share a couple of shots with a group at the end of the bar. Dylan drank only half the glass and then left a ten before heading out.

Lily pulled up to the house across the street from the bar just as he crossed over to it. He waited for her on the sidewalk and said, "Sorry, I know it's late. But I figured you'd want to be here."

"I do," she said, setting her car alarm and not looking at him.

"You sure? I know you had a thing planned with Jake. I wasn't going to—"

"It's fine, Dylan. Let's see what she has to say."

The house was square and beige with a yellowed lawn in front. Patricia Iden answered the door and told them Leena was gone before trying to slam the door on them. Dylan put his foot against the jamb.

"Move your damn foot!" Patricia yelped.

"I need to talk to your daughter for like thirty seconds."

Patricia grunted as she pushed the door, almost slamming Dylan's fingers. "She don't want to talk to nobody."

With a final push of her somewhat prodigious weight, she slammed the door closed. Dylan had to move his foot and fingers so they wouldn't get crushed.

"Just thirty seconds," Dylan shouted. "I'm Arlo's lawyer. He wants to take responsibility, and they're going to kill him for it. Do you hear me? He's going to die, and I'm trying to save his life. To save the life of your granddaughter's father."

There was no sound coming from inside the apartment. Lily watched quietly as Dylan said, "If saving his life isn't even important enough for you guys to open a damn door, then he's already dead."

As they turned to leave, he heard the door unlock.

———

The home was messy, filled with baby bottles, packages of diapers, toys, and clothes. It smelled like cigarette smoke and cheap perfume.

Patricia sat on the worn-out green couch. Dylan carefully sat on the edge of the solid wood coffee table without being asked. He leaned forward and put his elbows on his knees. Lily rested against the opposite wall with her hands behind her back.

"So when will Leena be back?"

Patricia lit a cigarette and watched him suspiciously as she pulled an ashtray near her. "Not long. She ran to the store. What you wanna talk to her about?"

"Anything, really. I need to know if there's anything she can tell me that will help Arlo. She refused to speak with the police, so we have no idea what she knows."

Patricia grinned. "Yeah, them pigs came by askin' all sortsa questions and then threatened to arrest her and take her baby away for . . . what was it . . . something with justice."

"Obstruction of justice. It means she's either lying to the cops, or she's purposely hiding something that could help in their investigation."

She nodded as she blew out smoke from her nose. "I said, 'Do your worst, pigs.' That's exactly how I said it, too."

The door opened. A younger woman, younger than Arlo by at least five or six years, came in. She wore a gray shirt with a green army jacket and had her hair pulled back with an elastic. Groceries were in her arms, and she stood at the doorway with her mouth open, clearly shocked her mother had let someone in.

"Leena, this here's Dylan. He's Arlo's lawyer, and he needs your help."

42

Leena stared at Dylan for a long while, and he got the distinct impression she was debating whether to run or call the cops. Her mother, luckily, took the two bags of groceries out of her hands and carried them to the kitchen. Leena didn't move other than folding her arms. She looked at Lily and then back to Dylan.

"Hi," Dylan said with the least amount of awkwardness he could muster. "Um, sorry for just showing up. I called probably—"

"I know who you are. What do you want?"

He noticed a round toy on the coffee table. Unable to figure out what to do with his hands, he picked up the toy and rolled it around in his palms. "You know he's facing the death penalty, right?"

A hesitation.

"Yeah, I know."

Dylan glanced at Lily, and they exchanged a look before he said, "And you know he was found covered in blood and confessed to doing this?"

"You ain't telling me anything new. Just tell me what you want and leave."

Dylan set the toy down and glared at her. "I want to save your husband's life, but apparently I'm the only person in the whole damn world who does. His brother won't help us, the prosecutor won't offer anything but death . . . even Arlo won't let me plead him not guilty and keeps saying in court that he did it. We're fighting for him completely alone. I reached out, hoping that maybe we're not alone. That maybe there's one person that knows what the hell is going on and can help us."

Lily said, "Do you want him to die, Leena? Tell us now so we don't waste each other's time."

"How the hell you gonna ask me that?" she barked. "He's the father of my child. The last thing I want is for my husband to die."

Dylan looked at Patricia, who didn't seem to be paying attention as she put groceries away. "Then why won't you talk to us? I understand not talking to the police, but why us?"

Leena sighed and shut the door. "He told me not to."

"Why?"

"I don't know. But he said it's important not to talk to anyone."

Dylan noticed scars on Leena's hands. They were faded and had the dull coloration of age. Some cuts were on her wrists as well, and they were thin and straight. Done purposely. "Well, he's in trouble, and he's going to die unless you talk to us."

She was quiet awhile and watched her mother in the kitchen. Then she lit a cigarette before sitting down in a recliner near the door. She watched them like she was expecting a question but said nothing.

"Does he keep any weapons here or at your house?" Dylan asked.

"No."

"No knives?"

She shook her head. "Not that I've seen."

Lily said, "When did he find out he had schizophrenia?"

"He was a teenager, but he'd had symptoms since as long as he could remember. His parents just didn't care enough to take him to see anybody."

Dylan asked, "How does it affect him on a day-to-day basis? Do you see a lot of unusual behavior?"

Leena inhaled smoke and blew it out through her nose. "Most days he's fine. Especially when he's taking his meds like he should. But when he gets off his meds, things change."

Dylan had seen the pattern so many times it wasn't a surprise that Arlo fell into it as well. Schizophrenia medications all had horrific side effects, but they would stabilize the patient enough that they were lucid and felt good. Maybe it was plain wishful thinking, but almost everyone believed that something other than the medication was the cause of their well-being. Then they would stop taking the drug because of the side effects. Within a couple of weeks, maybe less, their lives would begin to unravel again.

"What's he like when he's off his meds?"

She blew out a puff of smoke and stared down at the floor as she kept the cigarette in between two fingers. "He starts seeing things that aren't explainable."

Dylan leaned forward. "The demon."

She nodded. "The demon."

"When was the last time he saw it?"

"I dunno," she said, ashing into a can of soda on a side table. "I'd say a couple months before he got arrested. He woke me up one night and was standing over the bed with the phone in his hand and said the demon wanted to talk to me. Of course, there was no one there. I asked him when the last time was he took his meds, and he said three weeks ago. So I started givin' him his meds every morning myself, and he got better."

Patricia spoke from the kitchen. "Tell him about Richie."

Leena watched her mother and then turned back to Dylan. Dylan looked between them. "Who's Richie?"

Leena blew out smoke again and said, "Richie was a boy that almost got hit by a car. He was playing on his phone while he crossed the street. This car came out of nowhere. The driver was on his phone, too. Arlo was on the sidewalk and saw what was about to happen, so he jumped out into the road and pulled the boy outta the way. The car caught Arlo on the hip and broke his leg and hip and gave him that limp. But he didn't even stop to think about it or worry that he could die. He just ran out there and saved that boy's life."

Lily said, "So you don't think he killed those people?"

"No. I know that man better than anyone on this earth. He's never even raised his voice at me." She glanced down at the scars on her hands. "I've dated some real scum, and I know what a violent man is like. Arlo isn't one."

"Did he go to the cabin a lot?" Dylan asked.

She nodded. "It was where he went when he felt an episode coming on. Even with the meds, people with his illness still get episodes. They think things are after them. He doesn't like putting me and Amy through that, so he goes up to that cabin for a couple days until the episode passes. I tell him I don't mind, and I wanna take care of him, but he says he doesn't want Amy to see him like that." She gave a melancholic grin. "As if a baby knows what it means when he acts like that."

"What was he like before he left to go up there this last time?"

"He was fine. I gave him all his pills in candy bars and told him to eat one candy bar a day. Then I heard about all this when the police showed up in the middle of the night."

Patricia had stopped putting groceries away and was now leaning against the counter listening.

"Leena, there was a baseball bat found inside a cabin near where the murders happened. Did Arlo say anything about it to you?"

She shook her head. "No, he don't talk to me about that stuff. But I never saw a bat in the house and I know he don't play baseball."

"Did he say anything to you about a knife the police can't find?"

She shook her head. "No."

"After his arrest, what did he tell you about all this? Did he give any details?"

"All he said was everything was going to be okay and to not talk to anybody."

Lily said, "Has he ever mentioned to you that he has dreams about being famous?"

Leena took another pull off the cigarette. "So damn much I'm sicka hearing about it. He was interviewed on the news once about something stupid, like a new bridge or something, and he was just walkin' by when they were filming. He's made us watch that video like ten times."

"So do you think he's taking credit for these murders because he knows it'll make him famous?"

"I know he keeps sayin' me and Amy will never have to worry about money again. That he's gonna sign the rights to the book over to me and that maybe they'll even make a movie about him."

"Boy's a damn fool," Patricia said.

Lily asked, "What about his brother?"

"What about him?"

"What's Evan like?"

Leena shrugged. "We don't have anything to do with him. They hate each other."

Patricia said, "He's a bum. Been to jail over beatin' his girlfriends more times than you can count. That's what Arlo says anyway."

Dylan nodded. "Can you think of anyone else that Arlo could've been up in the woods with? A friend, a neighbor, cousin, anyone? Anyone that could do this and let Arlo take the blame?"

Leena shook her head. "No, he don't got any friends, and he likes to be alone up there."

There was only one next step that made sense. Dylan let out a long breath. "I need you to do something for me, Leena, and it has to happen right now."

43

Jails at night always unnerved Dylan. They were manned by skeleton crews, and the silence made him think of coffins.

They checked in at the front counter. Leena held Amy as the baby glanced around in wonder. Leena hadn't wanted to bring her, but Dylan, somehow, managed to talk her into it. The guard, who was half-asleep on a chair when they came in, only gave them a quick glance and sent them through the metal detectors.

They were seated in a common area with no glass barriers between the visitors and the inmates. When Arlo was brought in, he froze at the doorway, and the guard had to tell him, "Keep movin'."

He sat down across from them and stared at his child. "I told you never to bring her here."

"I wanted her to see her daddy before all this—whatever it is you're doing—finishes."

Arlo looked at Dylan. "Why'd you bring her here?"

"Look at me," Leena said. He slowly turned to her. "You need to do what these people tell you to do. They're trying to help you."

"You don't know anything about it, Leena. You shouldn't have come here."

"Arlo, look at Amy. She's gonna grow up without a father. You're not helping us. I don't care about money, I want you home." She gestured to Dylan. "He says that maybe he can get you off if you say you didn't do it, that you only said you did because of your sickness." She hesitated. "That's what happened, isn't it, Arlo? Someone else did this and you're just saying you did? If you ever cared about us, you need to tell me right now. I need to know."

Arlo watched his daughter. "Everything I do, I do for you and her. I'd gladly g-give my life to make sure you two have a good one."

"I know, baby. I know you would. But this isn't the way. What's Amy gonna think when she's older and she goes online and reads the horrible things people say about you? Is any amount of money gonna make her feel better?"

Arlo wouldn't look at her. Instead, he glanced back to the guard and then looked at Dylan before Leena said, "Look at me, baby."

It took him a moment, and it seemed like he had to build up courage, but his eyes finally locked onto his wife's. "I'm so sorry you gotta be married to me . . . you deserve better."

He reached out to touch her, and the guard said, "Hands off."

Arlo withdrew his hand. "I love you, but don't come here again."

Leena quietly sobbed as her husband went back to the guard and was led out of the visitor's area. She hurried out of the room with her daughter.

Dylan had hoped Arlo's wife and daughter could convince him to plead not guilty and say he made everything up. That someone else was responsible and he was as much a victim as anybody. Instead, Dylan had made things worse by upsetting both Arlo and Leena.

Dylan felt a dim nausea at the thought that the only way to save Arlo Ward's life might be to convince a jury he was insane. Something Dylan had never even seen done in a murder case.

After leaving the jail, he sat in the quiet of his car a long time before starting it and heading home.

44

Dylan and Lily sat in her truck and stared at the circus.

At least seven news vans were there, with reporters talking to cameramen and producers. They tried to grab anybody going into the courthouse who they thought was part of the case. When they couldn't get anyone, they would speak into the camera for a while. Probably editorializing about why no one would talk to them. He figured at least fifty spectators were there as well, sipping coffees and snapping photos.

When the bus arrived carrying the jurors, the frenzy intensified, and the media swarmed the bus to get shots of the people inside. It took several deputies to clear the way for the jurors to step off the bus and head inside the courthouse.

"I think we should go in through the back," Dylan said.

"No. Once you go in the back, you'll always have to go in the back. Just ignore them."

He blew out a breath. "This is going to be a shitshow. You know that, right?"

"It's what we signed up for. Because we certainly aren't doing it for the money." Lily glanced at him. "Besides, your big firm in LA is probably following the case. Maybe they'll offer you more if you win."

Dylan watched one of the reporters trip and fall while he clamored to shout questions at the jurors. "We could lose. How am I supposed to keep practicing law if he dies because we lost, Lil?"

"Same as we always do. You just keep moving forward. If you're going through hell, keep going, right?"

Dylan watched as the last juror tried to get into the courthouse and was circled by the reporters. She looked frantic, and he didn't want that to be the image on tonight's news, so they got out of the truck and crossed the street. The steps to the courthouse were narrow, and the reporters crowded them.

Dylan ignored their questions and pushed his way inside the courthouse. As he got past the doors, he looked over to see Holly Fallows waiting to go through the metal detectors. They exchanged a glance but said nothing.

Dylan waited until she was headed for the courtroom before going through himself.

45

"Ladies and gentlemen of the jury, we will now hear opening statements from the attorneys."

Kelly walked over to a projection screen. She had a small remote in her hand, and without a word, she hit the play button. An image came to life. Arlo Ward sitting at a table in the sheriff's station, two male detectives seated across from him. The video didn't start at the beginning but in the middle, at the most shocking part.

"I cut her head off," Arlo said. "It was much easier t-to do than you would think."

"Why cut her head off?" one of the detectives asked casually, like it was the most normal question in the world. "She was already dead."

"I wanted the other two to see it when they came back. I thought it would be fun to see their faces."

"But you said you attacked them before they got to the campsite."

He nodded. "Yeah, I changed my mind. I thought maybe they might run if they saw everything, and I wouldn't be able to catch them." He smiled. "But I was wrong. It w-was easy to catch up with her when she ran."

Kelly looked out behind the prosecution table at Holly Fallows, who sat with her father. Tears streamed down her cheeks, and her father put his arm around her.

"You don't realize how heavy a dead body is until you lift one," Arlo volunteered. "She felt like she weighed a t-ton. But I would never say that to her face, of course."

The detectives didn't smile or chuckle or have any reaction at all.

Arlo shifted in his seat and said, "I really wish I would've g-gotten that last one. I was close. But who could've guessed she'd jump? I thought she might beg me not to kill her instead. It would've been nice to hear one of them begging. Everything happened so fast the other three didn't have time to beg."

"Why would you want them to beg?"

A slow smile spread on his face. "To see their face when they realized I was going to kill them anyway."

Kelly stopped the image on Arlo's smile and set the remote down on the prosecution table. She stood in front of the jury with her arms behind her back.

She launched into the facts of the case, outlining who was where and at what time. From there, she detailed the actual injuries and mutilations. Showing the gruesome photographs of the scene to a jury who could barely look at them.

"Objection," Dylan said, rising to his feet. "Your Honor, these details are not relevant to the opening statements in this matter."

Kelly felt a small flash of anger. It was customary not to object during another attorney's opening or closing statements because you would disrupt their flow. In turn, that attorney implicitly agreed not to object during your opening or closing. The objection was nonsense; of course the details were relevant. So she knew that Dylan had purposefully done it to break her flow.

"What's the matter?" she said. "Why don't you want the jury to hear all the facts of what your client did?"

Dylan and Lily objected nearly simultaneously, with Madeline sitting wide eyed and shocked. Judge Hamilton said, "All right, all right.

Mr. Aster, your initial objection is overruled. Ms. Whitewolf, their subsequent objection is sustained. Let's just move on."

There were two more objections over the next hour, each as nonsensical as the first. And each time Kelly responded with a comment about them wanting to hide facts from the jury, despite the judge giving her an admonition not to do it again. Understanding that she would do it every time, they stopped making objections and let her finish.

More exhibits were put up, enlarged photos of pure horror. One of the jurors, an elderly woman in a beige sweater, covered her mouth with her hand and looked away.

Kelly stood in front of the jury.

"Arlo Ward burned and suffocated one beautiful young woman to death. Another young man, he bludgeoned to death. So violently that they had to have a closed-casket funeral. Another young man bled to death from injuries so brutal I can hardly describe them. Then, afterward, he mutilated and posed the bodies. Poses meant to shock the conscience of anybody who saw them, to shock the entire world. And as you've seen from the number of news cameras here, it has.

"Anyone willing to do that has to have some insanity. You can't be a normal person and do what Arlo Ward did. But that's not the question we're asking you to answer, and that's not the legal definition of insanity. The only question we're concerned about in this trial is whether Arlo Ward understood the nature of his actions and the quality of his behavior. What that means is, Did he understand right and wrong and do wrong anyway? Did he understand that he was murdering people? Yes, of course he did." She put her hands on the banister in front of the jury. "*Of course* he did."

Kelly paused and looked each juror in the eyes again before she went back to the prosecution table and sat down.

Judge Hamilton said, "We will now hear opening statements from the defense."

46

Hushed whispers came from the media benches as people hurriedly made notes and sent text messages. Lily's eyes were closed, and she was taking deep breaths, something she always did before addressing a jury for the first time. Madeline smiled at Arlo, who grinned at her shyly and looked down to the table.

Lily approached the jury. "The law says if someone is not sane, they are to be committed to a hospital for treatment and not sent to death row. Arlo Ward . . . is not sane."

She waited a beat before moving. The silence in the courtroom was palpable. She wanted those words to hang in the air and bounce around the jurors' brains.

With that simple statement, she sat back down, and no one in the courtroom spoke.

47

Kelly sat in an Italian restaurant with James. He ate with zeal, ordering an appetizer before their main course, but Kelly only lightly picked at the food. She lit a clove cigarette, but the server came over and asked her to put it out. She told him to make her and kept smoking.

"You okay?" James said as he cut into some chicken parm, his eyes on the food to make it appear a more casual question than it was.

"Fine."

"You don't seem fine."

She blew out a long stream of fragranced smoke. "I didn't like their opening."

He shrugged as he put a hunk of chicken in his mouth. "Brevity's a good tactic. The jurors actually remember what you said. But it didn't seem like anything special to me. What made you nervous?"

"They're homing in on the right issue. The jury might believe no sane person could do something this savage."

James gently wiped his lips with a linen napkin. "Look at it like this—worst-case scenario, they find him not guilty by reason of insanity, and he gets an involuntary commitment at the state hospital. He's up for review only once a year. We can offer statements to the review board every year about why he shouldn't be let out. It could potentially be a life sentence."

"He doesn't deserve a life sentence!" she said more forcefully than she meant to.

They sat in silence a bit after that, and James finally broke it by waving the server over and asking for their check. Kelly told James she would see him tomorrow and left cash on the table before putting out her clove.

"You didn't drive. I'll give you a ride home," James said.

"It's fine, I wanna walk."

It was a chilly, cloudy night with a light drizzle of rain. She strolled past the courthouse and stared at it. So much of her time had been spent in that building that it seemed like a second home. When she looked at it, a feeling of warmth and comfort came over her, like getting to lie down after a long day.

Right now, there was no warmth and no comfort. It didn't appear like a home at all but like an abandoned building. A structure with no soul, left to rot in time. She shivered with a breeze and folded her arms as she walked.

Kelly went up the block and came to Urban Classic Chic. A clothing store she had never been to.

The lighting was dim and the small space packed tightly with clothes, jewelry, shoes, and bags. A young woman with bright-blonde hair behind the counter said, "Hi."

"Hello," Kelly said, running her fingers along a flower-print dress.

"Anything I can help you find?"

The suit she had on was one she'd worn a couple of days a week for the past five years, and the words of the focus group ran through her mind: *mean and plain.* An entire lifetime spent fighting for people who couldn't fight for themselves—for people like those in the focus group—and they passed judgment on her in a second.

"I need something really impressive," Kelly said.

48

Dylan and Lily ate in silence at a hamburger joint. Dylan watched as Lily dipped a fry in ketchup, slowly took a bite, checked her phone, and then took another bite.

"You okay?" he asked as he sipped his Coke.

"Yeah," she sighed. "I suppose."

"What is it?"

"We're losing, Dylan."

"What? We barely had opening statements."

"You didn't watch those jurors' faces—I did. I think those photos made up their minds for them. They only had a vague idea that evil existed until today. Now they know what it looks like. Evil's just a word until you see it in person."

Dylan took another drink and said, "Well, congrats. That's the bleakest thing I've ever heard."

She gave a small grin. "It's true, though. I saw it all the time with young soldiers."

"Is that what happened to you? You saw evil?"

A pause. "Yes."

Dylan leaned back in the seat and looked over to the cashier, a teenage girl laughing with one of the customers. "There's horror in the world, but that doesn't make it a bad place. We only like the sunshine because there's rain."

Lily picked up a fry, dipped it, but changed her mind and placed it back down. "Did you ever read *Lord of the Flies*?"

"Like in high school. Why?"

"There's this scene that's always stuck with me. The kids kill this pig, and they put its head on a stick to honor these island gods they've started worshipping. This dark, black blood starts dripping down its mouth, giving it a terrifying appearance, almost like it's speaking to them, and some of the boys run away. But one of the boys begins to cry. When I was a kid, I thought it was because he was scared, but when I got older, I understood that's not why he cried." She swallowed. "He cried because he realized they weren't innocent anymore. That's a real moment people have, Dylan. The moment they see what people are capable of doing. If any of those jurors hadn't had that moment yet, they have now. And they'll hate Arlo for it."

Dylan pushed away his food and folded his arms on the table. "I know it seems that way, but we've got a shot. The extreme nature of this, his diagnosis, his lack of criminal history, the way he's acting, and how he confessed without any prodding . . . it gives us a shot."

She shook her head. "They're not going to put him in a hospital and risk him getting out. And I don't like how hopeful you are that it's going to happen."

"No one knows what's going to happen."

"Right. And that includes you."

He sighed. "Lil . . . do you believe him? I mean, really believe him that he did this?"

She shook her head. "I don't know. I think at the least he's so mentally ill he shouldn't be executed for it if he did. But I'm telling you, they won't find him insane. They're going to want someone to pay for what happened, and the only person they have is Arlo."

"You're looking at it like—"

Her phone rang, and she said, "Excuse me," and answered it.

Lily went outside, and Dylan could see her through the glass doors. She was upset and arguing, her free hand making gestures as though the person on the other end could see her.

She hung up after less than a minute and came back in flushed with anger.

"What happened?" he asked.

"Family happened. My brother's wedding is coming up and everybody has an opinion about it."

A man was standing in line and glanced at them and then did a double take. "Hey, you're the lawyers from that thing in the news, aren't you?"

Dylan said, "In the flesh."

He shook his head. "Shame on both of you."

With that, he turned back around and wouldn't look at them again.

49

The next day in court, Kelly walked in wearing her new skirt and blouse. They had cost entirely too much, and she would have to find someplace in her monthly budget to cut to be able to afford them, but she felt good.

She strolled past the cameras set up near the double doors of the courtroom, feeling mild exhilaration because she knew she would look good on the news tonight. She hoped her ex would be watching.

They had called it an equitable divorce, but there was nothing equitable about his yearlong affair before leaving Kelly. Something the male judge had dismissed as "boys will be boys" with a chuckle, thinking she would find it charming.

The first witness was Detective Hank Philips. He appeared entirely comfortable in court. He looked at the jury while he introduced himself and answered the initial questions. As Kelly ran him through the timeline of events, he kept an even tone and spoke dispassionately. Careful not to use inflammatory words that might make him seem biased toward one side. Kelly heard Lily lean over to Dylan and murmur, "He's good."

Dylan objected thirty-one times in three hours. Most of them were overruled, and one garnered an admonishment from the judge.

"Detective," Kelly said, "I'm going to ask you the most important question you're going to be asked. What was your impression of Arlo Ward's demeanor?"

"Objection," Dylan said. "Calls for expert testimony."

"I'm just asking his opinion of the general impressions he got as a twenty-four-year veteran law enforcement officer, Your Honor."

"The objection is overruled. You may answer, Detective."

"He seemed nervous, of course, but not unusually so. His body language indicated he was calm and comfortable. Perfectly aware of what was happening and why. He answered our questions succinctly and, as you saw on the video, didn't seem confused about any of them. In fact, if I hadn't been told afterward, I wouldn't have guessed that he had any mental illne—"

"Objection," Dylan said. He glanced at Lily, who should have jumped in with an objection as well. "Calls for expert testimony, Your Honor. He's not a psychologist and can't speak as to what someone with this mental disorder would or wouldn't act like."

"Sustained."

Kelly said, "Detective Philips, did Arlo Ward ever give the impression that he was out of control or didn't understand the nature—"

"Objection."

"Sustained."

Kelly put both hands on the lectern, the tips of her fingers turning white.

"Did Arlo Ward seem—"

"Objection," Dylan said, rising this time, "calls for expert testimony."

"Sustained."

Kelly drew a deep breath. "Did—"

"Objection, calls for—"

"Sit down," Kelly snapped.

"I would object to Counsel's remark and ask the Court—"

"And I would ask Counsel to sit down again," Kelly snapped.

"Your Honor!" Dylan said with a wounded tone that grated on Kelly even more than the objections. "This is completely unprofessional, and I am hurt, shocked frankly, that—"

Judge Hamilton interrupted him. "Counsels, approach."

The two attorneys went up to the judge's bench.

"You two need to tone it down," the judge said quietly. "This makes all of us look bad, and you might approach a place where I have to hold you in contempt."

"Tell *her* that. She's the one asking objectionable questions."

"Oh, please. The only thing objectionable in this courtroom is you. You make our profession look like it's here just to manipulate—"

"*Our* profession? Since when do you see yourself as an attorney and not a glorified cop?"

"Okay," the judge said angrily, "enough. If you two can't control it, I'm going to take the day and hold a contempt hearing for both of you. At some point, maybe I'd have to declare a mistrial. Ms. Whitewolf, do you want a mistrial?"

She glanced at Dylan. "No, Your Honor."

"Mr. Aster, do you?"

"No."

"Then I suggest you each take a breath before we get back on the record."

50

The attorneys went back to their respective tables, and the judge called a ten-minute recess.

As people left to hit the bathrooms and voices filled the courtroom from those that stayed, Dylan looked at Lily and said, "Can I talk to you outside?"

They went out to the courthouse steps. Dylan put his hands in his pockets and looked out over the street at the cars passing by. For a small town, the intersection seemed busy.

"Lil, you're a million miles away since you took that call last night. What's going on?"

"Nothing."

"It's definitely something."

"Well, if it is, I don't want to talk about it. And honestly, it's none of your business."

"It's my business when it affects our client. You realize he's on trial for his life, right? That jury looks to us to see how to act. You're staring off into space and not even paying attention. If his own lawyers think he's a lost cause, what chance do we have that they'll see him differently?"

She shook her head. "It's so easy for you, isn't it? So black and white. There's defending the client, and everything else comes after. But maybe for some of us, our own lives come first."

———

Kelly stood in front of the lectern and finished her questioning of Detective Philips. Dylan objected only twice.

"No further questions for this witness."

Before she sat down, she turned back to Detective Philips and said, "Actually, one more question, Detective: Based on what you observed, did Arlo Ward seem like a man that couldn't control himself that night?"

"Based on my observation of him and my training and experience, my opinion is that Arlo Ward was perfectly in control of his faculties that night."

"Thank you."

As the detective poured some water into a plastic cup, Judge Hamilton said, "Mr. Aster, your witness."

Dylan didn't stand in front of the lectern. To cross-examine witnesses, he preferred to stand in the well, the space between the lectern and the witness box. Throughout his questioning, he liked to slowly move toward the witness. As the pace and intensity of his questions increased, he would decrease the distance. Getting closer while raising his voice created an intimidating effect that resulted in a more flustered witness, and a flustered witness was a witness who made mistakes.

"You've been a police officer for over two decades, correct?"

"Yes."

"Seen a lot during that time, I bet."

"You could say that."

"You've come to know the ins and outs of criminal investigation, yeah?"

Philips shrugged. "I take my job seriously, if that's what you're asking."

"You've worked in a Homicide Unit before, correct?"

"Yes."

"In the Salt Lake City Police Department?"

"Yes."

"And in Homicide, practically every unit across the country has a homicide board, isn't that right?"

"I can't speak to other jurisdictions, but the ones I've worked in this state and Utah do, that's correct."

"What is a homicide board?"

"It's just a white or clear board up on the wall that lists all the open homicides a unit is working at a given time. It gives the detectives a quick visual estimate of the ebb and flow of homicides in a particular jurisdiction."

"It lets you know how behind you are, correct?"

"That's one of its functions I suppose, yes."

"What's a whodunit and a dunker, Detective?"

He did a slight clearing of his throat as he glanced at Kelly. "They're common terms that homicide detectives sometimes use."

"A whodunit is a murder in which there are no witnesses, no solid leads, and no suspects, correct?"

"That's correct."

"What's a dunker?"

"It's a nonsense little shorthand for a slam dunk. It means there's plenty of evidence, a suspect, and witnesses, and the case will probably resolve with an arrest."

"Arlo Ward confessed to this crime, correct?"

"Yes."

"He was covered in blood when he was pulled over?"

"He was."

"He agreed to give a written confession, too, yeah?"

"That is correct."

"Isn't it true you told the other detective interviewing Arlo Ward that this case was a dunker?"

Philips sat in silence a moment, his brow furrowing. "How did you know that?"

"I didn't, until just now."

The detective looked at Kelly, who leaned back in her chair and folded her arms.

"So you thought this case was a dunker right from the start, yeah?" Dylan said.

"It's just a term we use."

"A term that means slam dunk, correct?"

Philips swallowed, his eyes never wavering from Dylan's. "Correct."

"So when you called this case a dunker, you meant that you thought you had this case resolved and Arlo was the one that committed these crimes?"

Philips thought a moment. "I did call this case a dunker, that's true, but it's not a simple term saying the case is over. No case is over on the first night. There's always more investigation to be done."

"Oh, okay. Great. What other suspects did you investigate, then? Please list them for the jury."

Philips exhaled through his nose while holding Dylan's gaze. "None."

"Not one?"

"No, there were no other suspects."

"Did you talk to the surviving victim that night?"

"I did."

"On that first night, did you look into her background and the background of the other three people to find out if they knew anyone who would want to hurt them? For example, did you check to see if either of the two women had taken out stalking injunctions against anyone? Or if the boys had gotten into fights with anyone recently? Or even if someone had tried to kill any of them before?"

"No, not on the first night. The first night is—"

"You went up to the scene of the murders that night, correct?"

Philips blew out a breath through pressed lips. Frustration, for the first time, flashed across his face. Dylan now knew what his weakness was: Detective Philips didn't like being interrupted.

"I did, yes."

"Did you search for other campsites other than the murder scene?"

"It's not common for people to camp up there."

"So that's a no?"

Philips ran his tongue along the inside of his cheek. "That's a no."

"Did you scour the mountain looking for suspects?"

"We did a cursory search of the area, yes."

"Really? Coyote Canyon is about thirty square miles. You searched the entire thirty square miles?"

"That would've been impossible with the manpower we had."

"So again, that's a no, correct?"

"Yes, that's a no," Philips said, his tone barely holding back the contempt he was feeling.

"After Arlo's arrest, how many people did you interview as potential suspects?"

"We didn't have—"

"None, yeah?"

Philips nodded slowly. "That is correct."

"My client told you he suffers from mental illness almost as soon as you interviewed him, didn't he?"

"We were made aware of that—"

"Simple yes or no."

Detective Philips paused, and a flush came to his cheeks. Kelly must've seen it, too, because she was on her feet and said, "Objection, I would ask for Counsel to allow the detective to fully answer the questions."

"Overruled. I'll make a ruling for each question individually that you object to, Ms. Whitewolf, but a general admonishment would be inappropriate."

"Yes or no," Dylan said. "He told you he was mentally ill when you interviewed him?"

"I didn't know what type or how severe. He told us something was wrong with him, but there was no verification—"

"I'll ask you for the third time, Detective, yes or no? Did my client tell you he was mentally ill when you interviewed him?"

Philips gritted his teeth. "He told us he was, yes."

"So after learning this, you continued to interrogate him, yeah?"

"Yes, but I called Ms. Whitewolf and we—"

"Thank you, Detective, you answered my question. Now, after your interrogation, you went up to the murder scene?"

"Yes."

"But before that, you went to the hospital and interviewed Holly Fallows, yeah?"

"I did."

"And she told you the man that attacked her came out of the shadows near a grouping of trees."

"As I stated in my testimony, that is what she told us, yes. He was standing about sixty feet away and ran toward her after Mr. Turner was incapacitated by the trap."

"So they came out of the cabin because, as you said, they heard the front door slam."

"That is what she told us, yes."

"You didn't tell this jury how long it took them to leave the cabin after hearing the door slam."

He shook his head and gave a slight shrug. "I don't know the answer to that, Counselor."

"Because you didn't ask Holly Fallows, right?"

"No, it's not relevant to any—"

"So they hear a door slam, take the time to come out of the cabin, and assuming it was the killer who slammed the door, he was now standing sixty feet away."

"Yes."

"So what would you guess is the time it took them to leave the cabin? Ten seconds? Twenty?"

"I couldn't say."

"I had to object dozens of times when you pretended you're an expert, but now you're telling us you can't guess the amount of time it takes someone to walk out of a cabin?"

"Objection, badgering."

"Overruled."

"How many square feet is the cabin?"

"The criminalist estimated it at eight hundred square feet."

Dylan took two steps closer to the witness stand. "How long would it take someone standing at the back of an eight-hundred-square-foot cabin to walk out of that cabin?"

"I couldn't say."

"Couldn't or won't because it's me asking instead of Ms. Whitewolf?"

"Objection."

"Sustained."

Dylan didn't miss a beat as he said, "Pretend I'm Ms. Whitewolf. How long?"

"Objection," she said, on her feet again. "Badgering."

"Sustained."

"Since you won't tell the jury what you think, let's assume ten seconds. So it takes—"

"It wouldn't have been that fast."

Dylan took another step closer to him. "Oh, now you have an opinion about it? I would appreciate you not being evasive with this jury. They deserve the truth."

"Objection!" This time it was James on his feet. Dylan noted the anger in his voice and thought he could see his hands shaking. Not a man used to seeing an attorney who didn't care if he was objected to.

"Sustained. Mr. Aster, please refrain from commentary about the witness's testimony."

Dylan took another step closer. "Fifteen seconds, then. So this killer would've had to sprint sixty feet away in fifteen seconds to get to the trees Holly said he was standing by, correct?"

The detective's jaw muscles flexed, but his gaze didn't waver from Dylan's. "If you assume it took them fifteen seconds to leave, yes, he would have had to sprint to make it sixty feet away."

"I'd like to show you something, Detective. Your Honor, I'd like Mr. Ward to stand and approach for a demonstration, if that's all right."

"I'll allow it."

"Arlo, stand up and walk toward me, would you?"

Arlo glanced at Madeline, who nodded, and then he stood. He went around the table to the well and approached Dylan. His limp caused a dip down on his right side with each step.

"Thank you, Arlo. You can sit back down." Arlo stood silently a second, unsure what was happening, and Dylan gently placed a hand on his shoulder. "It's okay, Arlo. Go sit back down."

Arlo limped back to his seat.

Dylan turned back to the detective. "He walked with a limp, didn't he?"

The detective didn't answer for a moment. "Yes, he did."

"Do you know how he got that limp?"

James was on his feet again. "Objection, relevance."

"He saved a boy's life by pushing him out of the way of a moving car," Dylan tossed in.

James and Kelly both objected, nearly shouting, and Judge Hamilton held up a hand, letting them know he already had it under control.

"Mr. Aster, that's twice I've had to warn you about objectionable questions. I will not warn a third time, I'll just cut the cross-examination short."

An empty threat, since not being able to thoroughly cross-examine a witness on a death penalty case would be automatic grounds for reversal on appeal. But Dylan didn't say anything; he knew the judge just wanted to appear in control of the courtroom for the cameras.

Dylan took two more steps toward the detective. The detective's discomfort was growing. Dylan could see the sweat on his brow.

"Did you run that length, Detective?"

"What do you mean?"

"From the cabin to the cluster of trees about sixty feet away. Did you run it?"

"No."

"Would it surprise you if I said I did, and it took me ten seconds?"

"No, I suppose that's about right for someone that can run relatively fast."

"Could someone with a limp run that fast?"

"I wouldn't know, Counselor."

"Really? Ten seconds was me pushing myself as hard as possible, and you're testifying today that someone with a limp could do it just as easily as me?"

"I don't know how fast your client can run. You'll have to ask him."

Perfect, Dylan thought. Police officers hated conceding any point on the stand, and many times, if the point was obvious, the jury would wonder what they were trying to hide.

He took another step toward the detective.

"I'd like to show you another photograph that Ms. Whitewolf already put up."

Dylan moved the board with the photos pinned to it so the detective and jury could see it. He pointed to the corner at six photos of Arlo.

"Now, in these photos, Arlo's face is covered in blood, correct?"

"Yes."

"That wasn't the word you used, though, right? You never said *covered* in your reports?"

"I don't recall if it was or not."

"Let's take a moment, then, for you to refresh your memory."

Detective Philips sighed quietly and then picked up his report, which sat on the banister in front of him. He flipped through a few pages until he found what he was looking for. "I stated that the AP had blood smears running both vertically and horizontally across—"

"Smears. You said 'blood smears,' not 'covered in blood.' Correct? In fact, you used the term *smear* twice."

"Yes."

"*Smear* implies that you mark something messily, yeah? The way a child smears chocolate over their face."

"If you say so."

"If I say so or yes, Detective? If you have a different definition of the word *smear*, please share it with us now."

A beat of silence passed before Philips cleared his throat and said, "No, I suppose I don't."

"Okay, so *smear* implies that it was done purposely. If a paint can explodes from pressure, paint doesn't get smeared on the wall, correct? It spatters."

"I suppose that's right."

"Now, if you look at Arlo's face in these photographs, the blood is on his forehead, his cheeks, nose, and chin, right?"

"That's right."

"Does that look like blood spatter to you?"

"Objection," James said.

Dylan grinned. "The reason they're objecting is that Detective Philips is not an expert, something I objected to fifty times, Your Honor. They can't have it both ways."

"I'll allow the detective to testify as to what he directly observed. The objection is overruled."

Dylan took another step toward the detective and then another. "Does that look like blood spatter to you?"

"I suppose it could be, yes."

"But Detective, you wrote that he had blood *smeared* over his face and clothing. Isn't that right? So that implies you know the difference between a spatter and a smear. You do know the difference, don't you?"

Dylan took another step toward him so that he was only about five feet away.

"Yes, Counselor, I know the difference."

"And to smear something implies it was done on purpose, as we already said, right?"

"If you say so."

Dylan had increased the volume of his voice and took another step forward. The detective was feeling threatened. Dylan could tell because he was getting flushed and was answering quickly instead of taking time to think.

"So you have a man who is severely mentally ill, has a limp, and can't run fast, and the blood you find on him is purposely smeared as though to make it look like he had been randomly covered in blood—"

"Objection, stating facts not in the record."

"You have this man," Dylan continued before the judge could say anything, "who you know is sick with about the worst mental disorder you can have, and instead of random spatters of blood that would be consistent with butchery, you have someone who carefully—"

"Objection!"

"—smeared the blood over his body. You have all this, and you didn't look for other suspects, did you, Detective Philips?"

"Your Honor, I've objected twice now."

"Mr. Aster, please wait until the objection is ruled upon before continuing with your questioning. Ms. Whitewolf, your objection is sustained. Move on, Mr. Aster."

"Detective Philips," he said, taking another step forward, "you didn't even look for another suspect, did you?"

"Based on the evidence we had on hand—"

"Ah yes," Dylan said, so close now that he put his hand on the banister of the witness box. "The *evidence* you had. The evidence . . . you never found the murder weapons, did you?"

"We found a bat at a cabin in—"

"You found a bat in a cabin weeks after the murders, correct?"

He paused a moment. "Yes."

"And you didn't find it, did you? Someone gave you a tip?"

"That is correct."

"Has it tested positive for any blood evidence?"

"It has not to my knowledge, no."

"In fact, the bat looks brand new, doesn't it? Unused."

"I suppose it does."

"There was likely a knife used to mutilate the victims, correct?"

"Correct."

"You find this knife?"

"No, we have not at this time."

"Some organs were missing from the victims, isn't that right?"

"Yes."

"Were all those organs ever recovered?"

"They were not."

"One of Michael Turner's limbs was missing. His left arm. Did you find it?"

He shifted uncomfortably in his seat. "No, we never found it."

"One of the victims' hands was missing. April Fallows's right hand. Did you ever find it?"

"We did not."

"That's it. 'We did not'? Isn't that sentence usually followed by, 'We assume it was taken by the perpetrator'?"

"Not in every case, no."

"Not in this case because you allegedly caught the perpetrator, and he didn't have anything like that with him, did he?"

"No."

"In fact, the only thing he had that linked him to this crime was the blood on his skin and clothing, correct?"

"And his confession as to—"

"The only physical evidence linking Arlo Ward to this crime was the blood that was purposely smeared on his face and the blood that was smeared all over his clothing. Isn't that right?"

He hesitated, glancing at Kelly several times before answering. "Yes, that's right."

Kelly rose. "Your Honor, may we go in chambers to discuss a matter outside the presence of the jury?"

"Certainly. We will take a ten-minute break and return on the record at that point."

Dylan stared at Kelly, who wouldn't look at him. The only reason she'd ask to discuss a matter outside the presence of the jury was because it would hurt the State's case to discuss it in front of them. He looked at Lily and Madeline, who both appeared as puzzled as he did.

51

The judge's chambers smelled better than Dylan remembered from his last time there. No dust anywhere, everything arranged just right with vacuum waves on the carpet. The judge must've had it cleaned recently, probably in case someone from the media wanted to interview him back here.

Dylan and James sat, but Kelly folded her arms and leaned against the wall near the judge's desk. Lily took a spot across from her on the opposite wall with Madeline.

Kelly said, "This entire line of questioning needs to be stricken from the record, Your Honor."

"For what?" Dylan said. "'Cause your detective started sweating bullets up there?"

"Because it's all irrelevant. Mr. Aster has claimed an affirmative defense of insanity. As such, the question of whether Mr. Ward's actions add or take away from the impression of legal insanity presented to the jury should be the only focus of Mr. Aster's questioning. Instead, in essence, he is building a case that hinges on Mr. Ward not being the one that murdered those people."

Dylan gave Lily a look that said, *Little help*, and she said, "The prevailing case is *Hutchinson v. Scout*. There, the defendant was seen running from the scene of the crime. That defendant also suffered from schizophrenia, and the defense wanted to preserve the issue of diminished capacity. So they argued innocence, and in the alternative, not guilty by reason of insanity."

Kelly said, "That was a narrow set of circumstances involving evidence of a second culprit. There is no evidence here that anyone else was involved in these murders. What they're doing is shifting the burden of insanity back to us to avoid having to prove the M'Naghten standard to the jury themselves. They can't have their cake and eat it, too. He either didn't do it, or he did it and was insane at the time, and they have to prove that, not me. They have to make a choice, Your Honor, because otherwise it unfairly shifts the burden of proof to the State."

Lily said, "We certainly do not have to make a choice. The M'Naghten rules shift the burden to us to prove insanity, but there is no case anywhere saying we can't also argue that he didn't do it, but if in the alternative, you find that he did, we don't feel he had the requisite mental state to be held accountable."

The judge inhaled deeply, thought a moment, and then looked at James. "Mr. Halden, anything to add?"

"I think that about covers it, Your Honor."

"Mr. Aster?"

"This entire objection is academic, Your Honor. I'm simply exploring the groundwork for the insanity defense. Not once in that entire cross-examination did I say that Arlo did not commit these crimes, just that the detective rushed to judgment without doing a full investigation that could've provided—"

"Bullshit," Kelly interrupted. "You might as well have said, *Hey, we think he's innocent* and *insane and the State should have to prove it, not us.*"

Hamilton tapped his pen a few times and said, "Mr. Aster, I'm not going to strike the testimony that we've heard so far. I feel Ms. Whitewolf's objection to the entirety of the testimony is unwarranted. However, going forward, I'm going to limit you on what the jury can hear regarding the innocence of Mr. Ward. You have claimed an affirmative defense of insanity. Once such defense is approved, the burden then shifts to you to prove by a preponderance of the evidence the defense you have claimed. The defense of factual innocence is no longer an issue. I believe Ms. Whitewolf is correct in that the line of cases Ms. Ricci has cited can be distinguished from the present set of facts and do not directly apply. You have, so to speak, already agreed that your client committed these crimes, just that he shouldn't be held accountable."

"A client who is severely mentally ill and won't let me plead him not guilty, Your Honor."

"That's a problem between you and your client. I will do further research on this issue, but for now, let's assume you must go forward with the affirmative defense of insanity since that is the plea entered. Now let's get back out there and finish the day. I can already tell the jury is getting weary of the bickering, and fair warning, so am I."

52

Kelly was one of the last to leave the courthouse. She and James met outside on the front steps to talk with their "shadow jurors." Two men and a woman who'd been paid to attend court every day and later tell Kelly and James what they thought about the proceedings. Since she had fired the jury consultants, James had insisted they at least do this for some objective feedback.

Today, they stated that they liked Detective Philips, and he'd done a "pretty good job" in the investigation. But they were curious why he hadn't looked at other suspects.

"Seems like you'd want to at least look around and see if anyone else was nearby, wouldn't you?" the woman said. "I'm no police officer, but seemed like to me they hurried through everything."

Kelly wanted to grab her and scream, "There was no one else around, moron! It's a trick by the defense to make you think the police did shoddy work when they didn't."

Instead, Kelly politely thanked them for their time and headed to her truck. It was a Friday, which meant two days without the case taking up every waking moment. It lifted her spirits enough that she didn't even mind the press shouting questions at her as she marched past.

The media attention had grown from a mild annoyance to a downright pain in the ass. A woman even followed her into the bathroom to see if she could get a snippet for the news.

A few cameras were there in the parking lot, pointed in her direction. She held her chin up just a little higher, making sure they caught a full view of the new clothes.

———

When Kelly got home, her daughters were at the dining room table, eating hot dogs and playing on Bethany's phone. Aunt Noya was watching television and sipping tea.

Kelly kicked off her heels for the first time in sixteen hours. It felt like her feet were being released from vises. She rubbed her aching arches, and her aunt said, "You should wear better shoes."

"Those are the nicest ones I have."

"Nice don't mean better."

"We saw you on TV, Mommy," Bella said.

"You did? How did I look?"

"So cool! You were arguing with that guy, and the TV man said you were aggre—aggre—"

"Aggressive," Bethany said.

"Yeah, aggressive."

Kelly grinned as she turned to the fridge.

"And those mean women were stupid."

"Bella!" Bethany snapped. "You said you wouldn't say anything."

Kelly scanned the fridge and settled on a leftover chicken salad from yesterday. "What mean women?"

Bethany and Bella were silent. Kelly turned to them. "What mean women?"

Bethany wouldn't look at her. "Just on that show where they talk about stuff. They were talking about you. It wasn't a big deal."

Bella said, "But I really like Polly Anna Taylor."

"Who's that?"

Bethany said, "She's an Instagram model."

"And she sings, and she can paint, and she teaches people how to put on makeup and how to get bodies like she has. She's really muscly. She's my hero," Bella said, beaming with pride.

Kelly placed the salad on the counter. "What did they say?"

"Nothing," Bethany said.

"Now I'm curious since you don't want to tell me."

The two girls looked at each other. Her aunt didn't say anything from the living room, but Kelly heard her turn down the volume of the television.

Since her mother's death, Aunt Noya had been Kelly's protector. The woman in her life who taught her how to be a woman. During the divorce, Kelly had cried in her arms more than once, and Noya held her, rocked her slightly like she used to do when Kelly was a child, and let her get it all out. The fact that she turned the television down to listen meant she knew Kelly wasn't about to like what she was going to hear.

Kelly went over to the table where a laptop sat closed. She opened it, saying, "Let's see what these mean ladies said."

Bethany hesitated, her head held low, and then pulled up her Instagram account. There was a video of four women. All of them could be twins: buxom, blonde hair, long legs, skimpy clothing, lips puffy from Botox, and long eyelashes.

"It's nothing, Mom," Bethany said. "They're idiots. It doesn't matter what they said."

"Yeah, but Bella said she's her hero. I'd like to hear what her hero has to say about her mom. Which one is she?"

Bethany hesitated. "That one in the white skirt."

"Start the video. Let's see it."

She hit the play button.

The women were jabbering and chuckling. They were discussing the trial. A video came up. It was Kelly standing at the lectern, making an argument. No sound to actually capture her words, just the image.

"And look at that skirt," Polly Anna Taylor said. "I mean, not to knock someone when they're doing their job, but my gosh, like, get a clue. It looks like she bought it off the rack."

One of the other women said, "It matches the hair. Like, if you know you're gonna be in front of millions of people, you need to look sexalicious, or you're better off at home and just telling people what you would've worn."

"Honey, if you're out there watching, I will be your stylist for free. We can't let this disaster just keep goin' on like nothin' happened. And you clearly got the bod for it. We can make miracles with our—"

"And OMG, I have to say something; those shoes? Right? Like maybe if you're working at a car wash, but if you're flexing your guns on every channel, you need to look like a Kardashian. Not a Karen yelling at a manager in a tanning salon."

"Oh, totally. The first thing I would do is get a refund from Target for that suit, and then—"

Kelly closed the laptop. She stood in silence a moment before saying, "What they say doesn't matter."

She put the salad back. She'd lost her appetite.

53

Once the kids were in bed, Kelly sat outside on her back porch. Her home was in the middle of two acres of property, and the nearest neighbors were far enough away that they rarely ran into each other. Kelly had, at first, not liked the isolation, but once she'd grown used to it, she wouldn't have had it any other way.

In her lap was the new outfit: a skirt and blouse. She lifted them up and stared at them. She picked up the scissors she had brought with her and cut a massive gash across the blouse. Then another, and another, until strips fell over her porch. The movements became frantic—the actions of someone rushing through what they were doing so they wouldn't have to think about it.

A small voice behind her said, "Mommy?"

It startled her, and she jumped. The scissors nearly dropped out of her hands. She saw Bella standing next to her with a look of confusion on her sweet face. "What are you doing, Mommy?"

Kelly looked down at the blouse and pushed the remnants onto the porch. She picked up her daughter and sat her in her lap and said, "Bella, I want you to know something. That person you think is your hero, she's not a hero. She's fake. Empty on the inside because she only cares about what's on the outside." Kelly's throat tightened with emotion. "The woman who gets up every morning and goes to work and tries to raise a family by herself with everyone telling her she's doing a bad job, and after a while"—she felt tears in her eyes—"after a while, she believes them, so she cries by herself sometimes . . ."

She composed herself and didn't speak again until the tears had stopped.

"The woman who goes through that but still gets up every morning and does it over and over again, she's the hero. Do you understand?"

Bella watched her a moment and then nodded. Kelly wrapped her arms around her daughter and laid her chin against her head. A breeze blew, and a few scraps of cloth slid off the porch and into the yard. It reminded her of a video of the crime scene. Arlo Ward had cut their clothes off before doing what he did to their bodies, and the clothing flapped around the dirt and shrubbery with the wind.

Kelly held her daughter tighter.

54

Over the weekend, Dylan had wanted to meet with Lily and go over the upcoming week's testimony. They would be pulling a surprise on the prosecution by calling Evan Ward. Kelly would be expecting him to get up there as a character witness and talk about what a great person Arlo was: she wouldn't be prepared for Dylan's accusing Evan of being the killer. So Dylan wanted his questioning to go perfectly. Lily declined to meet.

"What do you mean, no?" he'd said into the phone while mowing his lawn.

"Not this weekend."

"Lil, what the hell is going on? I've gone from being bugged to being worried."

"Nothing. I'm fine. I'll see you on Monday."

That was the last they'd spoken the entire weekend. Dylan drove over to her condo once, but Jake answered and said she had been out all day and wasn't answering her phone.

On Monday, Dylan finished up with Hank Philips's testimony. Arlo had gotten a fresh legal pad and was making drawings of fish weaving in between coral reefs. Kelly had a brief redirect examination, and then Judge Hamilton told Detective Philips he was excused.

"You all right?" Dylan asked Lily on a break.

"I'm fine, Dylan. You really don't have to worry about me."

"That's usually what someone says when people should be worried about them."

"You're sweet, but I'm good."

After the break, when they were seated again, the judge said, "Next witness, Ms. Whitewolf."

"The State would call—"

"Your Honor," Lily said as she rose, "the defense has a motion we'd like to argue at this time. It's probably appropriate for the jury to be excused for this."

Judge Hamilton glanced at the cameras and then said, "Very well." He turned to the jury. "Ladies and gentlemen of the jury, at this time, we will take another short break. The bailiff will lead you back, and please feel free to use the facilities if there is time."

Once the jury was out, the judge said, "Ms. Ricci, go ahead."

"Your Honor, at this time, the defense would make a motion to call Evan Ward to the stand as a witness for the defense. He is Mr. Ward's biological half brother."

"I would vehemently object to that, Your Honor," Kelly said. "They can wait until the State has rested. There's no reason to call him now."

"Your Honor, in our initial interview with him, before Mr. Aster could get out a word, Evan Ward ran from him and our investigator. I fear we're at risk of him becoming an unavailable witness. Our investigator has escorted him here today with a lawful subpoena, but I'm uncertain if we could ever get him back. I would ask we get his testimony on the record now. It's a very minor inconvenience to the prosecution but will preserve testimony that will help this jury come to a just verdict."

"That's not what this is," Kelly spat. "She wants to interrupt the flow of the State's case to manipulate the jury and present evidence counter to what has been offered by the State."

"That is not what we're doing, Your Honor. He might run. If we don't get his testimony on the record today, we may never get it."

The judge tapped his pen against the bench while he thought. Dylan kept thinking, *Come on, come on, come on . . .*

"On what authority do you assume that he may flee the jurisdiction, Ms. Ricci?"

"On the authority of his parole officer. May I approach?"

"You may."

Lily picked up two signed affidavits off the defense table and gave one to Kelly and the other to the judge before going to the lectern. "In front of you is an affidavit from Mr. Evan Ward's parole officer stating that he has jumped parole twice in the past. He told me in private she believes he will not wish to cooperate with this case, and either not show up to court or simply abscond."

"And how did your investigator get him here today?"

"We sent out a valid subpoena, as had the State, and my investigator went to his favorite diner and convinced him, just barely, to be here today."

"Uh-huh," Hamilton said, eyeing Lily suspiciously. He looked at Kelly and said, "What's the State's position, Ms. Whitewolf?"

"Ms. Ricci is treating this witness as though he's already unavailable, but he is not. The State should be allowed to finish presenting our case, and then we can worry about which of the defense's witnesses we can or can't get here."

Hamilton looked over the affidavit again. "Due to the fact that his own parole officer states he is a flight risk, I am going to allow his testimony to come in at this time."

"Your Honor," James said, as he rose to his feet, "this is an attempt by the defense to interrupt the State's case and confuse the jury. They know that the order of witnesses is laid out logically for any trial of this magnitude, and they're attempting to break that presentation and divert the jury's attention."

"Mr. Aster, Ms. Ricci, if that is what you are doing, I will hold both of you in contempt. Is that clear?"

Lily said, "It is, Judge."

Hamilton nodded. "Having said that, this witness does seem like a flight risk, and getting his testimony on the record outweighs the risk of, as you said, 'breaking the flow' of the prosecution's case. I'll allow him to testify."

55

Brody followed Evan Ward into the courtroom. Lily stood at the lectern and reviewed her notes. Dylan and Madeline were discussing something with Arlo in hushed tones. It seemed Arlo was arguing that he didn't want his brother to testify, but they convinced him it was a normal part of the case. It certainly wasn't, and when she was done, Lily fully expected to get yelled at by the judge and her client.

Evan was sworn in. He wore a long button-up shirt, but even that was too tight, and his muscles bulged underneath. He kept stealing glances at the jury and looked like he'd rather be anywhere on the planet but where he was right now.

"Please state and spell your name for the record." Evan did so, and his voice cracked once as he looked at the judge.

"Do you know Arlo Ward?" Lily asked.

"Yes."

"How?"

"He's my half brother."

"Do you know what this case is about, Mr. Ward?"

"I do."

"You read or saw it on the news?"

"Yeah, I saw something on the internet about it. It's everywhere."

"And you're aware the murders of William Page, Michael Turner, and April Fallows occurred on May ninth?"

"I am."

"That was a Friday, correct?"

"I guess," he said.

"You work in mail delivery at a private company, correct?"

"Yeah."

"And you work evenings, correct?"

"I do."

"You work Friday nights as well."

"I do."

"Is there anyone that saw you that night that can testify you were at work?"

He shifted uncomfortably in his chair. "I don't know. My boss maybe."

"So if you were at work, you got off around ten that night, correct?"

"Yeah."

"What'd you do after work that night?"

"I don't know, probably watched TV."

"What'd you watch?"

He glanced at the jury. "I don't remember."

"Objection," Kelly said. "Leading the witness."

"Your Honor, the witness is being evasive. Permission to treat him as hostile."

Evan's eyes went wide at the word *hostile*, and he stared at the judge.

"Permission granted."

Lily said, "You remember you watched television that night, but you don't recall what you watched?"

"Some nature shows, I guess."

"Some nature shows?"

"Yeah. Some nature shows."

"You moved to Las Vegas close to six years ago, correct?"

"Yes."

"But you left home in North Dakota two years before that, didn't you?"

"'Bout eight years ago, yeah."

"And where'd you go?"

"Oregon. Up the coast."

"You worked for a company out of Midway, correct?"

"Yes."

"What company did you work for?" Lily said.

"It was called Herbert Construction, out of, like you said, a small town called Midway."

"It's called Construction, but they did a lot more than construction, didn't they?"

"I guess."

"They were primarily a logging company, correct?"

"Yeah, we did a lot of logging."

"What was your job with the company?"

"I was a logger."

"In fact, you were something called a brush monkey, is that right?"

Evan swallowed and looked at Arlo, who was staring down at the table. He wasn't drawing now. "Yes."

"What is a brush monkey?"

"It's what they call the newer workers."

"That's not entirely true, is it? It's what they call the workers that get the worst jobs at the logging site, correct?"

"Yeah, I guess so."

"And what's the worst job on the logging site?"

He cleared his throat. "It's called a haymaker."

"And what is that?"

"It's someone who clears trees with an ax before the guys with the chainsaws come in. We clear out the—"

"Thank you. So you swung an ax for two years?"

"Objection," Kelly said. "Relevance? Also, we addressed this in chambers, Your Honor."

"Its relevance will soon be made clear, Your Honor," Lily said.

"I'll allow it," said Hamilton.

"Answer the question, Mr. Ward," Lily continued. "You swung an ax for two years."

"That's not all I did."

"Yes or no; you swung an ax chopping down trees as your primary duty with the company for two years?"

He looked at the jury again and rubbed his palm against his jeans, the way someone would if they had touched something distasteful and wanted to get the feeling off. "Yeah, I guess."

"But that's not the only thing brush monkeys do, correct? What happens when there are animals in the area you're clearing?"

He looked at the jury. "We have to dispose of them."

"You kill them, right? Deer, moose, boar, whatever you find. Correct?"

"Yes."

"You carried a large knife with you as a brush monkey, did you not?"

He shrugged. "Yeah, we all did."

"And the knife was to stab the animals if they were shot and weren't dead, correct?"

"Yes."

"How would you kill them?"

"How?"

Lily nodded. "In what manner would you kill them after they were shot and helpless on the ground?"

"Objection! Your Honor, we addressed this already and the Court ruled—"

"The Court ruled that further research will be conducted. The defense should be allowed to question all witnesses that may have exculpatory testimony or knowledge as to the defendant's mental health."

"I'll allow it within reason, Ms. Ricci, but my prior ruling on this stands."

"Thank you, Judge. Mr. Ward, go ahead and answer. How would you kill them?"

He swallowed. "We'd either gut them or slit their throats."

"By 'gut them,' you mean you'd stick the knife into the belly of the animal and then slide the knife all the way across. Disemboweling them."

"Yes."

"And by 'slit their throat,' you mean you'd slide the knife across the throat to cut major arteries and allow the animal to bleed to death, correct?"

"Yes."

Lily put her hands behind her back and stared right into his pupils. "And you were a brush monkey with another gentleman named Tom Naples, correct?"

Evan folded his massive arms across his chest. "Yes, I was."

"And you and Mr. Naples got into an argument one day."

"It was just . . . we did."

"It became a physical confrontation?"

He hesitated. "It did."

"And you struck Mr. Naples with a weapon, correct?"

He ran his tongue along his cheek. "I did."

"A log of wood, right?"

He didn't answer at first. "Only in self-defense."

"Hitting someone with a log and hitting them with a baseball bat isn't that different, is it?"

"Objection!"

Evan said, "What? Whoa, wait a seco—"

"Withdrawn," Lily said before the judge could rule. "You're on parole right now, aren't you?"

Evan looked at the judge but saw he wasn't going to help him. "Yes."

"In fact, you're on parole for a violent felony. Robbery."

"Objection," Kelly said, on her feet. "None of this is relevant and Mr. Evan Ward shouldn't even be on that stand."

"He's here because he has relevant information as to the defendant's mental state, Your Honor."

"That's not what this is, Judge," Kelly said. "They're attempting to blame someone else in clear contradiction to the Court's ruling."

"Again, Judge, if the defense is not allowed to question witnesses who may have direct knowledge about the most important issue at hand, what's the point of having a trial at all?"

"If that's the case," Kelly said with a quick look at Lily, "then the defense should've waited until the State called him and they could cross-examine him. They're attacking their own witness."

It was true, and everyone in that courtroom knew it. But if they had told Evan they were bringing him to court to blame him for the murders, he never would've come.

The judge was silent as he thought it over. He clearly didn't want to contradict his earlier ruling that they had to argue insanity, but he also must've realized not letting the defense fully question a witness that might have direct knowledge about the case would be automatic grounds for appeal.

"I'm going to allow it for now, Ms. Whitewolf, and we can go over the testimony at a later date and curative instructions may be given to the jury, should they be required. The objection is overruled."

Evan Ward cleared his throat as Lily held his gaze a moment before continuing.

"So you were convicted of robbery, correct?"

"It was a cash grab. Nobody got hurt."

"Most robberies occur using a gun, don't they?"

"I don't know."

"You didn't use a gun, though, did you?" she said, ignoring his answer so she could tell the jury what she wanted to tell them. "What'd you use?"

He swallowed. Lily noticed the sheen of sweat on his forehead. "Just a small knife."

"With a six-inch blade, right?"

"Yeah."

"And you said to the clerk, 'Open the register, or I'll cut your throat.'"

"Objection, hearsay."

"I'm not presenting it for the truth of the matter, Your Honor, that he was actually going to slit her throat, just that he said it. It's nonhearsay."

"I'll allow it."

"Is that what you said, Mr. Ward? 'Open the register, or I'll cut your throat'?"

He didn't answer.

"I would ask the Court to direct the witness to answer."

Judge Hamilton said, "Mr. Ward, please answer Counsel's question."

Evan inhaled deeply, his surprise and frustration turning to anger as he realized what was happening. "I didn't kill those people."

"I didn't say you did."

"Yeah, but I know what you're doing."

"Well, let's forget that for a second and go back to my original question, which you're avoiding, Mr. Ward. You told the cashier you would cut her throat if she didn't open the register, correct?"

He shifted in his seat again and said, "Yeah, but I was never gonna do it. I just needed the money 'cause I was strung out back then."

"You realize one of the victims in this case had their throat cut, right? In fact, cut all the way through to the point they were nearly decapitated."

He didn't respond.

Lily placed both hands on the lectern, and the volume of her voice increased, the anger in it. She needed to jar him, shake a reaction out of him that would stay with the jury long after he was off the stand.

"Mr. Ward, you don't like your brother, do you?"

"I wouldn't say that."

"You wouldn't say you dislike your brother? Really? So you didn't tell Leena Ward, Arlo's wife, the very first time you met her, that she should leave him because he's, and I quote, 'just a crazy-ass loser.'"

"I may have said something like that. I don't remember."

"The last time you saw Arlo was at your apartment, correct?"

"I guess so."

"He came to your apartment to let you know he was getting married."

"Yeah, he did."

"And you opened the door and saw him."

He shrugged. "Yeah."

"And you told him to leave."

"I don't remember."

"And after you told him to leave," she said, ignoring his answers again, "you became violent with him."

"No, I didn't."

"You didn't grab him and throw him down?"

"No."

"You didn't get on top of him and punch him not once, not twice, but three times in the face?"

"No."

"So if Leena Ward was sitting in the car watching this occur, and she came in here and testified that's what she saw, well, she would be a liar, wouldn't she?"

He shrugged. "Can't say nothing to that. But I didn't hit him."

"In your history of prior convictions, you have one from North Dakota for assault, correct?"

He let out a long breath. "Yeah."

"It was against Arlo when you and Arlo were still living with your parents?"

"Yeah."

"I have here the police report for that incident, Mr. Ward. Do you need to read it to refresh your memory of what happened that day?"

Evan gave her a hard stare, a stare that said the second they stepped out of this courtroom, he was going to explode at her. Lily held his gaze without blinking.

"No, I don't need to read it."

"You hit Arlo that day, correct?"

"Yeah, I guess I did," he said quietly now, the fire in his voice dissipating as he realized he might be in real trouble.

"You hit him with something, right?"

"I guess."

"It was a baseball bat, correct? You hit your brother with a baseball bat so hard your parents had to call an ambulance."

"Objection!" James nearly shouted.

"Overruled," the judge said.

Evan swallowed. "I did, but only in self-defense. I was like nineteen, just a kid."

"He was unarmed, correct?"

Evan shook his head and looked away, as if he couldn't believe what he was hearing. "Yeah."

"He fell on the ground and started crying after the first blow, according to the police report, is that right?"

He didn't answer, and Lily lifted the papers. "It's here in the police report if you need to read it."

He bit his lower lip to the point it looked like it bled and then released it. "Yes, he was on the ground."

"So what'd you do then?"

A deep inhalation, a glance to the jury, and then his eyes went to the floor as he realized the implications of what he was saying. "I hit him with the bat while he was on the ground."

"You hit him in the head, right?"

"Yeah."

"That seems to be a common thing with you, doesn't it? Threatening to slit people's throats or bash their heads in?"

"Objection!" both prosecutors shouted.

"Withdrawn," Lily said without looking away from Evan. "You know where Coyote Canyon is, don't you, Mr. Ward? And please don't lie, because we've already confirmed with your parole officer that you've been there."

"Yeah, I know where it is."

"You've camped there?"

"I fly-fish, and it's good fishing there."

"In fact, I believe your parole officer said you go up there quite a bit, correct?"

"Like I said, best fly-fishing in the state."

She came around the lectern but didn't approach the witness box like Dylan did.

"You were there on May ninth, weren't you?"

"No, I wasn't."

"You killed those people."

"Hell no, I didn't!"

"Objection!" Kelly and James both said, shooting to their feet.

"You finally did what you've always been threatening to do: bash in people's heads and then cut their throats. But then you panicked when you realized what you'd done, so you called your severely mentally ill brother to come down and—"

"Objection!" Kelly nearly screamed.

"—and take the blame. I bet you just loved that he was willing to do it, too. The thought of him being executed for a crime you committed must've made your day, didn't it?"

Arlo stood up. "I did it. I did it, Ms. Ricci. Don't say I didn't."

Dylan had to grab him and force him back into his seat.

"Ms. Ricci," the judge said in his "shit has hit the fan" voice. "In my chambers. Now!"

56

"I had every right to accuse him," Lily said as soon as they were inside the judge's chambers. Judge Hamilton shut the door before marching behind his desk. He sat down and took a drink of what looked like cold coffee out of a mug that said *#1 Dad*.

Kelly said, "That wasn't questioning; that was an ambush. They convinced that man to come to court to support his brother, and then they sandbagged him."

Dylan said, "It's perfectly within our rights to blame whoever we want for these crimes as long as it's within reason."

"You think that was within reason?"

"Your Honor," Lily said in a placating voice, "the man camps near the murder sites, has a history of violence involving knives and bats, and is currently on parole for threatening to kill a cashier in the same manner one of the victims was killed. If the police had actually done their job, he would've already been a suspect."

James said, "The defendant himself stated his brother had nothing to do with these murders. There isn't a shred of evidence Evan Ward was anywhere near Coyote Canyon. This was all done in bad faith. I would ask that the entire testimony be stricken and the jury told to disregard it."

Hamilton let out a sigh and raised his eyebrows at Dylan, asking for his response.

"Again, Judge, I would ask the State to point me to one statute or rule of evidence that says we can't question another suspect about this crime."

Hamilton shook his head and looked at Kelly and said, "He's right. What they did is neither contrary to law nor to the Bar ethical rules." He looked back at Dylan and Lily. "But it is sleazy and borderline immoral."

No one replied. Judge Hamilton rose and said, "Let's get back on the record and excuse the jury for the day. I think everybody's exhausted and could use a break."

57

The next day, the first witness to be called was a forensic technician who was the assistant to the criminalist for the county. He had little to add, and Dylan figured he was there as a show of force to convince the jury the State had poured every resource they could into the investigation of this case.

When court was over for the day, Dylan went out onto the steps of the courthouse in front of the cameras. Lily stood next to him. They waited until all the cameras were pointed at them and the reporters had rushed up from all corners.

One asked, "Mr. Aster, do you honestly believe Arlo Ward's brother is the one that committed these crimes?"

"Murders are a simple matter of who is the most likely person to have killed the victims. Arlo Ward is severely mentally ill, he walks with a limp that prevents him from running, and he's never been arrested for anything. Evan Ward is a convicted felon with a long history of violence behind him, including violence against his brother, who he harbors a deep hatred for. He likes to camp at the site where the victims were murdered, he has an affinity for bats and knives and knows how to use them, and he's got a bad chip on his shoulder.

"I don't know why the victims were chosen by Evan Ward. Maybe he just wanted to rob them like he wanted to rob the convenience store that resulted in his latest arrest. Or maybe he just has so much rage inside him that he killed them because they were there, but either way, it's just Occam's razor: the simplest explanation is always best. And the simplest explanation here is that Evan Ward killed those people and then called in his mentally ill brother to take the blame. Now, if you'll excuse me, I have somewhere I need to be."

They hurried through the crowd of reporters, who followed them until Kelly and James stepped out of the courthouse. The crowd then turned toward them, and Dylan and Lily were able to make it across the street to Lily's truck without speaking to anyone else.

Once they were driving, Lily said, "That was good. Conjugal visits for the jurors are tonight, and their spouses will tell them everything they heard you say on the news."

"We'll see. I mean, we just need one of them, Lil. Just one to get a hung jury. It'll convince people this case isn't as clear cut as it seems, and our next jury, death qualified or not, will be much more favorable to us."

"Yeah, but we also won't be able to do what we just did. Evan will be prepared. This might be our only bite at the apple."

———

They stopped at a diner known for serving hearty country breakfasts all day and ordered pancakes, eggs, and hash browns with orange juice to wash it all down. As they waited for their food, Dylan flipped through the latest report Brody had emailed him.

"How's it looking?" Lily said.

"Brody still can't find the gas station attendant the vics spoke with before driving up the canyon. Police are considering it a missing persons case now."

"Didn't he show up to work at some point?"

Dylan shook his head. "Hasn't shown up to work—get this— since the day after this happened. Not answering his phone or email, nothing missing from his apartment, no contact with his family or friends. Just gone." He tapped his phone against his palm as he thought. "He gave the victims directions, so he clearly knew the area. He follows them up, takes them out, and then Arlo really does just stumble onto the scene after they were already dead." He put his phone down. "We've got to get Philips back on the stand. The jury will eat this up."

Lily shrugged as she looked down into her glass of juice. "Maybe. I don't know. We're running around in circles with complex theories when the most obvious answer is right in front of us."

"What obvious answer? That Arlo did it? You really believe that?"

"It would make the most sense."

He spun his phone slowly on the table. "I don't buy it."

Lily took a sip of her juice. "Dylan, there's three human needs we're all trying to fill. The need for intimacy, safety, and a sense of belonging. If we're not getting these needs met through normal means, we'll find other ways to do it. Ways that are barbaric but may seem perfectly rational to the person doing them. Arlo has been missing all of those needs his entire life. These murders and the fame that comes with them might be his way of getting them."

Dylan put his arms on the table and leaned on them. "There's another need you forgot."

"And what's that?"

"The need for immortality. No one wants this life to be it. That we all just turn into a pile of dust, and none of it meant anything. We want to believe we can be immortal. What if taking credit for this is Arlo's way of getting immortality? People will dissect and analyze what he claims he did forever, and he knows it. It gives him an incentive to take credit."

Lily folded her napkin on her lap as the food arrived. "That's just the Methodist in you talking."

He chuckled. "Doesn't make it less true."

"You really think he didn't do it?"

He nodded, moving his food around on his plate without taking a bite. "Yeah . . . I think I do."

58

Kelly sat in her executive chair while the shadow jurors sat on the couch. James stood against the wall and said little, letting the shadow jurors speak instead. Things like "I was convinced, but I don't know now" and "The brother just seemed so much more violent—I mean, he *looked* like a killer" were said over and over again in different ways. Kelly took the comments in passively, letting the shadow jurors finish before saying, "That jury's job is to convict someone of *being* a killer, not *looking* like a killer."

When they left, Kelly lit a clove cigarette and stared out of her office window at the buildings across the street. She remembered when they were open fields and how the wind would sway the tall grass and weeds. Now, nothing moved. Metal and brick and silence. More like a cemetery than anything else.

James sat across from her and unbuttoned his suit coat. Neither of them said anything for a while.

She shook her head, still gazing out the window. "Why?" she said, more to herself than him. "It was so clear it was a trick to get them to look at the brother when all the evidence points to Arlo. Why would it be effective?"

"Because he's not entirely wrong, Kelly. The cops had their guy, and that was it. No other suspects were needed. The brother's got a history of violence, and he just happens to fish and camp near where the victims were killed? It's more than a coincidence."

"Arlo discovered that place because of him. He followed him out to Oregon, then followed him out here, and I'll bet you he followed him up to that canyon, and that's how he discovered it. He wants to *be* his brother."

"Perhaps. Or perhaps Evan killed them and then realized he could get his brother to take the blame."

She rolled her eyes. "Not you too, James. This murdering little slug is now a saint doing all this for the sake of his family?"

"No, I'm not saying that. I think he's good for it. But we're talking about reasonable doubt. It doesn't matter if the jury believes he did it if they don't feel like we've proved it."

James took out his phone and checked a text he'd just gotten. "Arlo looks like a choirboy. His brother looks like a Hells Angel. Don't underestimate how much of an impact that makes."

She sighed. It was true. Appearances mattered so much to juries because the majority of people had the mistaken belief that they could tell what a person was like on sight alone. But it wasn't true: what was on the outside was usually the opposite of what was on the inside.

An idea struck her just then that made her stomach tingle with excitement. She looked at him with a smile, and James said, "What?"

She put her clove out. "They have a suspect they can point the finger at, but maybe we have a witness that can point the finger right back."

"Who?"

"His wife."

59

Dylan didn't feel like going home after his dinner with Lily, so he went to the Strip and walked around. Watching the people and the lights. A breeze blew trash over the streets.

When he finally did get home, chips and empty soda cans were spread over the couch, floor, and coffee table. Markie was passed out in the middle of them.

Dylan kicked off his shoes and lifted Markie carefully. He put her in bed and turned her ceiling fan on since the temperature was hovering around ninety.

When he went back to the living room and started cleaning up, he heard his mother from the kitchen say, "She tried to wait up for you."

Dylan glanced at her as he gathered potato chips off the floor. "You shouldn't let her do that. She gets groggy for school."

"Or maybe you can try to be home a little earlier and spend time with her."

He sat back on his haunches. "How the hell am I supposed to do that, Mama?"

"I don't know. She's your little sister and worships the ground you walk on. You should hear the way she talks about you to her friends. It's like you came down from heaven on a cloud. But she ain't spent time with you for weeks."

"I'm trying," he said, louder than he had intended to. "I'm trying to do every damn thing I have to do and still keep my sanity, Mama. Okay? I. Am. Trying."

"You always gonna have work, Dylan. But you only got this one time when Markie's still a child. When she's outta the house, she's outta the house, and you gonna see her on Thanksgiving and Christmas. You need to think about what's important in your life and what ain't."

He was about to tell her what he was planning on doing for them. Moving to a densely populated, massive city—the type of place he could never have imagined living in—while working for a soulless firm that would shower him with money and gifts. All so he could better support them. But for some reason, he didn't mention it. Maybe because he knew what she would say.

She turned to go into the bedroom and stopped. "We've only got so much time, son. And once it's gone, we ain't never gettin' it back. Not one second of it."

60

The coroner for Jackson County, Dr. Fredrich Cohen, was a lithe man of about sixty who came to court in a suit at least two sizes too big for him. James handled the direct examination, and the coroner kept his answers as short as possible. Lily and Madeline took a few notes, and Dylan noticed that Arlo wasn't drawing. He was staring down at the table and rubbing his fingers together.

"What's wrong?" Dylan whispered.

"I need you to do something for me soon."

"Let's talk about it later."

Arlo nodded but never took his eyes off the table.

When James was done with his direct examination, Dylan stood in the well. Dr. Cohen took a sip of water, and Dylan let him finish before starting.

"Dr. Cohen, could you please describe, in general terms, the protocols you follow during an autopsy? As far as the timeline of the steps you take."

Cohen set the cup down on the wooden banister in front of him. "In general terms, an autopsy starts with an external examination, where we're looking at the outside of the body, the injuries, noting anything remarkable like tattoos or scars and such. Then we move to the internal examination, where we look for injuries, examine the organs, and look for diseases."

"In your report, you gave a description of the victims in this case, correct?"

"Correct."

"And you described Michael Turner as a 'muscular, well-developed, tall Caucasian,' yeah?"

"Yes, that's right."

"So he wasn't disabled or physically handicapped, yeah?"

"No, he was not."

"He was muscular and probably strong."

"Objection, speculation," Kelly said.

"I think a doctor can give us his opinion on whether someone was strong based on their musculature, Your Honor."

"The objection is overruled."

"So, Doctor, muscular and strong, yeah?"

"Yes, he was quite muscular, so I imagine he would also be quite strong."

"Now you stated that blunt force trauma was not actually the cause of death, correct?"

"Yes, that's correct. I believe he was rendered unconscious by the blunt force trauma. Then the perpetrator mutilated the victims, and it's during the mutilation that the victim died by exsanguination."

"Mutilated with what?"

"Most likely a large hunting knife."

"Now, you didn't mention something in your reports. You never said 'stab wound,' correct?"

"No, I did not."

"Why?"

"A stab wound is, by definition, something deeper than it is wide, and I didn't feel the victims had stab wounds. Instead, sawlike movements were used to dismember them."

"You said in your report the injuries were consistent with a large knife. What does the word *consistent* mean to you when you use it in this context?"

"It means injuries on a victim could've been caused by whatever weapon is in question."

Dylan took a few steps toward the witness stand. "But there are other possibilities for the murder weapon here than a hunting knife, right?"

"Well, the thing with knife wounds is that it's not like trying to match a gunshot wound. I know on television they show coroners and criminalists matching knife wounds to various weapons, but in actuality, we cannot match a knife wound or traumatic gash to the weapon used. We must say whether a wound is or is not consistent with the dimensions of a particular weapon."

"So obviously there could be lots of weapons that cause injuries that look similar, yeah?"

"Yes."

"So when you say an injury is consistent with a weapon, you just mean that weapon is one of the possibilities that could've caused that injury, right?"

"Yes, I would say that's accurate."

"And that same reasoning applies to blunt force trauma, doesn't it?"

"Yes, it does."

"So these wounds on the victims, particularly Mr. Turner, could've been caused by a different weapon than a bat?"

"Though I think a baseball bat is the most likely weapon used, yes, it's possible it was something else."

"Like a thick, dull ax?"

"Not likely, but not impossible, I suppose."

"What about a slim log?"

"Yes, that's certainly possible."

"You're aware Mr. Ward's brother beat someone with a log once, correct?"

"Objection!"

"Withdrawn. What's an agonal period, Doctor?"

"It's the time near when death occurs after a fatal injury is imposed."

"So when someone is fatally injured, if he dies six minutes later, you would say the agonal period was six minutes, correct?"

"Correct."

"How long was the agonal period in Michael Turner's case?"

"It's difficult to nail down an exact time."

"In your report, you don't even take a guess, right?"

"No, I did not."

"Most people don't die right away from fatal wounds, do they?"

"No."

"In fact, there's been documented cases in the forensic literature of people who have been stabbed in the heart and still ran several blocks?"

"Yes, there have been cases similar to what you described."

"And there's been documented cases of people who had their frontal lobes crushed but still go about completing tasks, such as driving to a hospital?"

"Yes."

"Michael Turner was rendered unconscious by blunt force trauma and then died of exsanguination, correct?"

"Yes."

"And you don't know what the agonal period for Michael Turner was after he received his fatal wounds?"

"I don't have an exact time, no."

"What would you guess?"

"Objection, speculation."

"They qualified him as an expert, Your Honor. I'm asking for his expert opinion."

"Overruled."

Dylan said, "What would you guess was the agonal period, Doctor?"

"If I had to guess, based on the initial blow to the frontal cortex from a lowered position on the ground, since he was caught in a bear trap, and the fact that it was the only injury to the brain before the wounds to his throat, I would say he probably survived from two to three minutes."

"He had a massive injury to his right hand, correct?"

"Yes."

"In fact, it was almost split in half."

"Yes."

"This was premortem?"

"It was."

"There were other wounds on the limbs? Abrasions and cuts?"

"There were."

"And these were consistent with defensive wounds, weren't they? And by 'consistent,' I'm using your definition of within the range of reasonable possibilities."

"Yes, I believe they were consistent with defensive wounds against a sharp weapon, likely the same knife used to mutilate the corpses."

"But you can't be sure it was a knife, yeah? It's consistent with a knife, but also a whole host of other weapons?"

"Correct. I cannot be sure to a medical certainty that it was a knife, no."

"So during the agonal period, your expert opinion is that Michael Turner fought—as best as he could—with his killer for two to three minutes."

"It's possible, yes."

"And during this time, Holly Fallows was running away?"

"I wouldn't know. I only know what I read in the police reports."

"You read that she was running away."

"Yes."

"So they leave the cabin, Holly runs, and Michael fights with the killer for up to three minutes while Holly is running away. You realize my client has a leg injury that causes him to limp and couldn't possibly catch up to her if he fought Michael for three minutes, right?"

"Objection," Kelly said as she rose. "I would ask that be stricken from the record."

"Withdrawn," Dylan said. "Thank you, Doctor. No further questions."

61

It was a Friday when all the forensic technicians, the criminalist, the coroner, and the coroner's assistants had finished testifying. The only issue of note had been that the eyelashes found on April Fallows came back as unable to be matched to Arlo's. For all anyone knew, the eyelashes might've had nothing to do with the crime.

Judge Hamilton adjourned court at three to give the jurors a more extended break. Mostly because the minutiae of scientific testimony could wear out anyone's attention span.

Arlo looked at Dylan and said, "Can you come to the jail and see me? I still need to ask you to do something for me."

Dylan gathered his papers and files. "I'll come by as soon as I can."

"I have to be in another court," Madeline said. "You need me to do anything this weekend?"

"You've got some investigators, too, don't you?"

"Yeah, the State gives us an allowance for one on each case."

"Have your investigator focus on finding the gas station attendant. Might be good to have two people on it and see if we can turn anything up."

"You got it." She looked at Arlo. "I'll see you on Monday, Arlo."

"Bye, Ms. Ismera."

After Arlo was led back by the bailiff, Lily sat on the edge of the desk and said, "I, um, have a favor to ask, too."

"What's up?"

"It's my brother's wedding on Sunday. I know it's last minute, but Jake can't go and . . . I don't want to go alone. My family's not exactly . . . well, you know I'm the black sheep, so it's just sometimes easier if someone's with me."

Dylan saw a sadness in her eyes he wasn't used to seeing. The distance he'd noticed about her ever since she first mentioned the wedding hadn't gone away.

"Yeah, of course I'll come."

———

The flight to Topeka took several hours. Lily rented a car, and Dylan called Markie, since she had demanded he call her as soon as he landed.

As they drove, Dylan looked out over the flat landscape and wondered if a barren view would have adverse psychological effects on someone. For him, at least, he knew he needed the deserts and mountains and hoped Los Angeles would at least have some nearby he could visit frequently.

"I really appreciate you coming," Lily said.

Dylan looked at her. "I was hoping you'd tell me what's going on. You've been depressed for like a month and won't tell me why."

She shook her head. "Just the same old family drama. Nothing new."

———

Dylan knew Lily had been raised on a farm, but he had no idea how much of a throwback to the last century her family farm was. Red barn, large green pastures full of cows, chickens running around everywhere like they owned the place.

Her parents were already waiting outside for them, and her father, Ray, gave Lily a long hug. Ray shook Dylan's hand so vigorously it made his fingers ache, and Dylan wondered if he did it on purpose or just thought that was how men should shake hands.

After an extravagant dinner, complete with homemade beer, they sat on the porch, and her father smoked a pipe. The sun drifted down below the horizon, and the stars peeked out of the blackness. Lily sat next to Ray on a rocking chair, and he said, "I saw you two on the news. You looked good. You've been the talk of the town ever since."

Lily smirked and said, "I imagine I have. Good talk or bad talk?"

"Mixed."

She rested her head on her father's shoulder, and Dylan could see the comfort it brought her. Whatever had been bothering her dissipated, and her face relaxed into a happy grin. Her dog, a German shepherd, ran around the enclosure barking at the cows and made them moo and go to the other side.

Her parents went to bed early, and Dylan and Lily sat in rocking chairs on the porch and sipped beer. The night sky appeared like a black blanket thrown around the earth and then encrusted with glimmering jewels. There was no light pollution here, since the nearest big city was seventy miles away.

"It amazes me sometimes how free I feel out here," Lily said. "We're born with a nationality, a religion, and a culture, and then we spend our lives rebelling against them. Whenever I come home, I realize it's not a bad thing to slip back into where we came from sometimes."

"Speak for yourself," Dylan said, taking a sip of beer. "I was born to be a coal miner."

She chuckled. "Are you serious?"

"The town I was born in was a coal mining town. Like nine out of ten of our high school graduates went into mining . . . what? What are you laughing at?"

"I'm picturing you in the depths of a coal mine. You can't even shake hands without slathering yourself in hand sanitizer after."

"Woman, I am manly as hell. I'd dig the crap outta that coal. Or however it is you get coal out. Anyway, doesn't matter. The coal mine collapsed, and the town went broke. Half the people moved away, including us, and the rest probably stayed there and let life slip away from them." He finished his beer and leaned his head back against the rocking chair. "I can't imagine anything worse. Just sitting around waiting to die without any plans for anything."

"Is that why you're leaving to take the fat paycheck? You're scared you're going to fulfill your destiny of being mediocre?"

He shrugged. "I don't know. Maybe." He sighed. "We're gonna lose this case, aren't we?"

"I don't know. We'll have to see how Holly Fallows does. And we still haven't discussed whether to put Arlo on the stand or not."

"I say no. He's going to get up there and say he's perfectly sane and enjoyed killing those people. There's no benefit to it."

"He could insist, and we'd have to let him."

"Yeah," he said, glancing up at the moon. "I know." He checked to see if there was any more beer but found none. "I had a nightmare the other night."

"You covered in soot swinging a pickax?"

"No," he said, staring up at the stars again. "I was sitting in the viewing area at the prison in the death chamber. Arlo was getting strapped down. I had a dog once that had to be put down. I remember the injection. Every muscle in him instantly went limp, then there was a final whine, and he was gone. Arlo did the same thing. A soft whine, and then nothing."

"Wow."

He nodded once. "I know. It woke me up at two in the morning, and I couldn't get back to sleep."

"It's a dream, Dylan. It doesn't mean it's going to happen. Even if he's convicted, the appeals can take more than a decade. You won't have to be there for the execution."

He stared at the sky a long time before saying, "Yeah, I will. And I'll never forgive myself for it."

62

Lily's brother, Charles, had decided to have his wedding at the farm. In the open space of lush green grass, there was a platform for the couple to stand on. A hundred white chairs were set up in rows next to a stage for the live band. Lily introduced her attractive cousin September—"Because that was the month I was born," she said with pride—who was already drunk at two in the afternoon. September gave Dylan a hug with a kiss on the cheek instead of shaking hands.

"Aren't you the cutest little thing," she said with a wide smile.

"September, quit throwing yourself at my business partner," Lily said.

"I don't see a ring on his finger."

The ceremony itself was a quick affair. Charles was a big guy of at least three hundred pounds. His bride was little more than a hundred, and all the women were gossiping about how life in the bedroom would work.

Dylan couldn't get a seat next to Lily, since she sat with her family. September asked the person next to her to move and motioned for him to sit before putting her arm around his elbow. She would lean over and whisper rumors about everyone around them.

"Oh, and he cheated on his wife with her sister. You believe that? Her sister? I think I'd cut his frank 'n' beans off if my man did that. You're not a cheater, are you? 'Cause I won't hook up with a cheater."

"You should probably not mention cutting frank 'n' beans off before telling someone you want to hook up with them."

She laughed so hard she snorted.

Lily sat with a young boy on her lap, her nephew.

Camden, when he had seen her, sprinted into her arms, shouting, "Aunt Lily!" Her sister stood with her arms folded and a disapproving look on her face. Lily was great with kids, and he wondered what she could've done to garner such obvious animosity from her sister.

Lily had given Camden a gift she brought with her from Vegas, a set of water guns, and Dylan had heard her sister say, "I said no more gifts."

"It's just water guns."

"It's always *just* something. No more gifts, Lily."

The boy ran off to play with some other kids with Lily watching him.

After the ceremony, Dylan stood against the fence of the cow enclosure and watched the guests as they gave toasts. Lily went around chatting with relatives and friends, laughing and reminiscing. Whenever she could, she would hug or kiss Camden. To the point that her sister took the boy away and shoved him with the other kids, who were playing in the barn.

September came up to Dylan, drunker still, and rested her head on his shoulder. The thought of her with a knife looking for things to cut off occurred to him, and he decided to let her stay there.

She sighed. "You know, I've never been to Las Vegas. I would need a reason to go. Like someone who wanted to show me around town. You think you could show me around?"

"Yeah, I guess. You really haven't been to Las Vegas? I figured every American has been there at least once."

"Nope. I've never left Kansas. Not once. Been working since I was fourteen years old to help my daddy out and never found time to travel. What's it like there? It looks like a playground."

"That's one way to describe it. The first couple of days, you're overwhelmed with how much there is to do and how fun it is. But after that, you slowly start feeling something . . . odd. It's like the city has this veneer of fun painted over something darker underneath. That's why I live outside the city. I only work in Vegas."

"Wow. You're just a barrel of monkeys, aren't you?" September smiled. "I don't care. I still like you."

Dylan saw Lily at a table. She was staring at the children playing, Camden holding one of the water guns she'd brought him and chasing the other kids with it.

"Can I ask you something? Why's Lily's sister treat her like that?"

"Like what?"

"It's obvious she doesn't like Lily talking with her nephew. Did something happen?"

September hesitated and then let out a long breath. "I'll tell you something, but you gotta promise not to tell anyone. I mean really promise, not just say it."

He looked at her. Her playful expression had turned serious, and she wasn't smiling. "Yeah, I won't say anything."

"Because if you break your promise—"

"I'm putting my frank 'n' beans at risk, yeah, I know. I won't say anything, promise."

September looked out at Lily, and a sadness came over her. It was so pronounced it changed her posture, and she seemed to slump against Dylan rather than lean on him.

"What is it?"

"That's not her nephew. That's her son."

63

The flight home was scheduled for nine that night, and Dylan said goodbye to Lily's family. Lily hugged her father and mother, and Ray was teary eyed but blinked the wetness away so nobody would see. Lily hugged Camden for as long as she could before her sister told her they had to leave. September wouldn't let go of Dylan and took his phone and put her number into it, making him promise to show her around Vegas one day.

Ray said to Dylan, "Look after her. She's tough as nails, but she's also soft as soap, and she don't ask for help when she needs it."

The drive to the airport was filled with an awkward silence. Lily seemed like she was on the verge of tears. Dylan turned on the radio and stared out at the dark night.

After dropping the car off, they sat in the terminal and waited for their flight. Lily stared at the floor and didn't speak. She wore a necklace with a small locket and kept rubbing it.

"Why didn't you tell me?" Dylan said.

She looked at him, and her eyes went wide. They were both silent for a few moments. "September?"

"Yeah, but I knew something was up from the way you interacted with him. Why couldn't you tell me?"

She leaned back in the seat and stared out the massive windows as the plane pulled up to the terminal. "It's not something I talk about with anyone. I was young and wanted to get out of this town. You don't know how suffocating it is. You left your small town when you were ten. I was an adult and getting ready to leave, and then I found out I was pregnant."

"Who's the father?"

"Some piece of trash I thought I was in love with. When I told him I was pregnant, he told me it wasn't his. I told him it couldn't be anyone else's. He said it wasn't his and to never talk to him again."

She folded her hands in front of her and stared off into the dark through the windows.

"So I was alone and pregnant, with no education and no prospects anymore for leaving the town I wanted to run away from since I was a kid. Lucy knew all that. We had a family meeting about it, and everyone agreed she would be the better mom. She already had one child, and there were complications where she had to have her ovaries removed. They wanted more kids, and I wanted out. It just seemed so . . . perfect. At the time, anyway."

She shifted uncomfortably in her chair and played with the trinket on her necklace.

"I had him, gave him to my sister, and then signed up for the army." She swallowed. "What kind of person am I, Dylan? How could a mother give up her child?"

"You were basically a kid, too."

"Even a—"

"Lily, you were a kid. We're not the same people at twenty that we are at thirty." He listened to an announcement that their plane would be boarding soon. "Have you thought about getting him back?"

She shrugged. "As I get older . . . yeah. But my sister would never give up custody. And it might hurt him."

"It'll hurt him more when he finds out Lucy's not his mother because somebody slipped rather than told him." He paused. "Is that why you want us to be on the news every night and get more clients? To show more income for a custody suit?"

She stared absently at the floor and shook her head again. "I don't know. What kind of mother would I make anyway?"

"A great one."

She didn't respond. Instead, she put her head on his shoulder, and they watched the blinking lights of the plane flash in the darkness outside.

64

On Monday morning, there were so many reporters outside the court-house that a bailiff had to clear a path for Dylan. The case had gotten not just national but international attention. Court TV had set up permanent cameras and broadcast several hours of the trial every day. Reporters called, emailed, and showed up to Dylan's, Madeline's, and Lily's homes. One even tried to sneak into the jail with a fake Nevada State Bar card and said he needed to talk to Arlo Ward.

Holly Fallows was there with her father and sent Dylan a sharp look. Dylan felt like giving her a warm smile, saying good morning, or giving any type of acknowledgment, but he knew it would only upset her more, so he just turned away.

Arlo came out with a smile and shook Dylan's and Lily's hands and hugged Madeline. When he sat down, he pulled the yellow legal pad and pen near him and said, "You look tired."

"I'm okay," Dylan said. "Just goes with the territory."

"I'm sorry you have to do this. I know it's not fun."

"I don't have to do anything, Arlo. I chose to do this."

Judge Hamilton came in, and the chatter in the courtroom stopped. The room was always packed now, and the spare spectator seats were given on a first-come-first-served basis. When they were filled, a bailiff had to stand outside the doors to make sure no one else entered.

Once the judge was seated and everybody followed, he looked around the courtroom, stopping his gaze for a second on the cameras, and then said, "Please bring in the jury."

The jury was seated, and Dylan noticed they looked refreshed. It was like that on Mondays, but by Friday, they'd look like they'd been up for a week on a meth bender.

"The State may call their next witness."

"Your Honor, we'd like to call a witness out of order of the schedule we presented."

"Go ahead."

"We'd call Leena Ward to the stand."

Dylan and Lily were both on their feet. Arlo's eyes went wide, and he looked behind him as the doors opened and a bailiff led his wife in.

"Objection," Lily said. "We were not given notice Mrs. Ward would be testifying today. Also, she has claimed spousal privilege, and the State shouldn't have even been speaking with her, much less calling her as a witness."

Kelly calmly replied, "Your Honor, Mrs. Ward will be waiving spousal privilege and has agreed to testify today. She's on the witness list we provided to the defense and notice isn't required."

"That's ridiculous," Dylan said. "She's maintained spousal privilege throughout this entire case, and now she just happens to waive it without cause? The prosecution has clearly intimidated her into testifying."

"I resent that insinuation, Your Honor. We did no such thing, and once Mrs. Ward takes the stand, it'll become clear that she is here completely of her own free will and choice."

Judge Hamilton leaned forward and put his hand underneath his chin as though he were a philosopher. "She is on the witness list submitted by the State. If she is willing to waive privilege under oath, I see no problem with her testifying."

Leena was sworn in and sat in the witness box. She wouldn't look at Arlo, and he had an expression of pure shock on his face.

"What's she gonna say?" Dylan whispered to Arlo.

"I don't know."

After Kelly introduced Leena, she asked, "How well do you know your husband, Mrs. Ward?"

"As well as anybody could, I guess."

"Tell us what he's like. From your perspective."

She glanced at Arlo once. "He's a good provider. He always makes sure me and Amy have enough and are taken care of, even though he can't work much. He's quiet and shy. Doesn't like to talk. He loves that board game, Go, and video games. Things that take a lotta time. I think he likes the distraction."

"Distraction from what?"

"He's got schizophrenia and depression."

"Let's talk about that. When did he tell you he has schizophrenia?"

"After a few dates. He said he had something to tell me and then explained it to me. That his brain doesn't work like other people's, and sometimes he might act strange but to not take it personally."

"And you married him anyway?"

"I did. He didn't seem strange to me at all." She glanced at Arlo again. "And I loved him."

"In the course of the marriage, how many times did you see him visually hallucinate something that wasn't there?"

She was silent a moment. "Never."

A quiet murmur went up from the audience. Dylan looked at Lily and knew they both had the same thought: *Crap.*

Either Leena had lied to them when they visited her at her mother's house, or she was lying now.

They objected, and it was overruled.

"You didn't see him hallucinate even once?" Kelly continued.

"I mean, he does things other people don't do. Talks to himself sometimes, and gets weird thoughts in his head, but I've never seen him hallucinate anything in my presence, no."

"What about auditory hallucinations?"

"I don't know. He says he hears things sometimes."

"He's claimed insanity in this case, Leena, meaning the mental illness affects him so severely he shouldn't be held responsible for these murders. What do you think of that?"

"Objection! She's not a psychiatrist."

"Sustained."

Kelly went on and said, "I'd like to turn to something painful, Leena, and I'm sorry I have to ask this. But I looked up your medical history and saw that you've visited the emergency room four times this year."

Leena looked down and swallowed. Her eyes glistened, and she spoke quietly when she said, "Yeah."

"The first was for a broken arm, then a fractured wrist, then a broken jaw, and then the fourth injury, which occurred two weeks before your husband's arrest, was for internal bleeding and fractured ribs. All of which you stated were caused by accidents, correct?"

"Yes," she said without looking up.

"But that's not true, is it?"

"Objection," Lily said. "Leading and irrelevant."

"Overruled."

"Sidebar, Judge."

"Denied. Go ahead and continue, Ms. Whitewolf."

Leena swallowed. Tears wet her cheeks. Kelly took a box of tissues and handed it to her. Leena grabbed several and dabbed at her eyes before rolling them up in her palms.

"Take your time," Kelly said.

The courtroom was completely silent. Dylan watched the jury and saw all their faces turned to Leena with intense concentration.

"No," she finally said. "No, it isn't true."

"What happened, then?"

"Arlo . . . Arlo's got a temper."

"What do you mean by that?"

"I mean, he sometimes loses control and hurts me."

Dylan objected, and it was overruled.

"What makes him lose control?" Kelly asked.

She shook her head. "Nothing, really. There might be a dirty plate he gets food served on, and it sets him off, or we have to cancel plans he was looking forward to . . . nothing and anything, I guess."

"So you don't do anything to provoke it?"

"No, nothing. That broken arm, I was just sitting on the couch, and he came in screaming about the house being dirty. I told him I'd clean it, and he lifted me by the arm and threw me on the floor and said to do it now. He threw me so hard it broke my arm."

"So he just flies into rages for no reason?"

"Objection," Lily said. "Counsel is characterizing the witness's testimony."

"Overruled. You may answer, Mrs. Ward."

She nodded. "Yes. He's always had a temper. I didn't know it at first when we were dating. He hid it from me. But once we were married, he changed. It's like he could show me what he was really like then."

"Why didn't you leave him?"

She shrugged. "I don't have an education, I work part-time and have a daughter to support. If I left, he told me he wouldn't help at all. I'd be on my own. I stayed for Amy. I started school last year, beauty school, and I thought once I get my license and a good job, I would leave him."

"You know that a bat was found in a cabin near where the murders occurred, right?"

"I do."

"Whose bat was it?"

"It was Arlo's."

"Does he play baseball?"

"No."

"Then why did he have a bat?"

Leena glanced at Arlo and then quickly away. "He likes having it for self-defense, he said."

"No weapons were found in your home when the police searched it. Did he have any?"

Leena swallowed again and looked at the floor. "Yes. But that night, when the killings happened . . . he called me and told me to get rid of all the weapons in the house."

"Objection!"

"Overruled."

"Do you recognize this, Mrs. Ward?" Kelly said as she handed her a few papers.

"Yes."

"What is it?"

"It's my phone records for May."

"And on May ninth at a quarter past ten, did someone call your phone?"

"Yes."

"What number is highlighted at that time?"

"It's Arlo's cell phone number."

"Move for introduction of plaintiff's exhibit forty-one, Your Honor."

"We would object," Lily said. "We were not given notice of this particular piece of evidence coming in and—"

"We sent it to the defense as supplemental discovery, Your Honor."

That was true. Dylan had noted its importance immediately, but Arlo explained that he was scared and had called his wife to find out what to do.

"What did he mean by 'get rid of them'?" Kelly asked.

"Objection, she can't know his thoughts."

"Sustained."

Kelly rephrased the question and asked, "What did he say to you on that phone call?"

"He said to get rid of them. So I got rid of all of them by throwing them into a dumpster at a grocery store. I didn't know what else to do with them."

"He told you to get rid of them," Kelly said, looking at the jury. "That doesn't sound like what an insane person who doesn't know what they're doing would say, does it?"

"Objection!" Dylan said, on his feet.

"Withdrawn. No further questions."

Lily nodded to Dylan and then went to the lectern. She watched Leena a moment before speaking.

"You never talked to the police before now, did you, Mrs. Ward?" Lily asked.

"No."

"In fact, the police tried to speak with you several times, and you refused."

"I did."

"But you decided to testify today."

"Yes."

"When did you decide that?"

"On Friday."

"Did you meet with Ms. Whitewolf on Friday?"

"I did."

"What did she say to you?"

"Objection, hearsay."

"Falls under the public records exception, Your Honor, as it's part of the State's investigation."

"I'll allow it."

"So what did she say to you, Mrs. Ward?"

"She said she wanted me to talk about Arlo today. That he could hurt other people if he was let out, and she needed me to come talk to the jury."

"What did she offer you in exchange for your testimony?"

Leena looked at Kelly, who nodded once. "She said they would help me after he went away. That they could get me some government assistance for me and my daughter, and a place to live rent-free for six months."

"So basically, they offered you money."

"I guess."

"And you decided to testify only after they offered you this deal?"

"Yes."

"Before then you weren't going to testify?"

"I didn't want to, no."

"Do you remember when Mr. Aster and I came to your mother's home?"

"I do."

"Do you recall telling us that Arlo was never violent?"

"I do."

"Do you remember telling us that he didn't have any weapons?"

She swallowed. "Arlo told me to say all that if I ever have to talk about it. It wasn't the truth."

"So you lied to us?"

"Yes."

"I had no idea. Have you always been skilled at being untruthful?"

"Objection," James snapped.

"Sustained."

Lily put her hands behind her back and stepped out from behind the lectern. "Now, the four ER visits you made, there isn't a police report on any of them, is there?"

"No, I never called the police."

"The doctors in each instance let you leave the hospital without calling the police?"

"Yes."

"Did you know doctors are required to call the police when they suspect domestic abuse?"

"No, I didn't know that."

"But they never called the police, did they?"

"No."

"Mrs. Ward, you love your husband, don't you?"

"I do."

"And he loves you."

"Yes, I know he does."

"If he's convicted of this crime, he's told you he might get a lucrative book deal, correct?"

"Yes."

"And he told you he would sign over all the money earned from that book to you?"

Leena nodded and said, "Yes, he did."

"So in addition to the money and housing the government is giving you, you stand to make money from his book if he's convicted, correct?"

"I guess so."

"Thank you, Mrs. Ward, no further questions."

65

When court ended, Dylan, Madeline, and Lily followed Arlo back to the holding cells. They got a side room, and Arlo sat down at the table across from them.

"No way," Dylan said. "No way she changes her mind because she might get six months of housing."

Arlo shrugged. "I know she's scared of what will happen without me. I don't blame her for looking out for her and Amy."

Dylan shook his head. "I don't buy it. Not for that little does she flip on you. What did you say to her?"

"Nothing."

"Arlo, I can go through your visitor logs and phone calls. I can see if you talked to her. She called you after the prosecutor talked to her, didn't she?"

He looked down at the table.

"Arlo, answer me."

He nodded. "She called me on Friday and said Ms. Whitewolf came to see her."

Dylan shook his head. The anger was erupting from him. He had to take a breath and calm himself, or else he would start shouting. "And you told her to testify against you, didn't you?"

He nodded.

Madeline said, "Why would you do that, Arlo?"

"Because things were going good. I told you, I d-d-don't want to be let off for this. I need to be in prison to write that book."

Dylan nearly shouted, "Damn it, Arlo, you're not going to prison! You're going to death row. You're going to die. How many times do I need to say it?"

Lily said, "We're trying to save your life, Arlo. Don't you want to see your daughter grow up? Be there for her on her first day of school, see her go on her first date, get her driver's license, get married . . . don't you want that?"

Arlo swallowed, and his eyes glistened. "I'm getting sicker, Ms. Ricci. I don't know how long I can keep functioning on a normal level. One day, I won't be anything but a burden to them. This way, I can give them what they n-need, and Amy doesn't have to grow up seeing her father lose his mind."

He stood before any of them could respond.

"Eddie," he shouted, "I'm ready to go back."

66

"The State calls Holly Fallows to the stand."

She appeared fragile. Her hands were shaking, and she couldn't look anywhere but right at Kelly. The jury had nothing but sympathy on their faces. Victim cross-examinations were always dangerous. One misstep and the jury could instantly turn against Dylan and Lily in order to protect the victim.

Kelly ran her through the testimony, and Holly stopped several times because she choked up. One pause lasted a good minute as she wiped tears away.

"He was such a good person," Holly said, speaking about Michael Turner. "He helped anyone that needed it. Any spare minute he had, he was helping other people. He once missed a football game because his neighbor needed help removing a tree from his yard."

Kelly pretended to flip through some notes, but Dylan knew she was just letting that sink in with the jury.

"You said you couldn't see the assailant."

Holly nodded. "Yeah, he had something black around his face. Like a black hood or cloth, or maybe a mask. And he never got that close to me."

"Was he limping?"

"I don't know. I only saw him for like a second, and then I took off running."

"The defense has raised the issue that he couldn't have caught up to you in the time it took him to run from the trees to your position, kill Michael, and then chase you through the canyon."

Holly sniffled and dabbed at some tears. "I got lost somewhere along the way. I was just running so fast. I couldn't think. And so the trail broke off into these other paths. I took wrong turns and ended up in denser trees and had to turn around. That's how he caught up to me."

"When did you notice him behind you?"

Holly looked up to the ceiling and let out a long breath. The difficulty in getting each word out was tangible. "The trees opened up to, like, this clearing near the edge of a cliff. That's when I heard him behind me. I could hear his breathing, so I knew he was close. I turned around and saw him like forty feet behind me. Not far."

"What'd you do?"

"I got to the edge of the cliff and stopped. It was dark, so I couldn't see how far down it was. But when I turned around, he was almost to me, and I could see something in his hand. Like a baseball bat or a thick piece of wood or something." She paused as more tears came. "It looked like it was covered in blood."

"What did you do when you saw this?"

"I knew he was going to kill me, so I jumped. I hit the rocks and shattered my leg, fractured my ribs and hips, fractured four bones in my face, and had a bunch of internal bleeding . . . I almost died. But I knew I couldn't lie there because he was going to climb down and get me. So I crawled away." She stopped a moment. "I crawled for a long time, I don't know how long, and then when I got to some trees, I found branches on the ground and used a big one like a crutch. I found the road and flagged down the first car I saw. Then I woke up in the hospital. I don't remember anything in between."

"How has this whole ordeal affected your life, Holly?"

She started to cry and stared down at the tissues in her hands. "I have nightmares all the time. I wake up screaming. I fell asleep in the bathroom the other day because I can't sleep and I even had a nightmare in there. Sometimes it's so bad I think I'm having seizures, but my doctor doesn't know yet if I am or not. And I'm scared all the time. A man was going into the same store as me the other day and I almost ran away crying because I thought he was coming after me. I've just . . . I've lost everything. All I had was April and Mike." She wiped her tears away. "He took everything from me."

"I can't even imagine going through something like this, and I am so sorry you had to endure it." Kelly stepped closer to the witness box. "If you could say anything to Arlo Ward, the killer of your sister and future husband, what would it be?"

Dylan almost objected but stopped himself as the entire jury seemed interested in what she had to say and might not like him preventing her from saying it.

"I would tell him that the people he killed were good people who wanted to make the world a better place. That all he did was put out lights that should've shined for a long time."

"Thank you, Holly. And thank you for your bravery in testifying today."

Kelly sat down, and Lily went to the lectern.

67

"Holly, you said you never saw the face of the man that did this, is that right?"

"Yeah, I didn't see it. I think it was covered by something."

"Do you know what race he was?"

"No."

"Do you know if he had any tattoos?"

"No."

"The color of his eyes?"

Holly shook her head. "No, it was dark, and I was never that close."

"The color of his hair?"

"No."

"The sound of his voice?"

"No, he never talked."

"So you know nothing about him other than he was wearing black and maybe had a baseball bat?"

"It was dark, and he never got that close to me."

"Can you give us one identifying trait of his? Something that would show that Arlo Ward was the man that attacked you that night, and not his brother, Evan?"

Holly glanced at Arlo for the first time and then had to quickly look away. "No, I can't."

"Thank you, Holly. No further questions."

68

The State rested its case with the testimony of Holly Fallows. Dylan thought the prosecution's case had gone about like he had expected, except for Leena Ward. Her testimony was absolutely devastating.

Though he intended to put up Dr. Simmons to testify that Arlo likely didn't know right from wrong on the night of the murders, the prosecution had put up three other psychiatrists and psychologists who'd testified the opposite. The insanity defense, which Dylan had never wanted to go with in the first place, rarely worked, and Leena had made the jury hate Arlo Ward on top of it.

After court that day, Dylan decided to stop by the jail, as Arlo kept asking him to. He'd also requested that Dylan bring his phone, something Dylan had never had a client request.

The jail was quieter than usual when Dylan arrived. He was wanded and allowed through the metal detectors with his phone, since he said he needed it to record his client's statement. He'd asked for a private room, and when he arrived, Arlo was already sitting cuffed to a steel table. The guard checked the cuffs and then left. When the door shut, Dylan pulled out his cell phone and placed it on the table.

"You didn't seem happy today," Arlo said.

"No, I wasn't. We're losing, Arlo. You know that, right?"

He nodded. "I know . . . but it doesn't matter. I asked you here because I want you to record a video for me. It's for my daughter.

You need to give it to Leena, but also keep a copy in case she loses it. When Amy's old enough, I want her to watch it. Can you do that for me?"

Dylan glanced at the door, which had a square glass window at face level, and he saw the back of the guard's head. "Sure, Arlo." He lifted his phone. "Let me know when you're ready."

"I'm ready. I've been thinking about what to say for a long time."

Dylan hit the record button. "Go ahead."

Arlo swallowed and was silent for a bit. "Um, hi, Amy. I'm your father, Arlo. If you're watching this, it means I've been executed by the S-S-State. It will happen fast. I'm not going to appeal my case. I don't want to trouble anyone anymore, and I don't want to sit in a cell thinking about it. That's the worst part of it. Just imagining what it's going to be like."

Dylan felt like turning the phone off and yelling at him.

Not appealing it?

Without his appeals, he could be executed in as little as three months. Despite what he wanted to do, Dylan didn't say anything and kept recording. Arlo was choking up, and he didn't want to take this moment away from him.

"You're not going to remember me. You're too young. But I wanted you to know that your daddy isn't the terrible p-person they say I am. I never hurt your mother. She had accidents because of issues she has with drugs, but I told her to say I did it. And I d-didn't hurt those people. I could never hurt someone like that. But I have a mental illness that's getting worse, Amy. I can feel it. When it gets very bad, I won't know what's real anymore. I wouldn't be anything but a burden to you and your mom, and I won't do that. It's my job as your daddy to make sure you're okay, no matter what."

He paused.

"I'm so sorry for all this."

Dylan turned off the recording and slowly lowered the phone. Arlo quietly wept for a few moments and then took a deep breath and stopped.

"I only give you permission to show that to Leena and Amy. No one else."

"I understand."

He swallowed and wiped away the last of his tears. "Thank you for doing that, Dylan."

"Arlo . . . you can't do this. I won't let you."

"I have to."

Arlo shouted for the guard, who opened the door and came in. He unlocked Arlo from the table and took his arm as he led him out of the room.

Dylan heard the door close as he stared at the still image of Arlo on his phone.

69

Dylan drove around the city for a couple of hours. He cruised the Strip, as the glittering lights against the backdrop of darkness sometimes perked up his spirits, but it felt empty. Like light bulbs in an abandoned warehouse.

He drove through the nearby deserts on I-15 and got to a gas station in the middle of nowhere. He bought ibuprofen and a Mountain Dew. A family went into the gas station, the father teasing his two children, who pretended to hit him. Dylan thought about Arlo and his family, how Amy would never have that. She would have an empty hole in her life where her father should have been.

The thought made him feel heavy and tired. He started the car and drove home.

The lights were out when he got there. He checked on Markie, who was sound asleep in her bed. Dylan pulled the covers up to her chest and then kissed her forehead before checking on his mother.

She lay with her back to the door. He was about to head out to the porch and drink some beers when she said, "You're home late."

He looked at her, but she hadn't moved. "Just needed to drive and clear my head."

She turned toward him. "What happened?"

Dylan sat on the edge of the bed and stared out the only window in the room. "My client is going to die, Mama. They're going to kill him for something he didn't do."

"Are you sure he didn't do it?"

Dylan nodded. "I think it was his brother or this man that we can't find, and Arlo's taking the blame because he thinks he's helping his wife and daughter. They're going to kill him, and it's because I failed. I couldn't protect him." He let out a long breath. "But I'm done now, and I need to tell you something I've been keeping from you . . . I have a job offer. It's a law firm in Los Angeles. It's three hundred thousand a year, Mama, with a luxury car and a condo thrown in. I'm going to be able to hire a nurse for you and send Markie to a private school. We're going to have everything we ever wanted."

His mother pulled herself up and grimaced from the shot of pain it caused. She leaned against the headboard and said, "Listen to me, boy. If you think a rich man's gold is going to bring you happiness, then I haven't taught you a damn thing."

The words surprised him, and he sat silently, trying to figure out if what she had said was what she actually meant. She tried to sit more upright and grunted as she did so. "Money don't solve anything, son. It covers up problems for a while, but they're still your problems. They ain't goin' nowhere 'cause you got a fancy car."

There was a knock at the front door.

Dylan sat a moment in stunned silence and then said, "I'll get it. Good night, Mama."

Lily stood on the porch with a six-pack. "Thought you could use a beer tonight."

———

They sat out on the porch on a rocking bench his mother liked to use. The bench swayed lightly as Dylan pushed them back and forth with his heels. The beer was cold and tasted good, something foreign, which he never bought for himself. He guzzled half a bottle before saying, "How'd you know?"

"Just a feeling. I assumed whatever favor Arlo needed wasn't going to be good." She took a sip of beer and then picked at the label with her thumbnail. "Wanna tell me about it?"

Dylan sighed. "He had me make a recording to show his daughter after he's dead. He tells her he made everything up and convinced her mom to lie on the stand. And he's not going to appeal. Once he's convicted, it'll be a few months on death row, and that'll be it."

"Do you believe him?"

He nodded. "Yeah, I do."

She looked out over the tall grass, lit pale blue by a half moon in the sky. "Do you know what I admire most about you, Dylan? You never give up. Not until there's absolutely nothing else that can be done."

He shook his head. "And what does it get me? How did it benefit Arlo? We'll put up Simmons, but so what? They had three psychiatrists just as qualified say Arlo isn't insane. I don't know what else to do."

"Yeah, but maybe someone does."

"Who?"

"It's not like when we first started, Dylan, where it's just us and law enforcement and that's it. There's this whole community of amateur investigators. I guess you'd call them web sleuths. They dig into cold cases or interesting current cases and become obsessed with them. And they're good. A lot of times, even better than law enforcement. Maybe they know something about this case that we've missed."

"How have I not heard about them before?"

"Because you still like to use paper files and write with pencils like a caveman. I bet even Markie knows about web sleuths. Let's dig around and see what we turn up."

"Couldn't make the case worse for us, I guess."

She squeezed his hand and then stood up. "Better go. Just know I'm here for you. No matter what."

He watched as she got into her truck and drove away. Leaving him alone in the dark with the crickets. He rose and leaned against the banister of the porch, enjoying the rough texture of the old wood underneath his hands.

He finished the last beer, then went to the computer in his home office.

70

Lily had been right. After only a few searches, it became clear there were thousands of people who considered themselves online detectives. All working to find perpetrators for crimes law enforcement had given up on or diving into current cases in areas law enforcement wasn't exploring.

Dylan found a message board dedicated to Arlo Ward and saw that there were 1,412 posts, with almost 4,600 replies. He got an energy drink out of the fridge, sat back down, and began to read.

Many of the posts were a back-and-forth about whether Arlo had really committed the crimes, whether he was genuinely insane, and who was winning the trial so far. The consensus was that Arlo would be convicted, that it was his wife's testimony that would put him away, and that the defense attorneys should have done everything possible to prevent her from testifying.

I tried, jerkoffs.

One post did talk about how cute the male defense attorney was, and Dylan read all the replies to that one.

He scrolled through the dozens of posts about various aspects of the case, and one, posted by a user named Obzed Wit Crimze, had a single line that caught his attention:

Does anyone else find it weird how similar this is to the Angel Lake killings?

Dylan had never heard about the Angel Lake killings. He quickly went to Google and searched. Only a few pieces came up, all from several years ago, and he read the article in the *Las Vegas Sun*, then a post on a blog, then a report on the local news station's website. Two campers, a husband and wife, had been murdered near the shore of Angel Lake "with a blunt instrument." That was it. There was no other description in any of the sources about how they were killed.

No photographs of the crime scene, no autopsy photos, no pictures of coroner assistants hauling away bodies. The media lived for cases like this and described them in as much horrific detail as they could. The only time Dylan had ever seen stories sanitized of the particulars was when law enforcement requested it or a judge ordered it.

At the bottom of the *Las Vegas Sun* article, he read something that made his heart drop and quickened his breath.

The detective assigned to the Angel Lake killings had been Hank Philips of the Jackson County Sheriff's Office.

Dylan minimized all the windows on his computer and brought up a new document. He typed in the heading, *Motion for Finding of Prosecutorial Misconduct and Request for a Mistrial.*

71

"They purposely hid this from the defense in violation of every discovery rule known to man," Dylan said.

The courtroom had been emptied except for the judge, bailiffs, clerks, and lawyers. Even Holly Fallows had been escorted out. Arlo sat quietly and watched, looking like he didn't understand what was happening.

"The State withheld exculpatory evidence from the defense that would have greatly impacted both defense strategy and plea bargaining on this case."

Kelly replied, "Nonsense. The Angel Lake killings were an unrelated crime from six years ago that has no relevance to this case."

"Your Honor, I would direct your attention to the police report our investigator secured that I've added as an addendum to the defense's motion. You'll see that the two victims, Marty and Caroline Bennett, were killed, according to the coroner's report, with what was most likely a baseball bat. The bodies were then mutilated with a large knife or machete and posed in gruesome, sexually suggestive ways that are not only similar but identical to the posing of the bodies here. And Ms. Whitewolf is correct, this was six years ago. Several months before my client moved to the state of Nevada."

"These murders have nothing to do with this case. We did briefly look at this in comparison to the actions of the defendant. We found that there were dissimilarities that did not warrant further investigation. This was work product, and as such, we are under no obligation to turn it over to the defense. This is just an attempt—"

"This was exculpatory evidence that could've changed this entire case. The State had a duty to hand this over."

"The defense could easily, and should have, searched for similar cases in the state themselves. We're under no obligation to do their job for them."

"Your Honor, again, I would refer you to the articles attached to my motion. You can see that none of them, not one, mentions the method of death other than that the victims were killed with a blunt instrument. None of them mention the mutilation or the posing of the bodies. How exactly could I have found this when none of it was ever released to the public?"

Judge Hamilton said, "So why is it the State's malfeasance if these publications didn't release the details? Perhaps they simply thought they were too gory?"

Dylan spoke in a lower tone so the judge couldn't pick up on the anger he was starting to feel. "It is the defense's assertion that the State got a sealed court order demanding that these publications not reveal any of the details of what occurred. It is a tactic commonly used by law enforcement so they can separate those taking credit for crimes from those who actually committed the crimes. I had no reasonable way to find this case. As such, they had a duty to hand these files over to me and did not."

Judge Hamilton tapped his pen against the bench. "So the remedy you're asking for is a mistrial. I don't think that's warranted, Mr. Aster. The jury has heard nothing about this, and there's still time for you to present it to them. I'm going to deny your motion for a mistrial."

"Then, Your Honor, in the alternative, we would ask to change Mr. Ward's plea from not guilty by reason of insanity to straight not guilty."

"What?" Kelly said. "They can't simply change a plea once the prosecution has already rested, Your Honor."

Arlo tugged at Dylan's suit coat. "I don't want that, Dylan."

Dylan leaned down. "Honestly, Arlo, I don't give a damn what you want. I'm saving your life whether you want me to or not. Don't interrupt me again, or I'll have them gag you."

He said it with such force that Arlo seemed to understand there would be no argument. He put his head down and stared at the table.

"This was exculpatory, Your Honor. The Court knows it, and the State knows it. At the very least, we should be allowed to change our plea to better fit the case in light of the withheld evidence."

The judge looked between them. "Ms. Whitewolf, were the details of the method of death and postmortem injuries of the Bennetts withheld from the public?"

"At the time, we had no leads and no motive for anyone to harm the victims. But we felt we might be able to draw the perpetrator out. I was informed by a criminal psychologist I consulted that these types of perpetrators crave attention, and by denying them that, it would cause them to attempt to get it. Perhaps by sending letters to us or the media. We needed some way to know who was the real perpetrator and who was attempting to take credit, and the only way to do that was to withhold information from the public."

Dylan said, "And it also made certain that I could never have possibly linked these two cases together."

The judge took a moment to think. "I did read the entirety of the reports Mr. Aster provided, and I did find striking similarities between the crimes. So much so that I do believe it is not simply work product, as the prosecution claims, but in fact is exculpatory evidence that should have been given to the defense. I am therefore withdrawing Mr. Ward's pleas of not guilty by reason of insanity and entering not-guilty pleas on all counts."

Kelly bit her lip and looked at Dylan with venom. "So, what, now you're going to instruct the jury that he's claiming he's innocent?"

"What I am going to do," Judge Hamilton said, "is follow the law. If you'd done that from the beginning of this case, you would not now be in this predicament."

Kelly's face flushed with anger, but she said nothing. The judge turned to his bailiff and said, "Bring in the jury so Mr. Aster can call his first witness."

72

The gun store had a range in the basement, and she could hear gunfire.

Holly Fallows said, "Thank you," to a woman who held the door open for her. Though she still used a crutch, the pain had become much more manageable. She had stopped taking pain pills and instead relied on ibuprofen and Tylenol.

She had never been in a gun store before. A glass case held dozens of handguns, and behind them were assault rifles and shotguns. Knives and ammunition were on shelves in the middle of the store, and the entire place smelled like leather.

"Can I help you with something?" an older man with a white beard and camo hat said.

She swallowed. "I need something for protection," she said nervously.

"Okay, what you got now?"

"Just some Mace I bought, but I don't know, it doesn't feel like enough."

"You gonna concealed carry or use it for home protection or both?"

"I'm going to carry it with me when I can."

He nodded and put his hands on the glass case. "What you probably want is this." He pulled out a black gun. "Glock twenty-six. One of the more popular ones we sell for concealed carry. It's small, just over six inches, and has a ten-round magazine with one in the chamber. First firearm?"

She glanced shyly at the floor and nodded.

"Then I think this is the best option. Lightweight, works well, and has decent stopping power with the right ammunition. We can do a quick background check and get you going."

She reached out and touched the weapon before picking it up. Just holding it in her hand made her feel safer, but it also filled her with a sense of regret. If she'd had this on the night . . .

"I'll buy it. With some ammunition, please," she said, placing it back down.

"Sure thing. But first, you ever fired one of these things before?"

She shook her head.

"All right, well, we got a range in the basement. How 'bout we get this paperwork filled out, and I take you down there and show you a few things? You really wanna make sure you've fired this a lot, because in an emergency you're not going to be thinking clearly, and instinct'll take over."

She touched the gun again. "Okay."

73

"The defense recalls Detective Philips to the stand."

The change of plea had been announced to the jury and the jury instructions modified. The judge explained it for a good half hour before letting the defense call Detective Philips.

Dylan handled the cross-examination and spent the first few minutes lulling the detective into a rhythm with easy questions he didn't need to think about to answer. A tactic Dylan liked to use to jar the witness when he got to the meat of what he was attacking them with.

"I'd like to turn your attention to something, Detective Philips," Dylan said. "I've handed you a police report you wrote over six years ago. Do you recognize it?"

"I do."

"It's for the murders of two campers, Marty and Caroline Bennett, correct?"

"Yes."

"Tell us about their deaths."

Philips cleared his throat. "The victims were camping at Angel Lake here in Jackson County. The campsite was in a secluded area without anyone else nearby. At some point during their first night there, the perpetrator found them and attacked them. The tent was torn, so we assume he cut through it to get inside. Mr. Bennett was attacked first and killed. His wife made it out of the tent and ran about thirty feet before being killed."

"What did the coroner conclude they were killed with?"

Philips glanced at the jury and cleared his throat again. "Head trauma from a blunt instrument."

"So the murder weapon could've been, say, a baseball bat?"

"Could've been, yes."

"In fact, the coroner states a bat *is* the most likely murder weapon, yeah?"

"He does state in his report that the injuries that caused the deaths of both Mr. and Mrs. Bennett are consistent with the use of a baseball bat, yes. But no murder weapon was ever found to confirm this."

"What happened to the bodies after they were killed?"

"They were mutilated."

"Mutilated and then posed, correct?"

"Yes."

"Posed in obscene ways?"

"I would say so, yes."

"Did you find a knife or machete nearby?"

"No, we did not."

Dylan held up photos of the Bennetts' corpses. He showed them to Kelly and then slowly walked them past the jury. "Detective, do the poses remind you of anything?"

"Remind me of anything?"

"Do they remind you of any current cases you're working?"

Philips was silent a moment. "Yes, they do. They are similar to the poses in this case with Mr. Ward."

"Not just similar." Dylan took a large color photograph of William Page postmortem and a color photograph of Marty Bennett postmortem and held them up to the jury. "Not just similar, but the *same*, isn't that right?"

"There were some differences that I believe—"

"The jury is looking at these two photos right now, Detective." Dylan turned the photos toward him. "Are these poses the same, or aren't they?"

He glanced at Kelly, who was sitting with her arms folded, her jaw clenched.

"Yes, they are nearly the same."

"You and Ms. Whitewolf didn't release the details of these killings to the public, did you, Detective?"

"Objection, relevance."

"Overruled."

Hank Philips blushed and started sweating. Dylan stood right in front of him. Close enough that he could smell his cologne.

"We felt at the time that—"

"No, Detective. No, I don't care about your feelings. I asked you a question. Did you make the details of these killings public?"

He looked at the jury and then back to Dylan. "No, we did not."

"And you didn't hand these reports over to me, did you?"

"No, after investigation, we didn't feel they were relevant to the matter at hand."

Dylan took another step closer. "A couple killed with a baseball bat while camping, mutilated postmortem, and then posed, and you didn't think it was relevant for me or this jury to know about it? Boy, I would love to see what you think is relevant then."

"Objection."

"Withdrawn. Detective, you verified the whereabouts of my client going back years, correct?"

"Yes, we did."

"Where was he six years ago in July?"

Philips swallowed. "He was living in Oregon at the time after following his brother out there from North Dakota."

"And on what date were the Bennetts killed, Detective?"

Philips's jaw muscles flexed and relaxed. He looked over to the prosecution table, and he and Kelly exchanged a glance. "Six years ago, on July the tenth."

"Do you have *any* evidence, Detective, that Arlo Ward was in Nevada at the time the Bennetts were killed?"

"No, we do not."

"In fact, when you first arrested him, it reminded you of the Bennetts' murder, and you looked up where he was at the time, yeah?"

He hesitated long enough that Dylan was about to ask him the question again before he said, "Yes, I did."

"How do you know he was in Oregon on July tenth of that year?"

Philips coughed into his hand, then said, "We received verification from his employer that he had worked that day. He held a job as a cashier part-time at a thrift store. We also could not find his name on any flights, buses, or at any car rental agencies, and he had no vehicle of his own."

"Where was Evan Ward on July tenth of that year, Detective? Were you finally able to come to a conclusion?"

He wouldn't answer for a few seconds. "Yes, we did. He was living here at the time. His brother moved out a few months later."

People in the spectator seats immediately expressed disbelief—murmurs, guffaws, and *what the hell*s were heard. The judge had to tell everybody to quiet down or he would have to clear the courtroom.

"So Arlo couldn't have killed the Bennetts, could he have?"

"It's unlikely."

"An identical crime happening at a time when Arlo Ward couldn't have committed it, and you decided to hide all this from me and the jury. Anything for a conviction, right? Whether he's guilty or not."

"Objection!"

"You almost got an innocent man killed. You make me sick, Detective."

"Objection!" both Kelly and James shouted.

Dylan took a step away from Philips, holding the detective's gaze. "I'm through with this witness."

74

Dylan paced his office while Lily sat on the couch. Madeline returned text messages while sitting next to her. Chinese takeout was spread on the desk.

The moon was full tonight and gave the city an icy glow. He thought his office was starting to smell like sweat because of all the late nights with a broken air conditioner. He opened a window, and warm air bathed him.

"We have to put Arlo on," Dylan said.

"It's risky, and Philips's testimony was devastating to their case. It's enough for reasonable doubt."

"I agree," Madeline said, looking up from her phone. "That was brutal for them today."

"For us as lawyers maybe, but it might not be for the jury. Especially since his wife got up there and said he beats her because he's a violent prick."

"You'll just have to hammer in your closing that he's taking credit for the fame and money."

"Sure, but why would they believe me?" He shook his head as he continued pacing. "We have to put him up. They have to see what he's really like when he talks about the killings."

Lily drew in a deep breath. "It's dangerous, but it might work."

Dylan put his hands on his head and turned to the window, staring out at the city. "Then why does it feel like the wrong move?"

"Whatever we do here will feel like the wrong move." She hesitated. "We have to attack him on the stand. And I mean attack him hard. I know you like him, so you might pull back subconsciously and not even know it. It's best if I or Madeline do it."

"No, he's closer to me. I have to do it. He has to feel the betrayal up there to lose his temper and say things he doesn't want to say."

"Well, I'll leave that call to you." Lily rose. "I can barely keep my eyes open. I'm going to bed."

"I'll walk down with you," Madeline said, rising.

Madeline stopped at the door and turned to him. "Dylan? Whatever happens, you tried an amazing case. I'm proud to have worked with you."

She gave a melancholic little smile and left. He turned back to the windows and stared at the empty courthouse. The statue of Lady Justice lit up with the headlights of a passing car and then faded to darkness again.

75

Arlo looked terrified on the stand. Like a child at an assembly who had to give a speech in front of the entire school. He tried to pour some water into a plastic cup and spilled it, then tried to mop it up with tissues and just spread it around instead. The bailiff came over with paper towels and cleaned up the mess himself.

"Thanks," Arlo said.

The bailiff just grunted.

"Arlo, I want you to take me back to the night you picked out these particular victims," Dylan said calmly.

"Okay."

"Who did you notice first?"

"Um, the girl, April. She was really pretty. Like the kind of pretty you see on magazines. So she was the first. Then I noticed Holly and then the two boys."

"What was April wearing?"

"Excuse me?"

"What was she wearing? You watched them awhile, followed them up the trail, so what were they wearing? I noticed the police never asked you that."

"She was wearing camping clothes. I don't know how to explain it better than that."

"Jeans?"

"Yeah, jeans."

"Flannel shirt?"

"I think that's right, yeah."

"Your Honor, may I approach?"

"You may."

Dylan picked up one of the large color photographs Kelly had already introduced, clothing that had been removed from April Fallows and found crumpled on the ground. "You recognize this, Arlo?"

Arlo didn't respond.

"It's April Fallows's clothes. Please tell the jury what she was wearing." Dylan turned the photograph toward the jury and walked up and down near the banister so they could all get a good look.

"She was wearing shorts."

"Shorts. That's right. And not even denim shorts, but canvas."

"Yeah, I just forgot. It was really dark."

"What was Holly Fallows wearing?"

Arlo said nothing for a while. "I don't remember what they were wearing. I was more concerned w-w-with how I was going to do it."

"By 'do it,' you mean kill them, right?"

"Yeah."

"Let's talk about that for a second. You said to the police you held April Fallows down onto the fire with your boot on her back, right?"

"Objection, leading," Kelly said.

"Permission to treat the witness as hostile."

"I'll allow it."

Dylan turned back to Arlo. "You held her in the fire with your boot on her back, yeah?"

"Yes."

"There were no burn or char marks found on your boots, were there?"

He swallowed. "I guess not."

"Your hands and feet had no burn marks the night the police examined you, did they?"

"No."

Dylan stood in front of Arlo. "How many times did you swing the bat to crush William Page's skull?"

"Um, I don't know. I kept swinging until he fell down."

"So like two, three?"

"Probably two."

"Arlo, I'd like to refer you to the coroner's report, something you haven't read, right?"

"I haven't."

"What does it say right here? The highlighted passage."

Arlo was silent.

"Arlo, please tell the jury what it says."

He cleared his throat. "It says that William Page had at least four injuries to his skull from a blunt object, most likely a baseball bat."

"Four. So whoever killed him took four swipes to knock him out and crush his skull. It'd be pretty hard to crush a grown man's skull with two swipes of a bat, wouldn't it?"

Arlo swallowed. "I killed them, Mr. Aster. I did it. Just because I don't remember the details doesn't mean anything."

"What color hair did April Fallows have?"

"What?"

"What color hair did she have?"

"Blonde."

"All blonde?"

"Yes."

Dylan picked up another photo. A close-up of April's face, clearly showing red tips in her hair with a red streak going down the left side.

"It's not all blonde, is it?"

"That's too hard to see in the dark."

"Yeah, but you cut them up for, how long would you say? At least an hour, right? You claim you decapitated her postmortem, but you didn't notice she had red hair?"

Arlo said nothing.

"What kind of shoes was April wearing?"

"I don't know. It was dark."

"What kind of shoes was William Page wearing?"

"I don't know."

"What about Michael Turner?"

He shifted in his seat, and the first flash of anger appeared on his face. "I already told you it was really dark, and I couldn't see."

"These bodies were posed sometime after death, right?"

"Yes," he said, a slight smile returning now. "I thought it'd be fun to terrorize Ms. Holly Fallows when she came back and took it all in."

Dylan had to resist the urge to look back to Holly Fallows for her reaction.

"Right. And so when you posed these bodies, you had to lift the severed limbs, correct?"

"I did."

"That would include the legs. The killer cut off both of Ms. Fallows's and Mr. Turner's legs at the knees. The way they were arranged, he would've had to pick those up, correct?"

Arlo started nervously rubbing his fingers together. "Yes."

"So you take the clothes off but leave the shoes on, pick up the legs, hold them in your hands, take the time to arrange everything, and you can't tell us what kind of shoes they were wearing?"

"It's not like that. When you kill people, everything moves quickly. It's like your b-brain is on autopilot. You don't notice the details."

"Oh, but in your confession you do mention the details, don't you? You talk about how far you ran after Holly, about how the bat felt when it came down onto Mr. Turner's head, how you set up the bear trap to catch him . . . speaking of which." He turned to the judge. "Your

Honor, I would like permission to have Mr. Ward give a demonstration to the jury."

"You may."

Dylan went to the clerk and asked for two exhibits that had already been introduced into evidence. She went through a door behind the judge's bench and came out with the bear trap and the bat that had been found at the cabin, both contained in thick plastic bags.

"Arlo," Dylan said, taking out the bear trap and putting it down near the jury, "please come over here."

Arlo did. He stood next to Dylan with his arms folded, his mouth tight lipped as he stared at the trap.

"This is the trap you allegedly used on Michael Turner, correct?"

"Yeah."

"Then, if you would, please set the trap in the same way you did that night."

"What d-d-do you mean?"

"I mean, you have to set these traps before they can go off. Set it for the jury to see how it works."

Arlo stared at the trap and then bent down. He fiddled with it in various ways, attempting to open it, then trying to twist the spring, then turning it upside down and trying to open it that way. It became clear he couldn't do it. Dylan went to the defense table and got out a long piece of round steel.

"Maybe you need this, Arlo? It's the tool that, once you open it, you use it to push up the round part in the middle, which then sets it."

Arlo took the length of steel and stared at the trap. He tried two different ways before finally getting the circular steel pan in the middle up and setting the trap.

"That's fine, Arlo. Thank you. Please stand up."

Dylan unset the trap and moved it aside. Then he took the bat out of the plastic bag and handed it to Arlo. "Show us how you swung it."

"What?"

"Show us how you swung the bat that night."

Arlo glanced at the jury and then Lily and Madeline. He held the bat with both hands and stared at it a second before swiping it left to right. It looked like how a child who'd never held a bat might swing it. There was no power behind it, and the swing looked sloppy and uneven.

"Again, please. Swing hard."

Arlo swung the other direction, and it looked even worse.

"You claim you expertly killed the victims with precision swings. Please show us how you did it."

"I . . . don't want to."

"The jury would like to see it, Arlo. They need to get a sense of what the victims went through, and the best way is to show them exactly how they died. So swing exactly like you did that night."

Dylan took a step back. One of the bailiffs went around Arlo, his hand nervously tapping his gun. As though Arlo were about to jump on the jury and start swinging away.

"Your Honor," Kelly said, "I would object to this demonstration. It proves absolutely nothing. Not to mention that handing a bat to a defendant accused of committing murder with it is highly dangerous."

"We have bailiffs here ready to tase if necessary, Judge, and the jury should be the ones deciding whether Arlo actually knows how to swing this thing or not."

The judge tapped his pen against the desk. He was taking too long to think. For the cameras, Dylan added, "I think any judge would want to remain objective on this, Your Honor. If the Court is fearful for its safety, we can put ankle restraints on Mr. Ward and bring him farther away from the jury."

He nodded. "Yes, why don't we do that. Bailiff?"

They took the bat out of Arlo's hands and then strapped cuffs to each ankle connected by a length of chain. Short enough that if he tried to move quickly, he would stumble. Dylan moved him farther away from the jury and near the defense table.

"Go ahead. Swing."

Arlo swung. He swung so hard that he went off balance, creating a whiff of air that filled the silent courtroom before he stumbled and had to correct himself.

"One more time."

Arlo swallowed, his face red. "No."

"No? But you're an expert at swinging a bat. These people were fighting for their lives, and you still managed to take them down. I mean, it's really an amazing feat. Killing targets with such a cumbersome weapon while they're fighting you. Let's take another swing and show the jury how you did it."

Arlo set the bat down on the defense table. "No."

"You don't want to show them because you can't do it, can you, Arlo?"

"I killed those people."

"You killed those people, but you can't even swing a bat without almost falling over?" Before Kelly could get out an objection, Dylan said, "You can sit back down in the witness box, Arlo."

76

Once the ankle restraints were removed and Arlo was seated, Dylan came into his space and stared into his pupils, clearly unnerving him as he began to fidget and shift in his chair. "April Fallows was missing her kidneys. Did you take her kidneys?"

"Yes. But I left them there."

"How'd you cut them out?"

"With a hunting knife."

"What hunting knife?"

"Just a knife. I threw it over a cliff when I was done. That's why they didn't find it."

"See, that's interesting," Dylan said, taking a step back. "Because April Fallows only had one kidney, her left kidney. She'd lost her right kidney in an accident when she was sixteen, and her left kidney was found at the scene."

Everyone in the courtroom sat in dead silence; even the crowd of reporters in the media box didn't write anything or glance down to their phones. Arlo noticed the focused attention; he couldn't look up from the floor.

"I get confused sometimes. It happened so fast, and it was dark, and I get confused because of my illness."

"You weren't confused when you confessed. The detectives asked you for all the details and you never mentioned she only had one kidney, did you?"

"No."

"Now you say you remember she only had one, but you couldn't tell me what their hair was like, what shoes they wore, or what clothes they wore. You couldn't even swing a bat hard enough to hurt a child, much less a college football player."

"Objection!" Kelly said.

"It's not because you're confused, Arlo. It's because you didn't kill these people, did you?"

"Objection, Your Honor."

"No!" Arlo said. "No, I did. I killed them, and I'm famous now."

"You didn't kill anybody. Whoever killed the Bennetts killed these people."

"No," Arlo said, panic in his voice now, "no, that's n-not what h-h-happened."

"I have a recording of a phone call between you and your wife at the jail dated twenty-seven days ago. I'd like to play it for the jury."

Arlo glanced at the jury and then turned his eyes back to the floor. Dylan handed the disc to the clerk. Kelly objected on foundational grounds, and Dylan gave her and the judge a signed document by the clerk at the jail that the disc was an authentic recording made on the date stated.

Voices came through the speakers in the courtroom.

"I miss you."

"I miss you, too."

"Pause it, please . . . thank you. Arlo, that's your and your wife's voices, right?"

"It i-is." He was trembling now and had lost all the color in his face.

"Clerk, could you fast-forward to minute eleven and twenty-two seconds, please."

The clerk did as he asked. Arlo's voice came through the speakers and said, "You'll both be taken care of. Amy is never gonna have to worry about money again. I want you to put her in a private school. A good one. I want her to have everything I didn't have growing up."

"What she needs is her daddy, Arlo."

"Her daddy will be gone either way. I can feel everything slipping away from me, Leena. It comes in w-w-waves, but I feel it. You won't even r-r-recognize me anymore. I'll just be gone. It's better this way."

"Thank you, Clerk, you can stop it," Dylan said, folding his arms but not moving an inch away from Arlo.

"A man's first job is to take care of his family, right? You told me that once. You believe those words, don't you, Arlo?"

He nodded without saying anything.

"You love Leena and Amy and would do anything for them?"

"Of course."

"Even take the blame for murders you didn't do if it meant you could help them."

"I did this!" Arlo shouted, his face flushed with anger. "I did this! I'm famous. I killed them and everybody w-wants to t-t-talk to me now. They're going to give me money just to t-t-talk to them." Tears formed in his eyes. "I'm a good father! I'm not like the trash that raised me. I'm a good father, and I would do anything for my daughter, and I did this. I killed them!"

He sobbed now, his shoulders slumping as his hand covered his eyes. "Please, D-Dylan. Please don't take this away from me. I'll just b-become a burden to them. Please." He looked directly at the jury as tears came. "Please don't take this away from me."

Dylan watched him a moment and then turned to the jury. One of the jurors had tears in her eyes.

"We don't execute innocent people, Arlo," Dylan said. "No matter how much they want to be executed."

77

Kelly's cross-examination of Arlo went through all the details of his confession, and she played the video again, with her asking questions about it throughout and Arlo answering gleefully. It took several hours but introduced nothing new. It was just a tactic to force the jury to watch the confession in full again.

Dr. Simmons was next to testify and told the jury precisely what Dylan had hoped he would: Arlo Ward was doing this for the attention and likely hadn't murdered anyone. Kelly attacked him on the fact that he couldn't possibly know what Arlo was thinking and ended with, "Have you ever been deceived by a patient?"

"Yes, I have. All psychiatrists have."

"In fact, when you were on the board for a care facility for the mentally ill, you approved the release of a man named Ian Rupert Belle, correct?"

"Yes."

"And I have here your report about his release, where you state that he was ready to be reintegrated into society and had reformed, and I quote, 'as much as any patient in here can reform.'"

"I see what you're doing, but that particular case—"

"Did you say that or not, Doctor?"

He let out a breath, trying to hold back the frustration that was clearly showing. "Yes, I did."

"And Ian Rupert Belle was a model citizen on his release for . . . let's see . . . twenty-one days, correct?"

Dr. Simmons hesitated. "Yes, he was."

"Then what happened on day twenty-two, Doctor?"

"You're treating this as if it were an exact science like mathematics. The human mind is enormously—"

"I will ask you again, since you apparently do not want to answer my question. What happened on day twenty-two of his release?"

Dr. Simmons swallowed and glanced at Dylan. "He killed his wife."

"Wow. *Reformed as much as anyone could be.* I wonder how many other spouses are dead because you thought the patients were reformed?"

"Objection," Lily said.

"Sustained."

"It's fine, I'm done with this witness, Your Honor."

Judge Hamilton said, "You are excused, Dr. Simmons. The defense may call their next witness."

Dylan rose, looked at Arlo, looked at the jury, and said, "The defense rests."

"Any rebuttal witnesses from the State?"

"No, Your Honor."

Judge Hamilton tapped his pen a few times and said, "I believe we have enough time to begin the State's closing statements, if you'd like to proceed, Ms. Whitewolf. Or if you'd prefer, we can wait until tomorrow."

"I'm sure the jury is tired from a full day of testimony. I'd prefer to begin in the morning."

"I think that's best as well. Court is adjourned until morning."

While most everyone in the courtroom hurriedly shuffled out to use the bathroom and make calls they'd been ignoring, Arlo remained seated. Dylan sat on the edge of the table and stared at him until he looked up.

"That's not what I wanted, Dylan. You made them think I didn't do it."

"No, I didn't. We might lose, Arlo. You still might get that needle in your arm. But at least this way I know I did everything I could to save your life. Maybe you'll hate me, but you'll be alive to do the hating."

78

That night, Dylan, Markie, his mother, Lily, and Jake all went out to dinner. It was a quiet Chinese place Dylan had learned about because he'd defended the owner for tax evasion.

Soft music played through speakers, and the restaurant was crowded, but everyone seemed to speak in hushed tones. Jake was telling stories about his time traveling through Africa as an amateur photographer, a hobby, he said, he had picked up with Greenpeace while in some country Dylan had never heard of. Markie looked like she was staring at Superman, and even his mother kept saying, "Wow. That is so interesting."

"What about you, DA?" Jake said. "What exotic locales compelled you to visit?"

Dylan hated being called *DA* but didn't say anything for the sake of not making it more awkward than it already was. "I went to Niagara Falls once and threw a basketball over. It was sweet."

Jake stared at him a second and then asked if anyone wanted dessert.

———

After dessert, in the parking lot, Lily got him away from everyone else and said, "Whatever happens, you did amazing, Dylan."

"You too."

She looked over to Jake, who was making Markie laugh. "No, I've been distracted. You carried the weight of this, and it's not fair I did that to you."

"Hey, what are friends for?" He waited until she looked at him before saying, "He's your kid, and no one can ever change that."

Markie shouted, "We're going to miss the movie, Dylan!"

Dylan and Lily exchanged a look, one that told them everything they wanted to say to each other. He got into his car with Markie hanging out the window and tapping the roof and shouting, "On, Dancer! On, Prancer! On—"

Dylan pulled away from the parking lot. When he looked in the rearview mirror, Lily was still standing there, staring off into space. She didn't move until Jake came up to her and said something; then she got into her truck.

79

Before closing arguments, the jury instructions had to be reexamined and finalized. The process was painful for both sides, and terms like *likely* and *somewhat likely* were hotly debated. Lunch came and went, and nobody ate while the jury sat in the deliberation room and had pizza delivered.

It was five in the evening three days later before the instructions were finalized.

Kelly stood in front of the jury with her hands behind her back. She looked each one of them in the eyes. The judge had ordered everyone in the courtroom to maintain complete silence during closing statements under punishment of being removed.

"I've never had a trial like this," Kelly finally said. "The defense began this trial with the argument that Mr. Ward is insane, and that he killed those three wonderful people and"—she looked at Holly Fallows, who rested her head on her father's shoulder as he held her—"and nearly killed one of the kindest, most humble people I've ever met in my life. Holly, only through pure courage, survived that night. She will never be the same. Her injuries, physical and psychological, have permanently changed her. Not to mention that the life she had envisioned for herself with her husband and sister is gone forever."

Kelly took a step back and pointed to Arlo.

"He confessed to this crime and was found covered in the victims' blood not three miles from where they were killed. So he comes in here and tells us he's insane. He didn't know what he was doing, he didn't know it was wrong to crush someone's head with a baseball bat or to cut off arms and legs and pose them in the most horrific ways possible. He can't be held responsible because he just didn't know it was wrong.

"As if that weren't ridiculous enough, he then changes his plea at the very end of the trial and says, *Surprise, I'm not crazy. I just didn't do it.* It's a level of maneuvering that anyone would look at and say, *This guy must be insane to do all this. It's chaos.*"

She put her arms behind her again and looked each juror in the eyes.

"It is not insane. It is not random . . . it is not chaotic. It's genius. Absolutely genius. A stroke of inspired brilliance. Arlo Ward isn't some hapless victim of circumstance. He is a chess grandmaster who set this game up with sheer cleverness.

"He also isn't some sympathetic mentally ill savior who is doing all this to save his family. If he wanted to write a book, then just write a book, get an agent, and sell it. Maybe it would've sold, maybe it wouldn't have, but the point is he didn't try. He didn't try anything else. He went straight to taking the lives of innocent young men and women who did absolutely nothing to deserve the barbaric way they were killed.

"But the real problem for Mr. Ward is Holly's bravery and resourcefulness. He didn't count on anyone getting away. He probably wanted to clean the crime scene before he left, dispose of the bodies, find a change of clothing . . . but he couldn't do any of that because Holly got away. And he had no idea how long it would take her to flag someone down and get the police out there. He quickly double-checked the bodies to make sure they looked like the Bennetts' killings, which he no doubt learned about at some point, and then jumped into his car, covered in blood, and raced home as fast as he could. And that's where luck came into play. That stretch of highway is known as a speed trap, and a squad car was quietly waiting on the side of the road watching for speeders. They clocked the defendant at almost thirty miles over the speed limit, nearly a hundred miles an hour. Why would he possibly be traveling that fast on a highway known for having a police presence? This is where his genius really shines.

"He can't just say nothing happened, because Holly might've survived and there would be a report of a speeder covered in blood pulled over near where the murders occurred. So instead, he fully confesses. Tells them everything in detail and then insists that he's guilty and needs to be punished. He knew he couldn't give an alibi, knew the blood would match the victims', and he couldn't be certain Holly wasn't alive to identify him. So he had to think fast, and he did.

"He concocted this entire story, careful to give some details but not too many. Not details that only the killer would know. He gave just enough that it would seem like he was taking credit, but not enough that you would know for certain he did it.

"He went under hypnosis as you saw in the video Dr. Simmons played, and fabricated another story of him just happening to stumble onto the horrific scene and thinking, *Gee, three people are dead, how about instead of calling the police I smear blood all over me and then speed home at a hundred miles an hour.* This entire show, ladies and gentlemen, was put on for your benefit. To convince *you* that someone other than Arlo Ward killed Michael, William, April, and almost killed Holly. It's genius, and it almost worked.

"Mr. Aster and Ms. Ricci, both brilliant attorneys, have been nothing but pawns. Arlo Ward needed attorneys that would somehow get not-guilty pleas entered while he still maintained that he did it. He needed you to believe that he wanted to get convicted to provide for his wife and child. The wife who took the stand and told you about all the times she had to go to the emergency room because of him. And who knows how many times there were where she didn't go to the emergency room."

Kelly paused and intertwined her fingers, taking time to ensure her next words came out the way she wanted.

"When you go back there and discuss this case, think of what would have had to occur for his story to be true. He happened to be in the exact spot in Coyote Canyon where the victims were. He happened to come by right when they were already dead. He happened to be in a condition where he felt his mental illness was getting worse, and he needed to find a way to get a lot of money for his family. He just happens to not have either the baseball bat that killed the victims or the knife that mutilated them afterward, but a bat is found in a nearby cabin. If someone really wanted to be caught and take credit for this, wouldn't they have kept the bat and knife? Not if they were playing the long game. Because the murder weapons could've conclusively tied Arlo to these murders. He can't get away with this if you have no doubt he committed these crimes."

She shook her head and turned to Arlo, staring at him as she said, "Arlo Ward killed those wonderful people. Arlo Ward nearly killed Holly Fallows. Arlo Ward has been laughing at us this entire trial." She turned back to the jury. "Please, don't fall for it—because trust me, you do not want him back out here with us and our families." She stepped close to them and took the time to look each in the eyes. "He's laughing at us, and he's laughing at the victims whose lives he so brutally took. Don't let him have the last laugh."

80

When court had ended and everybody left, Dylan remained. Lily had asked him to dinner, but he said he was too busy finishing up his closing to go. It wasn't the truth. His closing had been completed and memorized.

Something dug at his guts and wouldn't let go, and he needed time alone to think. Kelly's closing arguments kept running through his mind over and over:

He is a chess grandmaster who set this game up with sheer cleverness.

Arlo's favorite game, Go, was an extremely complex game—a game of strategy that required thinking many moves ahead . . . exactly like chess.

Dylan went home and had forgotten to grab dinner, so he ordered a pizza for everyone. Afterward, he went directly to his home office and booted up the computer.

The first place he went online was the true-crime followers forum and into the subcategory about Arlo Ward's case. He began reading the posts. Many of the new ones were commenting on today's developments and how good the prosecutor's closing had been. But some were saying that she hadn't adequately addressed how Arlo would've learned about the Bennett murders when the police never released the details, and there was a debate about whether it was pure coincidence or if Arlo was simply a copycat of the Bennett murderer.

Minutes turned into hours without his realizing it. His vision blurred, so he had to take a break and go outside. The air was cool, and the stars were out. He put his hands in his pockets and watched them in the night sky for a long time before going back into his office.

He continued reading the forum posts. Some of the web sleuths had done research into Arlo's life. Dylan was surprised how many little pieces of information they had that the police didn't. Like the name of Arlo's previous girlfriend and a prior address that wasn't in his history. It was always someone who knew someone else that had the information. Crowdsourcing seemed to have a reach that law enforcement just wasn't set up to have.

Dylan guzzled energy drink after energy drink, and it gave him a nervous edge but kept his brain sharp. At least for a little while.

After hours of scrolling and reading, his eyes ached, and his lower back was screaming. He rose and stretched his arms above his head. He was debating getting some ibuprofen when he glanced down and noticed the topic heading for one of the threads way down on the list. It read, *I can't believe his rating!*

Dylan sat back down and clicked it. It opened to a screenshot of a list of names, each with a flag and number by it, in a column titled *Elo*. A word Dylan had to google and found out was related to the game Go.

Arlo Ward was around the center of the list with an American flag and the number 3,012. Dylan searched what that meant. It was a numerical score ranking the different Go players that had played in tournaments. One hundred was considered a novice . . . one thousand was considered an intermediate player . . . three thousand was considered a world grandmaster.

He googled more about Go scores and found a study that correlated Go scores with IQ and concluded that it was more accurate in predicting IQ than school grades or chosen profession.

Dylan experienced heavy nausea. It felt like a boulder was crushing his chest and stomach and growing heavier by the second. He had to take a deep breath and expand his lungs to make sure he still could.

The thought couldn't be denied.

Arlo Ward might have schizophrenia, but he was very likely also a genius.

81

The jail didn't have many visitors that night, and Dylan scored a private room. He sat at the steel table, rubbing his hands together. Only then, when he looked down at them, did he notice they were shaking.

Arlo was brought in and sat at the table. The guard cuffed him to the metal ring near one of the legs and said, "I can only give you fifteen minutes this late."

"We won't be that long," Dylan said.

When the guard had left, they stared at each other. Arlo started to say, "Must be important to wake me up in the middle—"

"The stutter was a nice touch."

Arlo sat there a moment. "Excuse me?"

"It's just you and me now. No cameras, no other lawyers, no prosecutor, no judge."

Arlo stared at him in bewilderment . . . and then a grin slowly crept to his lips.

"Her closing was exquisite, wasn't it? Did she convince you?"

"I found your Go score. You're a world grandmaster. Then it was just Occam's razor: the simplest explanation is always best. The options are, Did you stumble on this scene and want to get famous and you don't know who the killer is, or did the missing gas station attendant kill them and you followed them up there and watched, or did your brother kill them and then called you down . . . or did you actually do it?"

Arlo clicked his tongue against his teeth. "Ted Bundy once said it's never the big things that get you caught. It's always the little things you can't plan for."

Dylan swallowed but wouldn't move his gaze from Arlo's. "Did you kill the Bennetts, too?"

"No, I really wasn't in the state at the time."

"How'd you know how they were posed? That wasn't public information."

He smiled, and the smile was awful. "I was in group therapy years ago with a man that talked about the Bennetts, and a couple of others, frequently. He never admitted to the murders, of course, but he either killed them or knew who did. And what a masterpiece that scene was. So unique. Do you know he was going to use Marty Bennett for target practice before cutting his throat? He planned to tie him to a tree and shoot him at a distance. But he felt rushed and skipped it. It was his first time killing. I'm sure he's improved by now."

Arlo sighed and picked at some loose skin on his thumbnail.

"I, unfortunately, didn't have a firearm with me that night, but I did have some of my hunting gear in the trunk: a trap and my bowie knife. So at least I could pose them like he did. I thought the signatures would be too unique for the police to just write off." He chuckled. "But boy, they surprised us both when they hid that from you. That's just plain unethical, if you ask me."

Dylan leaned back, unable to blink or even have coherent thoughts. He couldn't speak for a minute because he thought he might vomit. His hands were trembling badly now, and he put them together under the table so Arlo couldn't see.

"Have you ever . . . have you ever killed anyone else?"

Arlo shrugged, still picking at his fingers. "It's amazing how the gas station attendant, who saw me in line behind them, vanished, isn't it? The devil's in the details, you know."

"What'd you do to him?"

"That's not really what you want to ask me, is it? What you really want to ask me is why. Go ahead, ask."

A beat of silence passed between them.

"Why, Arlo? You didn't rob them. You didn't sexually assault them. Why?"

Arlo inhaled deeply and thought a moment, running his fingertip along a scratch in the metal table someone had made with a pen.

"Before my father's psychotic break, he was an engineer. He loved physics and would tell us stories about the lives of the great physicists. He told me once about Heisenberg. The OSS, the equivalent of the CIA back then, was unsure what he could give the Germans. So they recruited someone to kill him. Moe Berg. He was a famous baseball player, so he could go places they weren't letting other Americans go at the time. And no one would connect him to the murder of a scientist who was a stranger to him. So they recruited Berg and trained him. He went to one of Heisenberg's lectures in Switzerland. If the lecture presented enough concerning evidence that Heisenberg could help the Nazis, Berg had to kill him.

"So he listened to the lecture and then went outside to the back door, where Heisenberg was going to come through to avoid the crowds. Berg stood in the shadows near the door, lifted his pistol, and waited. Soon, the door opened, and Heisenberg appeared. He actually stopped right there, with the gun pointed at his head, and put on his hat before he kept walking. Berg lowered the gun and left."

Arlo put his hands on the table, and cuffs clinked against steel. "That story stuck with me. I kept thinking, even as a child, Could I have pulled the trigger? Would I have what it takes to kill? Berg was an average man who disliked violence, and yet there he was with a gun pointed at someone's head."

He looked up into Dylan's eyes. Their gazes locked in a way they never had before, since Arlo always looked away. He was different now. His countenance, body movements, and posture were all different. He wasn't slouching anymore, and when he moved his hands, they had a soft gracefulness to them. It was almost like a costume had slipped off, and he was showing Dylan what was really underneath.

"I gave up on the thought around my teenage years because of my illness. I had more pressing things to worry about. Then—and this was random fortuity—in a used bookstore, I discovered the work of an obscure criminology professor. He describes the method by which a normal child turns into a violent adult who has the capacity to rape and murder.

"One of the phases you have to go through is virulency. It's where you commit violence, and your self-esteem is boosted by it, so it becomes a part of your personality. I had never committed violence, but I was curious to see what would happen if I went through this process. I started small, fistfights with neighbors and such. Hitting people with things when they were walking by, throwing rocks at cars with open windows . . . but it wasn't doing enough . . . and then I saved that boy's life. That story is true."

"What does that have to do with anything?"

"I had committed the ultimate virtuous act: risked my life to save the life of an innocent. Everyone called me a hero, but I felt nothing. No elation, no sense of justice, no feeling that I had done the right thing. There was nothing."

He inhaled deeply and put his hands together.

"That's when the story of Moe Berg came to me again. I felt nothing with virtue; would I feel something with vice? The violence I had been experimenting with was petty and small. I needed to commit the ultimate evil act and measure its effect on me. I needed to murder."

He chuckled to himself.

"You should have seen some of my early attempts. Break-ins at homes that had alarms that made me sprint through backyards, chased by dogs sometimes. Once, my foot was run over by a car when I tried to force a woman out . . . it was almost comical. Then, fortune struck again. I was at a gas station when four young, good-looking, likable people were there asking directions to the most secluded area in the state. They were everything that's good in the world. If I killed them, it would be the evilest act I could commit in my circumstances."

Arlo's eyes had a distance to them now, a coldness that wasn't there before.

"How'd you do it?"

"I knew the area well. When my episodes were severe, I would go to Coyote Canyon to be alone. It was a simple matter to follow them and wait for the right time." He shook his head. "But that speeding . . . it was such a childish thing to do. I rushed through everything too quickly. I didn't even have a change of clothing with me. In hindsight, I should've found someone else when I was better prepared."

"How'd you catch up to Holly?"

"The forest is unforgiving. That poor girl took every wrong turn she could. Then she ended up exactly where I thought she would. But I will give her this; it took enormous courage to jump. I think I did her a favor in that she found strength she didn't know she had."

The thought of Arlo thinking he'd done Holly Fallows a favor made Dylan physically sick. He had to swallow down the bile rising in his throat.

Dylan took a breath and looked away. "Leena's testimony was real, wasn't it?"

He nodded. "That was actually her sloppy attempt to get away from me. She's been trying for some time. That Ms. Whitewolf is persuasive, I will give her that. Leena thought I would go to death row and she would go live on the government's dime somewhere. Luckily, though, she knew practically none of the details to share. Though I have to admit, when she took the stand, I thought we were cooked."

Dylan leaned forward, keeping his eyes glued to Arlo's. "Are you going to hurt her, Arlo?"

"Good attempt, Counselor. If I tell you I plan on hurting somebody, you can break privilege and report it."

"I won't let you harm her."

"How can I harm her from in here? Don't be foolish."

Arlo sighed ruefully, as though remembering a pleasant but regrettable memory.

"I think we're doing rather well with the jury given the circumstances, don't you?"

Dylan stood up and nearly tripped over his chair. Arlo said, "You all right, Counselor? You look white as a ghost."

Dylan hurried out of the jail. He barely made it outside before what little was in his stomach came up onto the pavement.

Two men saw him as they were heading in. One of them laughed.

82

The pounding on the door woke Lily up from a dream she frequently had: picking her son up from school and having him tell her about his day. Such a minor thing that most parents took for granted, but that she would've given anything to have.

She instinctively looked at the clock on the nightstand. It was almost three in the morning. Jake stirred and mumbled, "Who's that?"

"How would I know?"

She put on a robe and slippers and, just in case, got the 9 mm handgun from her gun safe. She held it behind her back as she looked through the peephole. Jake yawned from the bedroom.

"What the hell?" she mumbled. She put the gun on a small table that had a potted plant on it and opened the door.

Dylan stood there, red eyed, swaying, his clothes disheveled and his hair messy.

"What are you doing, Dylan? It's almost three in the morning."

"Hey, the party never stops, right? Isn't that what you're always telling me? That I need to relax and have more fun?" He brushed past her and said, "Wake Jakey-boy. Let's make it a real party. You got any tequila?"

"How much have you had to drink?"

"I don't know, but there's always room for more."

"Sit down," she said, helping him to the kitchen table. "I'm making you some coffee."

"Only if it's got rum in it. Hey, hey," he said, lightly gripping her arm. "You got any weed? 'Cause I could really go for some right now."

"No, Dylan," she said, pulling away. "I don't have any weed. Just don't move."

Jake came out of the bedroom. He was wearing pajama bottoms but no top. He saw Dylan and said, "What's going on?"

"Nothing, man. I'm just here to party with my best friend. We are best friends, aren't we, Lil? Anyway, you should join us. I think we're gonna have tequila and try to score some weed."

Jake looked at Lily, and she said, "We most certainly are not. I'm brewing him some coffee."

"Spike it with a little bit of Kahlúa, please. Just a tiny bit."

Lily put on the pot and then came over to the kitchen table. "Jake, can you give us a minute?"

"Yeah, sure," he said, not taking his eyes off Dylan. "You take it easy, all right, Dylan?"

"Jakey-boy! I've always liked you. I thought you were kind of a douchebag at first with your red Porsche and dress shoes with jeans, but the more I get to know you, the more I like you."

Jake grimaced and left. Lily sat down at the table next to Dylan. He mumbled something about partying until the sun came up, then calmed and stared down at the table. She got him bottled water, opened it, and shoved it in his hand.

"Drink it. Now."

"I don't want water."

"I don't care," she said, tipping the bottle up to his lips. "Drink."

He took a few gulps and set the water down. His smile went away, and he stared at a spot on the table, a notch. He ran his finger over it while the two of them sat in silence. Finally, he said, "He f . . ."

He couldn't finish the sentence.

The coffee was ready, and Lily poured him a cup and brought it over. He drank a sip and set it down next to the water. Dylan's head hung low, and he couldn't stop swaying, meaning he had drunk so much he was likely to just black out.

"Did you drive?" she said.

He sloppily shook his head, as though his neck were loose rubber. "Uber."

"Well, you're sleeping here tonight. Finish the water."

He looked up at her. "He did it, Lil. And he bullied his wife into helping him. I've never . . ." He couldn't even get the words out.

"Who are we talking about?"

As if building strength, he took a moment to breathe and then sat straighter in the chair. "Arlo killed those people."

She leaned back in her seat after pushing the bottle of water toward him again. "We've been through this, and it could've waited until the morning."

"He told me he did it."

"When?"

"A few hours ago."

"He's been saying he did it this entire time."

"No, he *really* did it. What Kelly said about this being a chess game made me think about how Arlo has always played Go. So I went onto that forum about this case and someone found his professional ranking. He's a world grandmaster, one of the best there is at a game that requires thinking far ahead. Oh, and he doesn't stutter, the slick weasel."

She watched him as he took a sip of water and then lowered it again. Lily had learned to never question whether a client had committed the crime they were accused of. She withheld judgment and defended everyone the same. Dylan, she knew, didn't have that ability to avoid getting emotionally wrapped up in cases.

Dylan stared at the wall as if lost in thought and forgetting where he was.

"So I went down to the jail to talk to him. Feel it out. He smiled at me, and his eyes just got . . . distant. He didn't look the same. And he told me why he did it. That he thinks it's some insane process he has to go through."

Dylan waved his arm around the room.

"This whole thing was a way for him to get attorneys that could get him not-guilty pleas entered while he proclaimed he did it. It was the best strategy to convince a jury he didn't do it, and he came up with it in less than a minute after he got pulled over. That's just creepy-level smart right there." He took a sip of coffee, and some of it spilled onto the table. "He used us to get away with this, Lil."

Lily was quiet a moment and then said, "Full honesty right now?"

"Always."

"I never thought he didn't do it. Something about him gave me an uncomfortable feeling from the moment I met him. Of course, it didn't affect how I defended him, but I never thought he was innocent."

"Welp, you're the better lawyer, 'cause he fooled the hell outta me."

Neither of them spoke. A clock was ticking somewhere, and it was the only sound in the condo until a police siren went by.

"You wanted to believe," she said gently. "That's okay to want to believe the best of people. It's an admirable trait that many people lose when they go from childhood to adulthood."

He shook his head. "I'm not doing it, Lil. I'm withdrawing from this case tomorrow."

"You can't."

"Watch me."

"I'll do the closing."

"No," he snapped. "No, you can't do it either. You don't want this on you any more than it already is. We're not doing it. We're withdrawing."

She took a deep breath and stood up. "Dylan, I want to show you something." She went to her office and came back with a manila envelope. She laid it in front of him. "Open it."

Dylan opened it and pulled out the police reports from one of their first cases, along with an order for dismissal.

"Oscar Beltran. You remember him? He was facing life for the sexual assault of a twenty-year-old woman, and the only evidence against him was her testimony. One of the first cases you and I ever had at our own firm. What did you do?" He didn't answer, and she touched his hand. "What did you do, Dylan?" she asked tenderly.

He swallowed and said, "He said he'd been at a college ball game at the time, so I watched the game several times in slow motion until I found a shot of him in the crowd."

"Yeah, and it got his case dismissed, and then the real rapist was arrested a few months later and looked just like Oscar. If it wasn't for you, Oscar, a father of three, would have spent the rest of his life in prison for something he didn't do. You saved that man's life and spared his family torture I can't even imagine."

She took his hand. "If you want to defend the innocent, you have to defend the guilty, too. It's all or nothing. So you need to ask yourself, Do you believe in what we do or don't you? Is the Constitution something real to you, or is it a piece of paper that we can disregard when it's convenient? But," she said, lifting the file, "you will never have another Oscar if you quit because of one Arlo."

She set the file down and said, "Come on, I'll get you a blanket and pillow. That couch may not look it, but it's really comfortable."

After she retrieved the blanket and pillow, she helped him to the couch.

"He killed those kids, Lil. How can I look those jurors in the eyes and say he didn't? What kind of person can do that?"

"A person that believes in something greater than himself."

83

The judge instructed the jury on what would be happening today. Dylan stared at a spot on the floor and couldn't take his eyes off it. Though he didn't mean to, he sat far from Arlo and leaned away from him. He lightly tapped the pen in his hand against his lips.

"Mr. Aster, it's now time for the defense's closing statements."

Dylan didn't move, and no one in the courtroom made a sound. Arlo stared at him, Lily and Madeline watched him, Kelly and everyone at the prosecution table turned to him, and the jury gazed at him . . . everyone waiting. But his eyes didn't move from the floor.

"Mr. Aster," the judge finally said, "are you ready for closing statements?"

Dylan didn't budge, and his eyes never lifted. Arlo whispered, "What are you doing?"

A slight movement of Dylan's head, and the two were staring at each other, understanding and animosity in both their eyes. Dylan didn't blink, and Arlo didn't look away.

Lily got to her feet and stepped toward the jury.

Dylan said, "There's really only one question in this trial, and it's not about Arlo Ward, and it's not about the attorneys or the judge. It's about the twelve of you."

He put his pen down and slowly rose as Lily sat back down, the two of them exchanging a quick glance. He buttoned the top button on his suit coat and approached the jury.

"Sitting over there is a man who has a severe mental illness. As Dr. Simmons said, probably the most severe mental illness you could have. Acute schizophrenia with both auditory and visual hallucinations. Yes, the government put up three doctors that said he knows the difference between right and wrong and that his confession is genuine, but not a single medical professional from the State ever spent more than two hours with Arlo. Barely the length of a movie, and they're supposed to make a determination about who a man is and how badly an illness affects him?

"So that leaves us with Dr. Simmons, who spent over forty hours with Arlo, and who tells us that he's taking credit for this and he did not kill those people. That he's a man who has craved attention his entire life and never gotten it, and this is his chance to not only get it but to have it provide for a wife and child he doesn't believe he can provide for.

"I know you don't want to release him. I know that. I know you're thinking, *What if he really did do it? How many more people would he kill?* But we all have our jobs to do here today. My job is to defend him, the government's job is to prove he committed these crimes, and your job, well, your job is the worst of it. Your job is to decide whether the government has proved Arlo's guilt beyond a reasonable doubt. Have they made you almost certain, *almost certain*, that he committed these crimes?

"How can you be almost certain when we have other killings committed in a nearly identical, not similar, but nearly *identical*, way? You'll notice Ms. Whitewolf didn't talk too much about the Bennetts in her closing. The police didn't even notify us of the Bennetts. Why not? Why didn't they immediately say, *Hey, just so you know, there was another two murders like this one at a time when Arlo Ward could not have committed them?* They didn't do that. They didn't hand it over to us until I filed a motion to get the reports, and even then they fought us on it. Why? Why did they fight so hard to hide it?

"Because it is a fact that two people were killed by blunt force trauma to the head, possibly from a baseball bat, and mutilated and posed in identical ways to the victims in this case, at a time when Arlo Ward was in another state. That's almost by definition reasonable doubt. And let's not forget this is a death penalty case, so knowing about these other murders that someone else committed in a nearly identical way six years ago, crimes the government tried to keep from you, how can you kill him?" Dylan stopped and looked at each juror. "How can you *kill* him, knowing that?"

He took a step back and stared at the jury. Then he looked at Lily.

"The question you need to ask yourselves is, Do you believe in our Constitution, even though you don't want to follow it in this case, or do you not believe in it, and think not everyone deserves the same rights?" He made a point to look each juror in the eyes again. "You took an oath at the beginning of this trial that you would uphold the law. Are you going to uphold the law and acquit Arlo Ward because there's reasonable doubt, or will you not uphold the law because you don't want to? Are you going to honor your oath, or will you break it? Because if you're going to honor it, then you *must* acquit him of these crimes. But if you're not going to honor it, then nothing in our system means anything anyway."

He paused a moment.

"Everyone in this courtroom knows the government has not proved their case. So the only question is, Are you honorable people, or aren't you?"

He sat back down and stared at the same spot on the floor. Arlo was going to say something, but Dylan held up his hand. Arlo leaned back, and neither of them spoke.

84

The jury broke for deliberations at noon. Dylan and Lily went to a nearby café and ordered lunch, while Madeline had other cases to attend to.

Dylan picked at his food without taking a single bite.

"It was a great closing."

"Good," he said without looking up.

"Dylan, we all have a part to play in that courtroom, like you said, and you played your part. That's all you can do."

"And if he gets acquitted and kills another three people? How about then, Lil? Will you feel like we just played our part and it's no big deal?"

"What he does or doesn't do when he leaves that courtroom is none of our business. Our job is to make sure the government doesn't lock up or kill people without enough evidence. You made sure of that today. You did exactly what the Founding Fathers wrote the Constitution for."

He nodded. "Yeah. Well, if he goes free, you can quote Thomas Jefferson to Holly Fallows and see if it makes her feel better."

Lily's cell phone rang. Her brow furrowed as she answered. "Yes?"

She looked at Dylan and said, "Thank you" before hanging up.

"Jury's back with a verdict."

———

Jury deliberations in murder trials ranged from a few hours to a few days. Dylan had even had one take eighteen days before the jury stated they couldn't reach a verdict and a hung jury was declared. This jury had come back in just under two hours. Two hours of deliberation on the deaths of three people.

The courtroom was so packed that the bailiffs had to force people outside. At least nine or ten cameras were in the courtroom, and spectators crammed in wherever they could. Arlo was brought out, and once Kelly and James and the rest of her staff arrived, the judge came out and said, "Any preliminary matters to take care of, Counselors?"

"No, Your Honor."

"No," Dylan said quietly.

"Then let's bring out the jury."

The jury came out single file and filled the two rows of seats. None of them looked over to the defense table. The judge said, "Ladies and gentlemen of the jury, it's my understanding you have reached a verdict in this matter."

The foreperson, a tall man in a suit coat, rose and said, "We have, Your Honor."

"Please hand the verdict forms to my bailiff."

The bailiff took the sheets of paper and brought them to the judge. Judge Hamilton read them impassively, careful to keep his face as neutral as possible. He handed the verdict forms back to the bailiff, who gave them to the foreperson again.

"Mr. Ward," the judge said, "please rise."

Lily, Madeline, and Arlo rose, but Dylan remained seated. When he saw the judge staring at him, he slowly stood up and put his hands in front of him.

"In the matter of *the State of Nevada v. Arlo W. Ward*, what say you on count one to the charge of murder within Nevada state limits on May the ninth of this year?"

The foreperson glanced at Arlo and then looked at the first sheet. "We find Arlo Ward . . . not guilty."

The courtroom erupted. The judge had to hit his gavel several times and threaten to clear the courtroom before it quieted down. Dylan placed his hands on the table because he wasn't sure his knees wouldn't buckle.

"On count two of the information, murder committed within Nevada state limits on May ninth of this year, what say you?"

"We find the defendant, Arlo Ward, not guilty."

They read the verdict form for every charge, and for every charge, it was not guilty. Holly Fallows was crying in her father's arms, the media was shouting and running around, and the spectators were talking at full volume. Judge Hamilton gave up on quieting them and simply waited until the verdicts were all read and then thanked the jury for their time.

Kelly shouted over the din, "Your Honor, we would ask that the defendant immediately be taken into custody for obstruction of justice for lying to the police during this investigation and for—"

Lily said, "It's a lesser included offense to the charges he was just acquitted for, Your Honor. Jeopardy has attached."

"She's correct, Ms. Whitewolf."

"Then I make a motion for judgment notwithstanding the verdict and ask this court to render a just verdict."

Judge Hamilton looked pained but tried to hide it as much as possible. Dylan, at least, had to respect him for that. "To find for you," the judge said, "I have to find that no reasonable jury would have acquitted Mr. Ward, and there is no basis for such a finding here. Your motion is denied. Mr. Ward, you are free to go."

Arlo leaned over to Dylan, who still wasn't looking at him, and said, "Excellent job, Counselor. I think I'd like to sue the state for malicious prosecution if you're ready for it."

"Actually, Arlo, I think you need to find another lawyer."

Arlo chuckled and slapped his shoulder. "You gotta get more fun outta life, Dylan. You're too uptight."

Dylan watched as Arlo left the courtroom. Subtly, and so quickly few others caught it, Arlo looked directly at Holly Fallows and winked.

The wink might as well have been a punch. Holly lost her breath. If her father hadn't been holding her, she would have crumpled to the floor. She sobbed, and Kelly went over and held her, too.

"We should go out the back way to avoid all this," Lily said.

"No. Someone much smarter than me said that once you go the back way, you'll always be going the back way."

Dylan took a deep breath, picked up his satchel, and began making his way through the crowd.

85

Dylan didn't feel like going home, so he walked the Strip and gambled and drank. He ate a small meal at a café and sipped beer until evening fell. When it was dark, he started strolling again. His phone was off, and he liked the idea that nobody could reach him.

When he finally drove home, Lily was sitting on the steps of his front porch. He got out of the car and sat next to her without a word.

They were quiet for a few minutes. Then she reached into her bag. "I got you something."

It was the motion to dismiss on Oscar Beltran's case, framed in a smooth silver frame. Dylan held it in his hands and stared at it.

He grinned. "Thanks."

She kissed his cheek and then stood up. "I'll see you at the office."

"Lil?"

She turned to him.

"I think you should fight for him. Camden. I think if you don't, you'll regret it for the rest of your life."

She gave a melancholic grin. "I, um, cried myself to sleep the other night. When I woke up, I drafted a motion for custody . . . I would appreciate if you could help me with the case."

"You know you don't need to ask."

She nodded. "I know. Good night, Dylan."

"Good night."

When he was alone again, a deep breath escaped him, and he took out his phone. He turned it on and dialed a number and, still staring at the framed document in his hand, left a message:

"Mr. Hitchens, this is Dylan Aster in Nevada calling about the job. I really appreciate it, but I don't think it's the right fit for me. Thanks again for the opportunity."

He slipped the phone into his pocket, leaned back on the steps, and stared at the sky for a long time. Markie came out and said, "Dylan? Can we play video games?"

He looked at her and smiled at the chocolate smeared on her lips and cheeks. "Sure, be right there."

"Yay!"

He stood up and glanced at the moon and the stars, then looked out at the vast grasslands in front of him, and only one word kept coming to him as he did so: *home.*

He went inside and shut the door behind him.

———

In the morning, Dylan's alarm clock went off as it always did. He picked it up, threw it as hard as he could against the wall, breaking it, and then went back to sleep.

When he woke up, he texted Lily's cousin September and said he was taking some time off, and he'd like to show her around Vegas.

She said she would fly out the next day.

86

Kelly Whitewolf sat outside on her porch steps and watched the sunrise. It was going to be a hot day, and she wore shorts and a T-shirt.

After a cup of coffee, she got into her truck and drove to the one place she least wanted to go: Holly Fallows's home.

Kelly felt little but shame. Shame that she had let this girl down so profoundly. She had been so certain Arlo Ward committed these crimes that she hadn't wanted the defense to even know about the Bennett murders. Certain that it would—as it had—cast reasonable doubt in the jurors' minds and lead to an acquittal. James had been right: she should have offered insanity and at least gotten Arlo Ward locked up in the hospital. Maybe Arlo would've taken the deal, maybe he wouldn't have, but she should have tried.

Holly answered after a few knocks. She wore boxer shorts and a long shirt.

"Hi," was all Kelly managed to say.

"Hi. Um, come in."

They sat on the couch again, and Kelly found she couldn't speak. She stared at Holly Fallows's crutch.

"Are you okay?" Holly asked.

Being asked that worsened Kelly's shame, and tears slid down her cheeks. "I'm so sorry," she said, wiping away the tears.

"You don't have to be. You did everything you could do."

"You have to live your life knowing he's out there because of me. I just wasn't good enough, and I am so sorry."

Holly put her hand over Kelly's. Her calm, the warm smile, and the confidence that had slowly returned to her comforted Kelly. That a young woman who had gone through what she went through could still keep her head up made Kelly feel like she needed to be stronger.

"You did everything you could," Holly said softly, "and I am really grateful. I couldn't have gone through this without you."

Kelly composed herself and blew out a long breath. "If you need anything, if there's anything I can do, call me. Day or night."

"You don't have to worry about me. I'm fine. I knew there was a chance this would happen." She hesitated. "I wasn't entirely sure it was him, but when he was leaving the courtroom, he winked at me. It felt like . . . like a knife going into my chest. It was the worst feeling I'd ever had. But I'm not going to let him take away the rest of my life because of this. I won't. He's already taken enough from me."

Kelly nodded and wiped away the last of her tears. "I should go."

At the door, they embraced. When Kelly let go, she still held Holly's hands and then let them slip away as she turned to the porch and headed for her truck. She took out her phone and dialed her ex-husband, Travis.

"Hey," he said.

"Hey. I've thought about it, and I want you to see the girls more like you've been wanting."

A pause. "Really? What changed your mind?"

"Life's too short to hold grudges forever. Every weekend is fine. But not this weekend. We're going on a trip this weekend."

He chuckled. "You're taking a vacation? Did pigs suddenly grow wings, too?"

"Yeah, well, I may have been focusing too much energy in some of the wrong areas. But I'm glad I caught it while there's still time to fix it."

"Where you going?"

"I don't know. But I think me and the girls are going to get lost for a while."

"Well, I'm glad. I really am. You deserve it." Another pause before he said, "I read about what happened. I'm sorry. That can't be easy."

"No, it's not. I actually thought about quitting. In fact, I went to the victim's house to tell her I was quitting. But I don't know, she just showed me that you can't let people like him change you."

"If it's any consolation, I'm proud of you, and I bet the girls are proud of you."

"Thank you, Travis."

"Take care of yourself."

She hung up and got into her truck. A laminated picture of her girls hung from the rearview mirror, and merely looking at them put a grin on her face. She kissed her fingers and then touched the photo before starting the truck and going home.

87

Arlo Ward drove his car up Coyote Canyon and took the winding road slowly. He enjoyed the scenery: red rocks, white and yellow limestone, dense forest, wide-open plains. Coyote Canyon had everything. Just the right spot where shrubbery could grow in parts and not grow in others. It felt . . . whole. Complete by being incomplete.

For the past few weeks, the interviews had been coming almost daily. He never did them for free, even the big ones on the networks, and had made a tidy sum so far. This particular interview was paying him $4,500 for an hour of his time. *People* magazine, which he had heard paid well, had contacted him yesterday, and he had agreed to the fee, though they sounded desperate, and he wished he'd tried for more.

The photo shoot was at the campsite where the murders occurred and at the cliff where Holly Fallows had jumped. He thought it was tacky, but the assistant to the editor assured him it would be a tasteful piece about an innocent man in a system that presumed him guilty.

He had also secured an agent who was working on a book deal about his trial.

Arlo drove high into the canyons and parked in a clearing that had enough room for several vehicles. It was, in fact, where he had parked on the night of the murders. It made him smile as he got out of the car and began the hike up to the camping spot.

A breeze blew, and it felt good on his face since it was a hot day. Tomorrow, he had another interview in New York set up for a cable news network. They were even flying him out first-class so he could be at the studio in person. He hoped the temperature was cooler there.

The campsite wasn't far, but the writer and photographer were meeting him at the ledge where Holly had jumped from. It was a good ways away from the campsite.

Arlo went up to the ledge and looked out over the forest. It was beautiful. The purity of it. Nature untouched by man. And it would be here millions of years after man was gone. A snapshot of eternity, he thought.

He checked his watch. They should have been here already.

"Waiting for someone?"

He turned around and saw Holly Fallows standing there, leaning on a crutch. At first, he felt nothing but shock, and then it made him laugh. She had come to confront him, for whatever good that would do. He wondered if she was stupid enough to have come up here by herself. Just in case she wasn't alone, he decided he would ignore her and leave.

"Go home, little girl," he said, taking a step toward the trail heading back to his car.

Holly lifted a handgun. Arlo chuckled. "You even know how to use that thing?"

"I've been practicing. I see you in the targets when I practice, Arlo. I see you in my dreams. When I'm out of the house, I see you everywhere. Grocery stores, parking lots, office buildings . . . do you see them anywhere? My sister or Mike or Will? Do you think about them?"

"Not really, no. They all died so quick it wasn't that memorable, honestly."

They watched each other a moment. Her hand began to tremble, and tears silently slid down her cheeks. Arlo thought she looked like she might pass out. If she did, the question was what to do with her. No one else was up here, and it was unlikely she had told anybody where she was going.

It made him grin.

"Put the gun down. You aren't shooting anybody."

She pulled the trigger. The bang sounded like thunder in the quiet forest. It scared off nearby birds and caused a rustling in some bushes from whatever animal was hiding there. The pain in Arlo's thigh was immediate. A searing pain that radiated up his leg. He tumbled to the ground as blood soaked his jeans.

"You bitch! You shot me!"

"Does it hurt? I tried to hit your femur to make it really hurt."

"You stupid bitch. I'll reach down your throat and tear your heart out!"

"No, Arlo. You won't. You're going to make a choice. The same choice you made me make."

His eyes suddenly went wide, and he glanced behind him at the ledge. He felt his stomach in his throat as he observed the jagged rocks and the sheer distance of the fall.

"I'm going back to my car. Shoot me if you want to, I don't care."

He rose, took a painful step, and she fired again. The shot hit him just underneath the wound in his thigh. It made him scream and collapse again. Holly took a few steps toward him but stayed far enough away that he couldn't reach her.

"You really shouldn't have winked at me. It's always the little things that get you, isn't it?"

"You fu—"

"I'm going to count to three, and then I'm putting a bullet in your head. Or you can jump. Your choice."

Arlo growled, "When I get outta this, I'm going to—"

"One."

"Put the damn gun down! We both know you're not going to kill me."

"Two."

They stared at each other just long enough for Arlo to realize she was serious. She was going to kill him if he didn't jump, and not only that, but there was something else in her eyes . . . it was satisfaction.

"Three."

He crawled backward away from her and tumbled over the ledge.

There was little pain at first. Just pressure as his body slammed into jagged rocks and kept falling. He could hear his ribs being crushed and the bones in his arms snapping, and he tasted the ocean of blood in his mouth from his teeth getting knocked out. The world spun so furiously he vomited from vertigo. All he could see was sky and dirt and rocks, each taking turns flipping and spinning like he was inside a swirling tunnel.

It wasn't until he hit the ground at the bottom and looked up that he realized how far he had fallen.

The last rock he hit had sent a loud crunch through the air, so loud that he could feel it in his face, and he knew his spine had been broken. He looked down to his leg, and it had snapped in half at the knee. Bones were jutting out through flesh, and blood poured out of him and mixed with the dirt, creating a dark mud. Arteries and veins had been torn open. Suddenly, he felt so cold that he began to shiver. He opened his mouth to yell for help, but blood cascaded down his throat and made him choke, letting him release nothing but a deep gurgle.

The full pain hadn't hit yet, but the cold made the shivering so violent it hurt. It amazed him again, like it had that night, how much blood the human body contained, as he watched it spill into the earth. He tried to reach out to touch it, but his arm had been broken in so many places he couldn't move it. But he could, slightly, move his head.

He managed to tilt it up just enough to see one thing: Holly Fallows on the edge of the cliff, watching him die.

She turned away and disappeared down the trail.

Faintness was overtaking him, his vision swirling between brightly colored rings and pure blackness, the rings slowly being eaten up as darkness filled his vision.

Then he was gone.

ACKNOWLEDGMENTS

Thank you to my agent, Amy Tannenbaum, my editor Megha, and everyone at Thomas & Mercer. A writer couldn't ask for a better team to have his back.

ABOUT THE AUTHOR

 At the age of thirteen, when his best friend was interrogated by the police for over eight hours and confessed to a crime he didn't commit, Victor Methos knew he would one day become a lawyer. After graduating from law school at the University of Utah, Methos sharpened his teeth as a prosecutor for Salt Lake City before founding what would become the most successful criminal defense firm in Utah.

In ten years, Methos conducted more than one hundred trials. One particular case stuck with him, and it eventually became the basis for his first major bestseller, *The Neon Lawyer*. Since that time, Methos has focused his work on legal thrillers and mysteries, winning the Harper Lee Prize for *The Hallows* and an Edgar nomination for Best Novel for his title *A Gambler's Jury*. He currently splits his time between southern Utah and Las Vegas.